To Veronica and C arlie

Other Side of the Letterbox

Sometimes a Letter
Is Better

2.8.25

Published in paperback in 2024 by Sixth Element Publishing
on behalf of Steven David Wood

Sixth Element Publishing
Arthur Robinson House
13-14 The Green
Billingham
TS23 1EU
www.6epublishing.net

ISBN 978-1-914170-63-8

British Library Cataloguing in Publication Data. A catalogue record for this book is available from the British Library.

Printed in Great Britain.

The Other Side of the Letterbox

Steven David Wood

Also by Steven David Wood

Don’t Forget To Breathe

This book is dedicated to all of my family and
friends who I have yet to meet and those who
I will never have the opportunity to meet.

PS: You will find me somewhere between the words,
the lines, the pages and, of course, the letters.

Author's Note

The other day my four-year-old grandson ran into the living room where I was sitting on the couch, in my usual place, and excitedly announced that he'd written a story. He was waving a scrap of coloured paper and launched himself onto my lap.

"I've written a book, Grandad," he told me. I looked at the piece of paper and saw that he'd managed to write a few letters… l… o… and what looked like either a p or a q.

"Wow, that's brilliant! Can you read it to me?" I asked.

He thought about it then said, "No, I can't, Grandad."

I asked, "Why not?"

And he innocently replied, "Because I can't read…"

"But you wrote it," I said, smiling to myself.

"Yes, but I can't read it," he replied.

So we spent the next few minutes making up his story and speaking out loud.

It was his story… and the story that he'd wanted to write… and so then he read it out loud, and we both laughed out loud.

It was a great moment and it reminded me of the power of words, something about a pen and a sword! And it reminded me also of the power of letters, not just the alphabet but the actual written message from one human being to another which can impact more powerfully than an atomic bomb exploding as we struggle through our daily drudge, and what can happen when that totally random unexpected handwritten envelope lands on the doormat… which unfortunately doesn't seem to happen very often these days, but it's always exciting when it does!

WELCOME TO THE OTHER SIDE OF THE LETTERBOX

Prologue

In the attics of our minds, when sometimes we pluck up the courage to investigate what's really going on up there, the spiders can be unexpectedly disturbed and that is when the demons are awoken.

It is at this point in time when the angels will try to find their way home.

So, let's try and pick the bones out of that one, my friend. I'd really appreciate your company on the journey because I fear that it will be a long and lonely one without you by my side.

So onward we go and if you need a guide… well, here I am. Please turn the page… and by the way, hello!

Oh! And one more thing… before we start the journey, don't forget to suspend your disbelief because everything that you're reading now is true… I know that because I'm the one who is writing it down for you. If I could put it in an envelope, write your address on it and put a stamp on it, I would post it to you… but then again I'd have to find a letterbox to post it into. If it was possible then I would, but there aren't any up here, as you'll find out. I'll see you on the next page… let's just get on with it… so, without further ado…

Chapter 1

The brown leaves were chasing each other through the air on the turbulence of the chilly wind and the shadows were getting longer every day. He shambled his way down the cobblestone road between the old crooked buildings as he reflected on the fact that the flowers and blossoms of springtime were now just a distant memory.

In every narrow pathway that led off the main street he noticed that there were many individuals who looked to be of dubious character and who were observing his passing with the potential of menacing intent. He was sure that it was the clinking sound of the metal tools in his backpack, which he'd needed in order to carry out an important task outside of the village boundaries, that was arousing their curiosity. He'd managed to complete his job, but now he just wanted to get home before it got dark, and this was the only way back. He didn't like coming to the village and so he quickened his pace in order to return to where he'd come from earlier in the morning.

His name was Artichoke Underwood and he resided in a treehouse two hundred feet up in the air, deep in the forest, way beyond the village.

The world in which he lived was called the Land of Khartoonz, where nothing seemed real, but everything actually was!

•

Artichoke entered the treehouse a few hours later just as the two suns were setting. He'd ascended to his lofty residence using a wooden platform, which he could move by using a series of ropes and pulleys. He closed the door behind himself and addressed the voice that came from the chair near the stove.

"Did you manage to do it?" asked Nelly.

"Yes, I've done it," replied Artichoke.

"Good, because he'll be arriving tomorrow. His name is Nathaniel and you have to show him the way," said Nelly, a black and white cat who'd lived with Artichoke for decades. He was very wise and a constant source of information for Artichoke, who was a Samaritan who acted as a guide for the lost people.

He removed his backpack, placed it on the floor, then he took off his hat, which had large white bird feathers inserted into one side of the headband. The hat had nearly blown off several times during his walk and he placed it onto the wooden table. He pulled up a chair and sat next to Nelly. He warmed his hands by the stove and waited for the cat to speak.

"I know you're feeling anxious about tomorrow," said Nelly. "And you don't always succeed in achieving a good outcome. But this is your job and you know what you're doing, so you can only try your best. Has everyone been informed?"

"Yes," Artichoke replied.

"That's good, so now you need to rest, and I will let

you know tomorrow when it's time for us to leave." Nelly got off the chair, jumped onto the only bed in the circular room and curled up at the bottom.

Artichoke rose from his seat and prepared himself to get into the bed.

The wind was whistling through the eaves of the treehouse and somewhere in the distance a pack of wolves were howling. He was glad to be home safe in his sanctuary, and as he pulled the blankets over himself, his thoughts turned to those who might not be as lucky as he and Nelly were tonight.

Chapter 2

Nathaniel Phischermann had spent the previous night trying to sleep on the back seat of his car, which he'd parked near the old pub… the pub that used to have a huge ship's capstan attached to its side but which had recently been removed by the new owners. The vehicle itself wasn't much to look at but it served its purpose as a run-around (when it actually managed to start that was). The Mini was very old and had had three previous owners; the rust was so bad that there were even small holes in the footwells in the floor where you could clearly see the road beneath. Nathaniel's *now apparently ex-girlfriend* Judy had sarcastically commented that Fred Flintstone himself would have been proud of it. He didn't get much sleep, because alongside the constant battle with his confused thoughts, it was both very cold and extremely uncomfortable. So, he'd got up early.

His first thought, once again, was to read the note that he'd found on the mantelpiece of their rented flat the night before.

It was a Dear John letter, or, in his case, a Dear Nathaniel letter. The words on the notepaper hadn't changed since the last thousand times that he'd read it and he knew that the sentiments wouldn't have either. To cut a short story even shorter… she'd left him. Apparently she didn't love him anymore.

He reached forward and turned off the song on the cassette player, which was Pink Floyd's *Comfortably Numb.* The music had been playing at a much slower tempo, due to the dwindling energy supply from the car's battery, and it was making David Gilmour sound like a tired and lonely drunk sat in a deserted bar… on his own… in the dark.

Nathaniel abandoned his breakfast remains of empty beer cans, along with a half-smoked packet of cigarettes, which had a lighter tucked inside of it. He also left his mobile phone; he'd have no further use for that. Then he got out of the car, leaving the keys in the ignition and made his way to the steps that led to the top of the cliff.

As he slowly ascended the steps, another song came to him. It was a song that *he'd* written. He'd always wanted to be a successful singer/songwriter, as he knew that he had a talent for it, but the pressures of everyday life and finding the means to survive had stolen the time away from him. That, combined with an inherent lack of self-confidence, meant his dreams had been frustratingly confounded. He'd taught himself to play the guitar early on in his life and the lyrics to this particular song, along with the chord shapes, slipped stealthily into his troubled mind. The song was entitled *When I Am Yesterday…* and it went like this:

It's more than just a photograph,
It's more like lemonade than laughter.
What is that you're telling me?
Results of strange biology.
Listen to my contradiction,
Adding fuel to my addiction.

Little child has gone away,
All in all, it's just like yesterday...
Feels just like yesterday!

Why did I do all that's stupid?
Could've lived my life like you did!
Please don't tell me it's too late,
Tomorrow I won't hesitate.
No more happy ever after,
Trying to derail disaster.
Please don't take this child away,
No more tomorrow when I am yesterday...
When I am yesterday.

Making the peace is not mine, you say,
While wrecking the future is not yours.
I'm ready to reach out and go far away,
For all these reasons now,
Hang your head upon my shoulder and cry.

Time and time I fooled myself,
Forget the words you spoke to help me.
Lighting candles while I wait,
Resigned to penance, resigned to fate.
Habit forming guns reloading,
I am a time bomb, I am exploding.
Little child is on his way,
Too late tomorrow when I am yesterday...
When I am yesterday, when I am yesterday,
when I am yesterday...

By the time he'd sung the song in his head for one last time – the fingers of his left hand instinctively forming the chords – he'd reached the top of the steps and had walked quite a long distance along the footpath. There'd been a young woman heading in the opposite direction to him, they passed, she smiled, he didn't. But now here he was… alone, standing motionless and lacking any hope for the future, as he simply didn't care about anything anymore. The reflection of the sun, which was rising on the right hand side of the horizon, began to stretch out onto the surface of the sea, and he was determined that he would not live through this day to be a witness for it setting later on.

He found himself stood six feet away from the edge of the towering cliff. As he looked down at the sea, he observed the old pier to his left, now much shorter than its original length from when it had been constructed over a hundred years before. The structure had been the victim of many storms and collisions with ships, which had resulted in its present condition, a very poor version of its former self… and Nathaniel knew how that felt.

Far in the distance beyond the pier, he could see the former steelworks that were long since redundant and were currently in the process of being demolished.

A large seabird landed behind him… it was a Black-Browed Albatross that just stood there staring with curiosity, head cocked to one side at Nathaniel's back. He was oblivious to its presence. That particular species of bird can spend decades mainly living out at sea, only making landfall in order to breed or if there was bad weather coming, and this particular bird had sensed a big storm brewing.

It had only been a few months earlier that Nathaniel's mother had suddenly died from an undiagnosed heart related illness. His father had left them both when Nathaniel was a lot younger for reasons that had never been explained to him, and now Judy, the only person who had kept him focused and given him a reason to live, had decided to leave him too.

At this moment, as if cruelly summoned up from the distant past, the scathing comments from one of his old schoolteachers came to mind and he recalled what Mr Hardcastle had written on one of his school reports many years ago:

'Nathaniel is a truly unremarkable boy with a limited attention span and the inability to resolve even the simplest of tasks which are put before him. I have no idea where his path will take him in the future, but I fear that he will come to nothing and achieve very little, to say the least. He is the one lad in the class who just can't sit still.'

He could hear the sarcastic tone of his so-called teacher's destructive tongue, a monster of a man who ruled the classroom with the slipper and the cane, which was an obvious indicator to his true failings as a leader of education. The man was a fraud, who unfortunately everyone believed. He was also a religious nutter who would constantly rant and rave about the values of Christianity and the penance of eternal Hell as a punishment for any small wrongdoing.

"This one's for you, Mr Hardcastle. Thanks for your words of encouragement and all that... you vicious bastard. At the end of the day though, I guess that you were right."

The bird behind him blinked twice, then Nathaniel closed *his* eyes and with arms outstretched as if he were about to be crucified, he walked forward and swan dived into oblivion.

Chapter 3

"Wake up!"

Artichoke opened his eyes to see Nelly standing on his chest. "He's coming earlier than I thought. We have to go… now," said Nelly.

Artichoke leapt out of bed and rushed to get ready. He emptied the tools out of the backpack, which he then placed onto the table and Nelly climbed inside.

They rushed to the wooden platform and it wasn't long before they'd made their way down to the forest floor.

"We must go quickly," instructed Nelly.

Artichoke started to jog along the pathway.

•

Nathaniel had taken several steps forward and had zoned out into a trance-like state, prepared for the sudden fall and the inevitable shattering of his body on the rocks below. However, he became aware that he was actually walking further than it would have taken him to have reached the sheer drop at the cliff edge, so… he slowly opened his eyes. He found himself walking along a path in a forest. He stood still, put his arms down and looked at the gigantic pine trees that were taller than any he'd ever seen. The track was covered with pine needles and scattered with pinecones… some as big as pineapples. The smell was fresh and pungent.

'I must be dead,' he thought. 'I must be in Heaven.'

He then became aware of the sound of footsteps behind him… someone – or something – was getting closer… and it was running. He turned around and noticed that there was a bend in the path, so he waited to see what was coming. It wasn't long before the figure of a man, wearing a hat with feathers on the side of it, appeared running towards him.

'Oh my god,' thought Nathaniel. 'I'm going to get mugged.'

The man stopped running and walked up to Nathaniel.

"Don't come any closer," ordered Nathaniel.

The man, who was considerably shorter than him, stood still. "Don't worry, I won't hurt you," the stranger tried to reassure him.

"Where am I? Who are you? And what do you want?" asked Nathaniel.

"You're in the Land of Khartoonz. My name is Artichoke Underwood and we have come to help you."

"We? But there's only one of you!" Nathaniel had noticed that the man was wearing a backpack and was very surprised when a cat poked its head out of the top. The cat put its front paws on the man's shoulder and stood up on its hind legs in order to get a better view of the person in front of them.

"Hello, my name is Nelly," announced the cat. "And it's a pleasure to meet you."

Nathaniel took a step backwards and he looked with

disbelief at Artichoke. "That cat just spoke. Are you some kind of ventriloquist?"

"No, he is my familiar and companion. He won't harm you," Artichoke assured him.

In order to reaffirm this, Nelly said, "Artichoke is the guide for the lost people who find themselves here, and I am going to help him to help you."

"I must be dead," said Nathaniel. "Either that or I'm in Hell or in some kind of traumatic coma."

"You're in neither," answered Artichoke. "The path that you are standing on is the Path of Second Chances and I am going to guide you along it."

"What's the point in that?" asked Nathaniel, sounding depressed.

"Because it's exactly where this path leads. At the end of it is a place called The Point and that's our destination, but first… you must complete the journey. So, if you follow me, I mean *us*, we'll take you there."

Artichoke passed by Nathaniel, who, with a degree of dubious reluctance, followed the strange man and his talking cat.

Chapter 4

Hello my friend and thank you for having rejoined me. I am sat here at a desk in a dark attic and, although I am in front of a small window – which is long overdue a clean – my main source of light is being provided by the solitary candle which only flickers when my breath catches it. Close by, in the rafters above me, I am surrounded by a multitude of spider webs, whose occupants hang there observing me with a silent motionless suspicion. In my hand is a quill, an albatross feather to be exact, and as I dip the nib into the inkwell, I will proceed to scratch out the words of the tale on the parchment before me. So, without further ado, I'll continue. Let's see what they are up to now… oh and by the way, don't let all of those spiders hanging above you in the dark make you feel anxious… they're more afraid of you, than you are of them. I think!

Chapter 5

The three travellers soon came upon a fork in the road. The way to the left led into a dark and foreboding place that looked to be both cold and lonely. It seemed that it would probably lead to the kind of an area where you wouldn't want to be left on your own. It oozed with negative emotions, like a vacuum sucking the goodness out of everything. The path on the right was blocked by a very high stone wall covered in ivy. There was an arched wooden doorway in the wall, and the path stopped there.

"So which way now?" Nathaniel asked Artichoke.

"You choose, it's your journey," replied his guide.

"What's behind the door?" said Nathaniel.

"Go and take a look," Artichoke suggested, gesturing towards the path on the right.

Nathaniel paused for a few moments then stepped forward. He stood in front of the doorway and looked back over his shoulder for reassurance.

"Go ahead," said Artichoke. "Try it."

Nathaniel turned back and took hold of the rusty door handle. It was the type that was circular like a ring and had to be twisted to lift the catch, but twist as he might, the door wouldn't open.

"It's shut tight," he called back. "So, what's on the other side?"

Nelly popped up from out of the backpack. "Take a look through the letterbox and tell us what you see," the cat instructed.

Cautiously, Nathaniel crouched down and opened the flap. What he saw was quite amazing… it was a scene of tranquil beauty and colour with an overall effect of peace and happiness. He could see butterflies of all sizes and species dancing between beautiful flowers of all descriptions. The grass was bright green and lush, and there wasn't a single cloud in the clear blue sky above. He was sure that he could smell the powerful aroma of roses, and, as a small deer entered into the frame of the enchanting picture, the haunting sound of melancholic chamber music drifted over to him.

It was a surreal image. He glanced downwards and could plainly see a large pile of envelopes stacked up against the foot of the door. Some of them looked fresh, with names and addresses written on them, although he couldn't read them from this angle; some had postage stamps and postmarks; some of them looked ancient and covered in mildew, and some of them were just blank. He became aware that there was maybe someone on the other side of the door, someone hiding to the right of the doorframe, out of his line of vision. He felt the person's presence but, try as he might, he couldn't see them.

"Hello," he whispered. There was no answer. "Hello, is anyone there?" He called out a little bit louder, and waited. There was no response. Only a quiet shuffling of feet.

He stood up straight and, to his surprise, the letterbox snapped shut.

"Can we get in there?" he asked Artichoke and Nelly, who solemnly shook their heads in unison.

"I'm afraid we have to go that way," responded Nelly, nodding towards the dark route on the left.

"But why?" asked Nathaniel.

"Because it's the way that you have already chosen, quite a long time ago actually," replied Artichoke.

"What do you mean?" Nathaniel enquired.

"It's called The Path of Least Resistance. The easy way forward, if you like," explained Nelly.

"I'm not going down there. It looks dangerous," said Nathaniel.

"The problem though is that you're already on it, and you have to keep going in order to get to The Point," explained Artichoke. As he spoke, the light went out of the sky and a cold wind blew through them all.

Nathaniel looked around and discovered that miraculously somehow, they were now on The Path of Least Resistance deep inside a dark, menacing and threatening forest that offered no sign of a way out.

Chapter 6

It was a place of tangles. There were nettles, brambles, bushes and thorns. The black roses were devoid of any scent and they painfully scratched Nathaniel's weary limbs. Sometimes the path was completely overgrown, and it was only because of Artichoke's experience that they managed to push their way onwards. Intermittently, strange noises came at them out of the murky darkness. Howls, screams and growls permeated the otherwise deadly silence.

"If this is The Path of Least Resistance, I'd hate to walk the path that resists the most," said Nathaniel.

Neither Artichoke or Nelly responded, choosing instead to ignore his protest… or was it that they knew something that he had no knowledge of yet? Something that they weren't quite ready to share with him at this moment in time?

"Can we stop, please?" Nathaniel shouted at Artichoke, who seemed to be getting further away from him. The small man with the backpack and the feathery hat stopped and turned around. "Why are you doing this? I mean trying to help me? I never asked for your help… as a matter of fact, I don't need your help or anyone else's. I've already made up my mind where I want to be, or *how* I want to be, but you're stopping it from happening. I should be dead now, erased from existence. That's what I want, not *this.*" He gestured at the landscape around him. "This bloody masquerade, this pantomime of pretence. This isn't reality, none of this exists. You don't exist. I don't want you to exist, just go away and leave me alone."

Nelly had emerged from the backpack after hearing the beginning of Nathaniel's rant and was now staring at Artichoke, who was looking back at him. They both nodded to each other in silent but seemingly reluctant agreement and turned their gaze towards Nathaniel.

"We are very sorry to have troubled you," said Nelly, and with those parting words they both disappeared into thin air.

Nathaniel looked on in disbelief, as if the situation couldn't have got any more bizarre, it just had.

And once again, he was all alone.

Chapter 7

As Nathaniel stood by himself on the path, a wave of emotion came over him. It was a feeling that he'd successfully managed to subdue and to deny himself recently… it was a subtle urge to survive. Here he was in the semi-darkness of a strange land in an alien environment surrounded by hidden threats; there were things in this forest that he was sure meant him harm, that probably even wanted to kill him, but wasn't that what he wanted to happen? To die? He was now starting to doubt himself, to doubt his original intentions and that thought just confused him even more. Now he was alone, the situation was becoming more acceptable to him as being real. So, what to do now with no-one to guide him along? That was a no-brainer really, the choice was simple: to either stand there and become a victim of whatever unseen menace was out there, or to keep moving along the way that Artichoke and Nelly had been showing him before they had disappeared (and he was already beginning to regret his childish outburst that had caused *that* to happen).

It reminded him of the time that he'd finally decided to leave home. He'd left under a black cloud after a particularly nasty outburst when he'd made the decision to plough his own furrow in life… and he never returned home or got back in touch again.

Ever since making that move, he'd resigned himself to drifting from dead end job to dead end job until today when he'd finally come to his ultimate dead end… but had he?

He took one step forward and continued on his journey.

It wasn't long before the path gave way to a more obscure route, with the surrounding undergrowth merging together until it was totally unrecognisable as a pathway at all and the ground eventually just became a wild overgrown area with no discernible direction to take at all… when he looked behind, the path was gone. He was now totally lost. He was stumbling around unsure of which way to go, just moving from tree to tree, hoping that nothing was going to jump out from behind them, but he knew that it was important to just keep on moving. He cursed himself for being such an idiot and upsetting his helpers in the way that he had. He really did need their help now, but what could he do? There was no way that he was going to call out for them and attract the attention of the beasts and monsters that he was now convinced were tracking him with malicious intent.

He decided to take a rest and nervously sat down upon the exposed root of a large tree. He sighed and regretted that he hadn't brought the cigarettes and lighter with him. In the depressing gloom of the forest he began to think of the reasons that had brought him to this place. It had been a steady build-up of circumstances and events that had finally got the better of him. Small loans had grown into a mountain of debt, lack of work and too many broken relationships had gradually pushed him further and further towards his choice of conclusion. His self-confidence was non-existent, shattered by too many hard efforts to improve his place in the world and equally too many harder failures, which had only compounded his increasingly dire situation. He'd disappeared down a boiler hole into the fiery furnace of no return and the heat had become overwhelmingly intolerable. Enough had eventually been enough and so, not being able to take any more mental suffering, he'd finally decided to take his future into his own hands. It was the only answer that he could think of, the only answer that made any sense. He hadn't left a note to be found, he'd just wanted to disappear.

•

It's a sad fact that when someone takes their own life, it is those left behind that are forever asking the unanswerable question of WHY?

Why didn't they just ask for help? The answer never comes, the answer never does… it is stolen away forever by the unfortunate victim who has been exposed to life's cruel truths, and lies, resulting in tragic consequence!

•

Nathaniel was snapped out of his deep thoughts by someone tapping on his left shoulder. He immediately spun his head around.

"Arti…" he began to say, then jumped to his feet in

disbelief at what he was looking at. He was staring at a huge construction made out of Lego bricks of all different colours and sizes, and as he craned his neck upwards in order to take in the incredible height of the thing, it in turn craned its body forward to take a look down at Nathaniel. The thing appeared to be a man or robot made entirely out of Lego. It must have been at least twelve feet tall, and, as it leaned down, it also creaked an eerie plastic-like sound. They both stared at each other… the thing with curiosity, Nathaniel with absolute terror. The Lego thing spoke first and when it did it was in a low booming tone that vibrated through Nathaniel's body.

"Don't be afraid, I was warned that you might come by this way, and so I am prepared to help you. If you want help, that is?"

Nathaniel was shocked at this bizarre turn of events and was confused about how to answer, but the answer came out of his mouth nevertheless, without him even having to think about it. "Yes please, I'm lost… and alone."

"Very well. By the way, they call me Tiny Toppings."

"Okay, if you say so. I'm Nathaniel."

"Yes, I know," said Tiny. "Artichoke told me yesterday."

"Where have they gone?" asked Nathaniel. "You know… Artichoke and Nelly?"

"They have gone to where you wanted them to go… away! And now you're on your own, that's what you asked for," replied Tiny.

Nathaniel sighed and turned his gaze away from the Lego man.

"Will they ever come back?" he asked.

"It's your turn to find *them* now, if you really want to. And remember, you still haven't got to The Point yet, so follow me, if that's what you want to do." Tiny Toppings confidently strode forward, creaking his joints.

Nathaniel followed on behind the giant, grateful that he now had a new escort to guide him through this strange place.

Chapter 8

As they carried on walking, Tiny crashing through the undergrowth and Nathaniel behind him, stumbling like a blind man attempting to do an obstacle course, it became apparent to that they weren't alone. Every now and again Nathaniel would see movement out of the corner of his eye, to his left. There was something moving swiftly between the trees about thirty feet away, but every time he quickly turned his head, the shadow would disappear behind a tree trunk. They were certainly being followed, and in the murk of the dim forest light amidst the howls and screams of creatures unknown, it put Nathaniel's nerves on an extremely sharp knife-edge. He was desperate to shout up to Tiny, but he didn't want to attract any more unwanted attention. The ominous shadow thing kept pace alongside of them, as eventually the undergrowth once again, thankfully, became a pathway, this time much wider than before. The trees became less dense, which allowed more light to penetrate the canopy of leaves above them, although the surrounding atmosphere was still one of anxiety and uncertainty. Nathaniel could walk properly on this path and Tiny, although still creaking, was creating a lot less noise and disruption with his bizarre Lego footsteps.

The minutes passed by and Nathaniel was aware that

the Shadow Stalker had not shown itself for quite a while now. He thought that maybe it had given up the hunt and they had left it behind. It was then that Tiny Toppings stopped dead in his tracks.

Nathaniel plucked up the confidence to speak. "What is it?"

"Be quiet, and listen," Tiny replied.

Nathaniel did as he was told, and soon became aware of a strange sound in front of them, coming from around a bend in the path. It sounded like a multitude of castanets being clacked together… and it was getting louder.

The source of the noise soon made itself clear, as racing around the bend came dozens and dozens of small creatures scuttling towards them. As they got closer, Nathaniel could see that they were about eighteen inches long.

"What on earth are those?" Nathaniel asked, quite alarmed by what was approaching. "Are they dangerous?"

"No, it's just the Wood Lobsters. They don't mean us any harm, just be careful that you don't stand on them, that's all. They don't appreciate that kind of thing."

Nathaniel wasn't convinced, and as they swarmed around him on the floor, running across his feet and occasionally nipping at his trouser legs, he could see that, yes, they were lobsters – like the kind that live in the sea – but these ones were actually carved out of wood. The grain of their shells was quite beautiful, having been well sanded down and varnished, their legs were going ten to the dozen propelling them at quite a speed, and the clacking of their claws was both quite deafening and equally annoying at the same time.

"They're excited to see you," boomed Tiny. "Artichoke told *them* that you were coming yesterday too."

The Wood Lobsters were running around like overactive puppies and Nathaniel saw that they each had a different number carved into their backs. There was one particular individual, who was larger than the others, that possessed the number one. It stopped at Nathaniel's feet and shook its tail with a tremendous rattle. The herd of creatures immediately stopped racing around and stood still.

"This is the leader and he is called Mr Slater," Tiny informed him.

Mr Slater began clicking and clacking his claws together in what seemed to be an effort to communicate with Nathaniel. This went on for quite some time and then Mr Slater became silent.

"Is he trying to tell me something?" Nathaniel asked Tiny.

"Yes," Tiny replied. "He says, 'hello!'"

"Is that all?"

"Yes. Their language is quite long-winded, I'm afraid," Tiny told him.

Nathaniel thought it was a bit like a complicated Morse Code system, but nevertheless he returned the welcome. "Hello, Mr Slater," he said. "It's good to meet you as well."

Mr Slater started chattering away with his claw language and, after a very lengthy speech, Tiny interpreted, "He's asking permission to come with us and help along the way? You see, I'm a lot like you, Nathaniel... sometimes I fall to bits too, but these little fellows help me to pick up the pieces and they put me back together again. And they also make damn good bodyguards and can be excellent guard dogs as well when required."

Nathaniel was taken aback by this honest information that Tiny had shared with him.

"Of course, it would be an honour to have you travelling with us," he told Mr Slater.

So, with Tiny Toppings leading the way and Nathaniel Phischermann close behind, the Wood Lobsters, led by Mr Slater, joined the parade and they all marched forward to wherever they were destined to end up.

Chapter 9

They had been marching for a long time and the daylight was quickly disappearing. It was strange when the two suns set because it got very dark and then slowly light again and then suddenly totally pitch black.

It was Tiny Toppings who called, "HALT!"

The column stopped and some of the Wood Lobsters crashed into each other, which resulted in an exchange of clicking and clacking expletives.

"There's a clearing over there in the middle of that copse, and that's where we're going to sleep tonight. Tomorrow's another day," said Tiny. "It's a day that you have to witness and address, because it's the first day of the rest of your life, or the first day of your death, which may or may not be celebrated forever by people who may or may not have cared... you might never know. Your life *is* worth living... because there are young people who hopefully will rely on you. Please, don't forget about *them.* I know that's not easy because how can you forget people if you haven't even met them yet?"

Tiny was talking in riddles and Nathaniel was too tired to care about solving them.

They entered the clearing and Tiny stopped in the middle, the Wood Lobsters formed a defensive circle around the giant, claws pointing outwards and upwards, at a distance of about twelve feet from him. Nathaniel sat down and rested his head against one of the Lego feet of the tall, strange, plastic giant, and it wasn't long before he fell asleep secure in the knowledge that he was being well protected by his new friends, even though he'd just met them, and as of yet didn't fully understand them, but, at this point in time, that didn't seem to matter at all.

•

He didn't know if he was dreaming or awake but he found himself lying down on the side of a formidable looking mountain. The sparse moorland grass and heather was interspersed with grey coloured boulders of various sizes, some as big as his fist and some as big as a car. The air was fresh, and the night sky was clear but there was a chill biting wind that whistled across the landscape.

Nathaniel realised that, once again, he was alone.

Where were Tiny Toppings and the Wood Lobsters? This wasn't the clearing where he'd fallen asleep in the darkness. He sat upright and surveyed the area in front of him and it was then that he once again felt a hand on his shoulder.

"Dad! What're you doing here?" he blurted out in surprise.

His father, who he hadn't seen in years, was looking down at him with an expression of sympathetic understanding on his face. "Don't worry, son, I won't stay for long. It's just that I have something to tell you, something important. It's a secret that I've carried all my life, and it's something that has distanced me from everyone, from the ones that I love the most... especially you, and I apologise for that."

Nathaniel was confused. "What is it? And where are we?" he pleaded.

"This place is called the Two Sisters and we're in the Falkland Islands."

"Why?" Nathaniel asked.

"It's something that happened long before you were even born. So, it certainly wasn't your fault." His father sat down beside him and pointed towards one of the larger boulders nearby. "Look at that and tell me what you see."

"It looks like the rock is crying tears of blood," Nathaniel replied.

"Yes, and that's because there are two bullets buried inside it. Rounds that were fired a long time ago. What you can see on the outside are the traces of rust that have wept out over the years and trickled down the face of the stone. I was the one who fired those bullets... from my rifle... but the rock wasn't the first thing that they hit." His father looked away and bowed his head while Nathaniel sat listening intently.

"It was war and I was a professional soldier... in fact, I was in the Royal Marines and it was what Her Majesty and her government paid me to do, to protect her and the interests of our country. We were the first ones in and the last ones out. I just did what I was told, I was young. At the time I just followed orders, and looking back now I wish that I'd had the courage to walk away from the whole bloody business, but that was impossible. I was in it up to my neck and we were all in the same boat, all relying on each other to protect each other, to fight… to the death, if need be." His father paused and sighed before carrying on. "It was a dark and cold night, but the flares up above were lighting up the battlefield like a football pitch and the sheer physical exertion of getting up the mountain made me sweat like a pig. The tracer and live rounds from the Argentinian machine guns were ripping through the air towards us and I could feel them warp the air as they whizzed past me. I'd never been so scared in all of my life… and I've never been that scared since… apart from in my dreams… or in my nightmares."

He looked back towards the rock that bled the tears of blood and then he said, "Now and again the illumination flares would burn out or drift away and there were times when we were plunged back into the dark of night. It was at this very spot, where we're sitting now, that I realised that I had become separated from my section. All around was chaos, the plan had gone to rat shit, it was so confusing… gunfire, shouting, screaming, explosions… fear… shadows running in all directions. Nothing made any sense, although everything that I was seeing was just black and white images, no colour. I hadn't shot a single round, I hadn't been able to identify a legitimate target, but then it happened… I was laying down, hugging the ground, willing my body to melt into every small indentation in the earth in order to avoid the intensive, fierce, relentless onslaught of enemy fire. He was running towards me, screaming… it was dark, my rifle was made ready, safety catch off. I reacted. I aimed and pulled the trigger twice, a double tap, the screaming silhouette was instantly silenced and spun around like a… like a demented ballerina before crashing to the ground, moving no more." Nathaniel's father once again looked away from the bleeding rock and closed his eyes while shaking his head.

Nathaniel could see that tears were streaming down his father's face, dripping off his nose and his chin. His shoulders were shaking and he was wringing his hands together. He'd never seen his father like this before, he'd always been distant and cold, and Nathaniel had often thought that maybe it was himself who had put his father in the state of detached emotion that he'd grown up with. Listening to him now, that was obviously not the case. He wanted to reach out and reassure him, but just didn't have the courage to do it. He was shaking with adrenaline himself and just decided instead to wait for the conclusion of the story… if there was going to be one.

"Another flare lit up the scene," his father said, as he continued sobbing. "So, I slowly edged forward… I couldn't believe that I had actually shot a man… another human being. I didn't even know him… I didn't know anything about him. I wasn't angry at him, he was just a soldier like me, just doing a job, sent by *his* government to do *their* dirty work, a puppet of the Argentinian Junta… brainwashed into believing that his cause was just and right… at least that's what I thought." Nathaniel's father looked back at the rock. "The fog of war is a terrible thing you know… it's confusing and it's easy to lose your track of thought… but that's no excuse, some people might say. I needed to look him in the face, I needed to see him. I needed to know that at least he was dead, and he wasn't in some kind of terrible agony. I had no argument with him, I was just a scared kid." He paused for a long time before he turned and looked at Nathaniel straight in the eyes. "When I was close enough… I could see what I had done. It wasn't an Argentinian soldier after all!" At this point he fully broke down and burst into more floods of tears. He then slowly stood up and once again put his hand on his son's shoulder. "I'm so sorry," he said.

Nathaniel was totally confused.

His dad sobbed as he walked away towards the rock that was bleeding the tears of blood, and then he turned around and addressed his son for one last time.

"The person that I had shot, and killed, was my best friend… my mate… Chalky White. We went through training together and we were down here together, we were so close and, apart from the bravado of it all, we were both terrified… but I'd killed him. I never meant to… and you're the first person I've ever told. I think he was so petrified that he'd started running in the wrong direction… or maybe he was running away… I'll never know. I noticed afterwards that he'd lost his rifle. You know if I could change that one moment in time then I would give anything to undo it, but I can't… sometimes in life things can never be undone. So, what I'm trying to say to you, son, is that if you think someone is trying to hurt you… actually they might be screaming out for help. You can get things wrong sometimes… but then it's too late. I'm sorry that I got things between you and me wrong.

I'm so sorry and secrets aren't good… sometimes you need to ask for help… I wish I had now. I never wanted to see you here, not like this… I'm sorry, son. PTSD wasn't even a thing back then, it was never diagnosed or recognised, you just had to get on with it, stiff upper lip and all that shit. I'm sorry that I wasn't there for you… I wish that I had been."

His father turned and walked to the rock. He reached out and touched it, and when he did, he faded away, along with the desolate and lonely mountainside.

Nathaniel never got a chance to respond, he was too choked up to speak.

Chapter 10

Nathaniel woke up with a start… with a deep feeling of sadness inside of him, tinged with an element of shock. And then he suddenly realised where he was. The clearing in the copse had been lit up with a peculiar tone of light from the rising sun, or suns (he wasn't sure how that actually worked yet). Nevertheless, here he was, still in the Land of Khartoonz, lying on the grass at the foot of the Lego giant. The Wood Lobsters had maintained their defensive stance, and, as he looked up at Tiny Toppings, he could see the drops of morning dew that were covering the giant's multi-coloured plastic body, and which were steadily trickling down his towering frame. Nathaniel struggled to move his own body, being chilled to the bone as he was by the night time coldness. His clothes were damp and uncomfortable from the dew-laden grass, but he finally managed to get to his feet. Everything was still and quiet, and unusually for this time of the day, in the middle of a wood, he noticed that there were no birds singing… not even one chirp! It was then that he once more caught a glimpse of the shadow figure darting behind a tree.

'Who is that?' he thought. Maybe it was Artichoke? "WHO ARE YOU? WHAT DO YOU WANT?" he shouted out.

The Wood Lobsters instantly came to life and started scurrying around, clicking and clacking, alarmed by the sudden outburst.

Tiny Toppings creaked and groaned a deep groan. "What's going on?" he asked in his deep rumbling voice.

"There's something out there in the woods, following us. It keeps hiding," Nathaniel explained.

Tiny didn't answer straight away but then he pointed upwards with a creak of his arm and said, "It's time to start moving again, but don't worry because Albie's looking out for you." Then he turned back to the pathway and strode forward.

The Wood Lobsters obediently followed him and, as they disappeared from sight, Nathaniel turned his head to the sky and saw a large bird circling above him.

He was still reeling from his father's confession so he didn't immediately follow the group out of the clearing, but as he stood there contemplating his next move, something painfully struck him on the top of his head then bounced off into the grass. Rubbing his head in pain, he walked to where the object had landed and picked it up. It was an old penny, one of the big ones from before decimalisation was introduced back in the early 1970s. The date on it was 1962, but the strangest thing was that someone had gone to the trouble of engraving some words onto it, simply:

To FLO

From

MAM

And whoever the engraver was had taken the trouble to intricately underline the word Mam with curls on the end of the underlining. They were engraved onto the Queen's head side of the coin and not onto the tails side of Britannia, who was proudly sitting with her trident in her left hand, a shield by her side and a lighthouse in the background. He didn't know it, but the lighthouse depicted was one of the Seven Wonders of the World… it was the Pharos of Alexandria, a mausoleum, a place where the dead were kept… forever.

Chapter 11

Nathaniel stumbled out of the copse, a bruise on his head and a penny in his pocket. No longer could he hear the clacking of the Wood Lobsters or the creaking of Tiny. However, there was a clear path that he could walk upon, so he just decided to follow it and see where it would lead him.

•

After a while, he noticed a thinning of the trees to his left and a decline in the landscape, which led towards a view of something that seemed to resemble a flooded swamp-like area down below. He stopped and peered through the trees. Not only could he see the swamp, but he could also detect the sound of a constant swishing noise coming from the right. He moved further forward and craned his neck around one of the tree trunks. In the distance, he could clearly see a waterfall cascading majestically over a cliff face, a cloud of mist rising from the destination of its descent. The waterfall seemed to have no effect on the swamp, as it remained as still as a millpond. However, a few ripples on the surface of the swamp caught Nathaniel's eye. He concentrated his gaze and could make out a shape emerging from the water.

It was a long distance away but he could see that it was covered in hair and was muscular in build… and that it was moving slowly in his direction. Its movements were purposeful as it waded through the water. It was soon joined by other similar beings that, in turn, surfaced from underneath the marsh. Their faces were sad, and they emerged behind their leader and joined in the slow trudge through the marsh waters towards Nathaniel, who was now attempting to hide behind a tree.

They were moving slowly, but the most disconcerting thing was the stench emanating from them, which travelled towards him on the gentle breeze… they stank like a Benidorm sewer. There was also a depressing, subhuman, mournful, chant-like drone that began to penetrate the forest as they edged their way closer towards Nathaniel's position. It was very unnerving. They would soon make landfall and endeavour to seek him out.

He watched on intently, clinging to the tree, crouched down as the creatures got closer and closer. It wasn't long before the first of them reached the shore. It crawled out of the swamp and stood up, shaking itself in order to rid its long black fur of the stinking water.

Nathaniel peeped out to take a look… the creature was ape-like, resembling a chimpanzee but larger, and stood on its two legs quite comfortably. Its legs were longer than a chimp's, and, even from this distance, he could see that its long fingers had menacing talons that nearly reached to the ground. The animal was scouring the area and sniffing the air in an obvious attempt to locate its target. The depressing droning noise had become very painful to Nathaniel's ears, and as more of the creatures began to haul themselves out of the swamp, he absolutely realised that whatever had happened before, it was now that he really did need help.

The first creature, which was larger than the others, located him and fixed him with a stare that felt like being plunged into a bath full of icy water. Its demonic red lizard-like eyes were unforgiving in their malicious intent… and that's when Nathaniel reached out for help. The creature's gaze was terrifying and, after first looking away because he was so afraid, he felt compelled to look back at it and very quickly in his state of terrified paralysis… Nathaniel blacked out.

Chapter 12

Life in the treehouse had been tense since Nathaniel had told them to go away. Nelly had told Artichoke not to dwell on it, he would probably come back... sometimes they did, sometimes they didn't.

Nelly was curled up asleep on top of the table in the centre of the round room, while Artichoke was wide awake, sat in front of a very large glass screen and nibbling on a bowl of chestnuts and brambles. The screen enabled him to view the live images that were projected back to him by a series of mirrors and lenses that he'd secured to tree trunks and other places around the vicinity. This system was known as a camera obscura. He'd worked out that by using the light of the two suns at various times of the day, and the several moons at various times of the night, when he followed the correct angles of ascent and descent, the images reflected back were a perfect real time scene of what was happening at that place, at that exact moment.

He was now staring at Nathaniel cowering behind a tree. He put the bowl of fruit down and craned forward to look closely at the mirror.

'Oh no!' he thought. Then "OH NO!" he shouted out.

The mute image of Nathaniel's terrified face turned to the screen and, before anything else happened, Nathaniel, unaware of exactly what he was seeing coming towards him, managed to mouth the words "Help me someone… please!"

Artichoke immediately jumped up. "NELLY WE'VE GOT TO GO… NOW."

The cat jumped off the table in a state of shock. "What's going on?"

"Nathaniel's recalling us. He's at the Grim Valley Mires near to the Razorfish Falls… in the grip of the Grimpanzees. There's no way we can let them get a hold of him or else that'll be the end of it."

So they raced to the wooden elevator and rushed to the aid, once again, of Nathaniel.

"Look before we leap," said Nelly, pulling Artichoke up short by gently clawing on his ears. "Look up there, over there."

Artichoke looked up to where Nelly was pointing his paw and in the distance he observed what looked like a large bird circling in the sky.

"It's Albie… he knows exactly where Nathaniel is. He's making it easier for us to find him," explained Nelly.

Artichoke leapt onto the elevator, the platform creaking and groaning on its ropes and pulleys as it descended to the forest floor. It hit the deck, and Artichoke, with Nelly in the backpack, made a good clean dispersal and darted off into the forest in the direction of the Grim Valley Mires.

Chapter 13

Nathaniel opened his eyes and immediately realised that he was lying on his back, but also that he was no longer in the woodland staring at the strange beasts.

He was staring at a blue sky littered with white clouds, and he was in motion… he was slowly rotating. The air was warm and heavy with the scent of blossom, and, as he began to acclimatise himself to his new situation, he felt like he was an astronaut staring down at planet Earth, at the blue oceans beneath him… and he felt enraptured by the awesome scene below him.

Mesmerized by the image, he was suddenly jolted by a memory that took him right back in time to when he was a child.

It was summertime, he was in a small playground in his hometown of Saltburn-by-the-Sea and he was alone, lying on his back on the roundabout… not the magic one on the telly but one that felt much more magical than that… it felt like real magic. It propelled him, using the power of his curious imagination, miles into the air and allowed him to observe the enormity of the planet he knew as his home but that instilled in him a yearning and wanderlust to explore every inch of its mysterious places with the promise of a million new experiences and adventures. He felt like a time traveller and wondered where his reality would lead him in the future, he wished for adventure and wondered what that would be like.

It was early in the morning and he was the only kid in the playground. Eventually, the roundabout stopped rotating and he lay there for a while contemplating his next move… which would be the real reason why he'd come here.

A couple of weeks ago, he'd accidently discovered somewhere. It was close to the playground but it was somewhere he wanted to keep a secret from anyone else. He sat up and looked cautiously around to make sure that he wasn't being spied upon. He wasn't, so he dismounted from the roundabout and made his way to the edge of the woodland which started at the top of the valley and eventually led to the stream below. He made his way into the undergrowth, through the nettles with his arms held high, and proceeded down into the dark seclusion of the woods. He knew that it wouldn't take that long to reach his objective but still he'd have to be cautious with his footing as the terrain was on an incline and covered with tripping hazards of overgrown plants and slippery soil. The last steps were always the most precarious because of the steepness of the slope, but he went for it and, just as he thought that he might overshoot his target with his feet slipping beneath him, he reached out with open arms and crashed into his newest best friend, embracing it… embracing its solid trunk… and with its distinctive pungent bitter smell, Nathaniel knew immediately that it was the right one… it was a crab apple tree, and it was his sanctuary.

He stayed still for a time, regaining his breath and composure while thinking of the challenge ahead of him. He knew that in order to reach his secluded place of peace and solitude, he would have to take courage and risk life and limb to get there. He'd done it before and he knew the route but each time he attempted the ascent, it never got any easier or any less terrifying. The first challenge was actually managing to get onto the first big branch which just outreached his grasp, so he'd devised a method of taking a run up then launching himself into the air with his feet on the trunk and his arms outstretched above his head in order to grab the limb. So, taking a few deep breaths, he went for it and, totally committing himself to the task, he got it first time. Quickly though he knew that he'd have to pull himself up or else his energy would fail him. He clambered upwards and managed to haul his body onto the security of the first branch. Gasping for air, he clung on for dear life, straddling the branch and staring at the woodland floor which seemed to be a very long way below him. He took his time and stole himself because he knew that this was just the start and that he had a long way to go yet.

He regained his composure and sat up with his back against the tree trunk, then he looked up. In order to progress, he'd have to continue climbing, up above to his left was another branch and in order to reach it he would have to stand up. This particular manoeuvre always took more balls to achieve than you'd find on a dozen snooker tables, but he knew that he'd have to do it in order to get up to where he wanted to be. The first thing that he'd previously learnt was that he had to move slowly, no knee jerk reactions. Tentatively using the trunk as a support for his back, a foot and leg at a time he slowly raised himself into a standing position, just like a gymnast on the four-inch beam. Once he was upright, he fixed his sight on the branch to his left. It was reachable... at a stretch. He looked at it then focused on his next move, which he would have to execute quickly using his gained momentum. It would be a quick right arm grab, spinning himself in order to grab the next highest branch while placing his feet in a secure position. He knew that once he'd succeeded with this it would be relatively plain sailing to make it to the top of the tree... as long as he didn't look down.

So once again he thought about it, but not for too long... then he launched himself skywards... and he made it. He clung on for a while, then looking upwards, he ascended the comparatively easier route up through the branches and canopy of the tree until he reached the top.

The view up there was breathtaking. He was perched very comfortably and safely in his lofty position, like an eagle in its nest, and he had no interest in moving at any time soon. Surrounded by leaves, small green crab apples and various types of insects, he was at peace with the world and, from up here in his total isolation, he could observe the comings and goings of the busy people below him, who were so busy at just being busy... and for what reason? And what did he care anyway?

The blue North Sea was clearly visible, as was the profile

of the majestic Huntcliff, a familiar geographical feature that was going to play a massive role in his future, a future that he could never have dreamt of at this point in his life. He stared at the horizon like he'd previously stared at the sky above him on the roundabout and wondered what all the busy people were doing on the other side of the sea, in another country, in another life, in a different world to the one that he knew and lived in.

At that point, a busy honeybee landed on his hand as if in acknowledgement of his thought and then, just as quickly, it took off again.

He loved it up there. Nobody knew he was there; he could happily spend the rest of his life up there.

The problem was the thing called reality… the things at the bottom of the tree, the roots of problems, and he'd always found that it was easier climbing up than it was coming down. He never wanted to come down but he knew that eventually he would always have to, and face whatever reality was put in front of him.

It was then that a beautiful butterfly landed on the branch he was sitting on, within touching distance. He observed its beauty and then tentatively reached out to it. The creature fluttered away but then he saw that the space it had just occupied had been replaced by an envelope. And the envelope had his name on it, as well as an address – 121 Crab Apple Street – which made no sense to him at all.

So he tried reaching even further, astounded that someone else had actually managed to get up here, somebody who obviously knew him and had discovered his private sanctuary. And he was even more perplexed that they'd left him a letter, and had placed it out of reach.

He would never remember what happened next, because it was then that he lost his balance…

Chapter 14

He awoke from his dream with a start. He was flat on his back but someone was on top of him.

"I'm sorry," said Artichoke. "I tried to catch you but you came down so hard."

Nathaniel blinked and tried to make sense of things. Artichoke Underwood was lying on top of him, and they were back on the path that stank of sewers.

He looked over Artichoke's shoulder and saw the Grimpanzee. It had stopped dead in its tracks, snarling and frothing at the mouth, saliva dripping off its viscous incisors, but seemingly distracted from Nathaniel. The rest of the troop had stopped at the water's edge, quite a long way back looking on, and they had begun to hoot and holler in unison, in support of their leader.

The beast was looking down, and it was then that Nathaniel noticed Nelly standing his ground at the foot of the monster, back arched, fur on end, and hissing and screeching. It was a sound so horrific that even in this situation it made Nathaniel's blood run cold.

"Just lie still," said Artichoke. "He knows what he's doing. It's not the first time he's had to do this."

Nathaniel said nothing but just lay still and observed the scene that was unfolding before him. The Grimpanzee looked furiously angry and frustrated by what had come between it and its intended target. It was now nervously moving sideways from foot to foot and changing its gaze from the ferocious cat at its feet and the two hapless individuals lying on the forest path.

Nelly took a step forward and increased his menacing wailing, baring his teeth like a sabre-toothed tiger. The Grimpanzee grunted with a sound of reluctant disdain and then Nelly launched himself at the creature's leg with his paws outstretched and claws fully out. He wrapped himself around the animal's limb and bit deep into the hairy flesh of the beast.

The reaction was immediate… the monster stumbled backwards, screaming in shock and pain, trying to retreat back in the direction of the swamp whilst attempting to remove the attacker from its leg.

Job done, Nelly jumped off and raced back to join the others. The Grimpanzee hobbled back down to its morbid abode, continuously looking back over its shoulder. As it got closer to the mire, the hollering and hooting of the others died down and the depressing droning resumed until it got quieter and quieter and eventually ceased. The ape-like creature slowly waded back into the swamp, followed by its troop of fellow Grimpanzees.

"You've had a close call," said Artichoke. "That was Grimaldi, he's the chief of the Grimpanzees and, whenever he gets the chance, he will gladly drain the very soul from your body, laughing as he does it. Don't let him. We're here to help you *remember*, it's our job… but only if you want us to help you. It's your call, and you called us."

Nelly wandered up beside them, and squaring up to

Nathaniel's face, he looked him in the eyes. "You shouldn't drift off on your own… unless we ask you to, that is," he said, panting out of breath. "Just because you think that you're on your own. You're *never* on your own… *we're* here. Your friends are here… your family is here… right in there…" Nelly put a paw on Nathaniel's chest over his heart. "You might not feel it *all* of the time it, but it's true. Sometimes you just have to suck it up, be humble and accept the fact that you can't do it all by yourself."

Nathaniel didn't respond as Artichoke got off him, picked up his hat and stood up and regained his composure as Nelly jumped up onto his shoulder and into the backpack.

Nathaniel struggled to his feet and brushed himself down.

"So, this is your second chance in the Land of Khartoonz," Artichoke informed him. "Are you coming or not?" And without waiting for the answer, he set off up the path that led away from the Grim Valley Mires.

With no hesitation at all, Nathaniel followed … hard on Artichoke's heels.

Chapter 15

Hello once again, my friend. Thank you for staying with me and welcome back to the attic. From the last time that we spoke, our poor distressed hero of the unknown has become educated with things that are now known, by some who have already been there and walked up the lonely path of life. Whatever happens to him next will be totally dependent on his ability to see the wood from the trees, a lie from a fake, a day from a night, a reason to live.

And by the way, some of the spiders above me have started to descend on their silken threads, curious as to what is happening. Don't be alarmed, I'm sure they mean us no harm!

My dear friend, one day the daylight will turn into blackness forever, and you won't have a choice about it. The blinds will shut and the curtain will finally come down. The end. Everything that you ever wanted to achieve will never happen, all of those dreams will never come to fruition, and nobody will ever get to know about your ambitions… you know, the ones you never talk about. But at this point in time, he does have a choice… most people never do! He is very, very lucky. And he has the lucky penny!

The candle is burning shorter but I will endeavour to continue, so I dip the nib once more into the ink and resume my scratchings on the parchment.

And don't let the spiders spook you… surely they are friendly? Aren't they?

Chapter 16

Nathaniel trudged on, resigned to the fact that he needed someone to lead him onwards. God only knew what had happened to Tiny Toppings and his scuttling wooden entourage. He was relieved though that he'd been rescued from the Grimpanzees and he was glad that he had company that he thought he could trust.

What choice did he have? Lost in a strange world with even stranger people to guide him, the only thing that he could practically do was to put one foot in front of the other and try to get to The Point as soon as possible, and then maybe all of this madness would start to make sense.

They'd travelled a long distance in silence, Artichoke leading the way with Nathaniel following obediently, like a subordinate pupil following his teacher on an unwanted but necessary nature trail. They were still in the woods and the path seemed to be endless, every time they approached a corner, Nathaniel's hopes were raised, hoping that he might see a different landscape before them, but time and time again it was relentless, until they eventually came to a place where the trees thinned out and they found themselves at a crossroads.

Relieved at the pause in the mundane yomp, Nathaniel stopped when Artichoke ceased walking and pointed at a road sign before them. "You now have a choice, once again," he told him.

Nathaniel stepped forward so that he could read the words on the raised and weather worn wooden sign that stood at the crossroad's corner. And although they were stood at the meeting of four separate roads, there were only three clear choices, none of the signs pointed back towards the way they'd just come from:

The sign pointing to the left said 'ABANDON ALL HOPE'

The sign pointing to the right said 'I DON'T CARE'

The sign pointing forwards said 'THE VILLAGE'

'Abandon All Hope' sounded like an appalling choice, the 'I Don't Care' made him shake his head and actually smile – the first time in a long time – but the idea of 'The Village' actually raised his spirits… that there might be a community of different individuals that could possibly shed more light onto his strange predicament.

"So what do you think?" asked Artichoke.

"I'd like to go to The Village," Nathaniel replied.

"Good choice," shouted Nelly, without making the effort of emerging from the comfort of the backpack.

"Why not the I Don't Care?" asked Artichoke.

When Nathaniel just froze and didn't speak a word, Artichoke immediately knew that he really did care, but he wasn't willing to admit it… just yet.

And so they set off again moving forward in the direction of The Village.

"Without meaning to bore you," said Nathaniel, "when

are we going to get to the point of all of this? I mean, when are we going to get to The Point?"

Artichoke stopped, turned around and looked up at Nathaniel. "You have to understand that you have done something that catastrophically impacts not just on yourself but all of your family and friends and anyone who has ever met you. So, taking that on board, I think that it might be good of you to stop whinging and thinking about yourself and maybe realise that you are getting a second chance here to put things in order. Whether or not you choose to do that is entirely up to you, but this is my job, so once again I say let's just keep moving forward and see what happens… okay?"

Nathaniel was impressed and slightly shocked with Artichoke's outburst, but the honesty of his sentiments were appreciated, so he just nodded his head and replied, "Okay."

And so they moved forward on the path that would lead them to The Village.

Chapter 17

As they advanced up the path Nathaniel observed that the ground that he was walking on was becoming muddier and the plants at the side of the path were beginning to look like weeds. The word 'weeds' immediately sparked a memory within him…

He was transported back to a time when he was a small child and he found himself in a garden. It must have been spring or early summer because it was warm and he was wearing shorts and a T-shirt. He had a garden fork in his hand, which he found large and unwieldy, but he was on his knees at the side of a flowerbed trying his best to turn over the soil. He looked up and noticed some plants that probably weren't supposed to be there, at the point where the flowerbed met the hedge. He stopped what he was doing and turned his head around to address the person who was accompanying him on his gardening duties… after all, it was this man's garden.

"Grandad," he called out.

The old man with the long white beard and the thin white hair, who Nathaniel had always thought looked suspiciously like Father Christmas but in normal clothes, stopped hoeing the soil on the opposite side and turned to face him.

"Yes, vot is it?"

"Should I dig these weeds up and get rid of them?" Nathaniel asked, pointing at the plants with the fork.

The old man looked to where he was pointing, and sighed and paused. Then he took a step toward the boy, and then he paused again and looked at the so-called *weeds*, then back at Nathaniel. He leaned on his garden hoe then began to speak. "You're doing a good job, and I zhank you for zat. I appreciate you helping me out, it's important zat you know zat. Ve all need to help each other out during our lives."

Nathaniel, even though he was young and used to his grandad's strange way of speaking, sensed that there was a lesson coming, like the ones that he had to endure at his infant school, nevertheless he remained still and silent in his respect for the old man. Still on his knees, he looked up and listened.

"You have to understand zat just because some people label zings as one zing, it doesn't mean zat you have to accept zheir definition of it." The old man glanced down at the boy and realised that he was struggling with the explanation, so he tried to make it simpler. "Look at ze flowers on zose so-called veeds." Nathaniel did. "Are zey not as pretty as ze rest of ze flowers in ze garden?"

Nathaniel looked and nodded, some of the flowers on the so-called *veeds* were even more delicate and coloured than the ones on the proper ones that his grandad had planted.

"Vhen I vas your age, maybe a little older, a black cloud moved over ze place vhere I lived. Zhere vere evil men who decided zat *I* vas a veed and that *I* should be pulled out of ze ground and disposed of, just like unvanted trash." The old man looked away and took a few deep breaths, and when he looked back Nathaniel noticed that that there were tears in his eyes and one was actually running down his cheek.

It was at that point that Nathaniel saw that the sleeve of his grandad's shirt had risen up and he observed a strange blurred arrangement of letters and numbers on his grandad's forearm. It was an observation that Nathaniel wouldn't make the connection with for many years to come.

"Vhat you have to remember is zat everything in zis garden has a right to be here and who are ve to judge vhat should stay and vhat should go?"

Nathaniel had no answer.

His grandad looked away and then up at the sky, then after a while he looked back at the boy. "So who am I to make that decision in my own garden? Am I God? Am I the god of zis garden? Vhat do you think?" he asked.

The question was fired directly at the young Nathaniel, who was totally perplexed, and it was only by the *grace* of God that his grandma shouted out from the backdoor. "Alphonse, Nathaniel, your soup is ready."

Nathaniel always thought this strange because everyone else, apart from his grandma, who addressed his grandad actually called him Albert!

His grandad took a deep breath. "Von more zing, never let anybody put you in a cage and tell you who you are and how *you* should behave. Never let ze oppressor vin.

You are a young boy as I vas vonce and I have been lucky… I mean look at me now, I am old and I am a free man but vhen I was a boy I vitnessed too many lives being cut short, people who never had ze chance to grow up, innocent people, innocent children… too many. Let me ask you a question, do you believe in reincarnation?"

The young Nathaniel innocently but respectfully shrugged his shoulders at the old man, he had no idea even what that word meant.

"Let me quickly explain, and I'm telling you zis because I do believe in it. You see vhen a person dies, or any living zhing for zat matter zey can come back to life as anozer person or animal or I suppose as any living zing. Maybe zose so-called veeds over zere, vere vonce people and zey have been reincarnated as zose plants… for vhatever reason."

Nathaniel just stared at his grandad in wonderment and confusion at this revelation.

"So have you any idea vot I vould like to come back as?"

Nathaniel shook his head, he had no idea what his grandad's choice would be.

The old man took a step toward him and, with a grin and a sparkle in his still bright blue eyes, threw his head and hands towards the sky and announced, "Before I eventually come back as anozer person I vant to be a bird of course, a high flying bird zat is free from everything zat ties us down. Free from the vorries and concerns having to live next door to each other in each other's pockets and compromise on how ve have to behave and conduct ourselves." He lowered his arms and gazed at Nathaniel. "You are lucky, you are still young, so be yourself and be vhatever you vant to be and don't let anybody tell you any different. Zhere are too many who vent before you who never got ze chance. And another zing, on your journey zrough your life, if you ever lose your shadow zen zat means zat ze sun has disappeared and zat's vhen you lose hope. You have to seek out ze sunshine and ze daylight and try to avoid ze darkness and ze cold of ze night time, because vithout your shadow you have no light, and without ze sunshine you have no hope. Always turn your head towards ze sun."

Just then, his grandma's scolding voice shouted from inside the kitchen. "Your soup's getting cold, stop all this yakkety-yakking and come inside!"

"Come on, let's go," Nathaniel's grandad gestured with his head towards the back door which led to the kitchen.

Nathaniel stood up and his grandad put his hand on Nathaniel's shoulder. "Just remember zat life is short… very short sometimes… and even zhough it can be hard as you go along, don't take it too seriously… enjoy ze good times and ze good zhings. C'mon, let's go and have some zoop. I think it's leek and potato today, and I know zat there's fresh varm bread just out of ze oven."

"Yes, I can smell it, Grandad," smiled Nathaniel, as they made their way into the house with the promise of fresh soup and bread.

"And do you know vhy I know that zhe bread is fresh?"

"No," Nathaniel replied.

"Because I got out of bed, even zough it was dark,

before ze sun came up zhis morning to start making it because I knew zhat you vere coming here, and I know how much you like it, and because you always bring sunshine into my life."

On occasion Nathaniel would sleep over at his grandparent's house and he'd observed that when he went up the stairs to bed, at the same time as his grandma, his grandad would be left sitting in his place on the sofa, and when he awoke in the morning and went downstairs his grandad would once again be sat in his place on the sofa, wide awake. Nathaniel pondered on the question of 'Does Grandad even go to bed?' Or even go to sleep, as if he was the nightwatchman on sentry duty… guarding them all from the monsters that lurked in the darkness in the dead of night? Or was he always the last one up and the first one down the stairs when everyone else was sleeping? He never asked. He could never be that rude and disrespectful.

At that point Nathaniel felt like crying, he loved his grandad, and, even at his young age, he knew that he wouldn't be around forever, sharing his words of wisdom… and love. And he was right, because shortly after that incident his grandad sadly passed away.

And so it was a shame that at the moment when he'd recently been stood on the edge of the cliff, he hadn't managed to recall his grandad's words that day back in the garden. Sadly, along the way, they'd been lost amidst the clutter and fog of his dysfunctional present existence, although now they were as clear as day to him… he hoped that it wasn't too late. And he also hoped that somehow he might be able to do justice to the memory of his grandad and his priceless and timeless advice.

Chapter 18

It was only when he stumbled over a rock on the path that he was shaken out of his childhood recollections… the memories that had unfortunately slipped his mind when they were definitely most needed.

He was back in the Land of Khartoonz and Artichoke was still in front of him. He looked down and realised that the path beneath his feet was changing from mud into cobblestones, and the further they walked forward the more pronounced and structured the cobblestone path became, until it was no longer a path but a narrow road. The daylight was starting to dim as the unusual sunset began to take place.

"We're nearly there," announced Artichoke. "When we get there you'll have to proceed on your own."

"Why?" asked Nathaniel.

"It's just the rules of The Village. But be careful, the locals are very wary of strangers."

"So what do I do?" Nathaniel was now feeling extremely anxious and concerned.

Nelly popped his head up. "All you have to do is make it to the other side of The Village and we'll meet you there. We'll be waiting for you."

It soon became dark and then light again, but shortly the second sun finally set plunging them into total darkness, and, as they wandered further up the road, the first streetlights of The Village came into view. They advanced forward until they were at the end of the woods and the start of The Village.

"This is where we have to leave you for now," explained Nelly.

"You just have to do what you have to do," offered Artichoke. "And hopefully we'll see you on the other side."

They stood there in silence for a few moments and then Artichoke slapped him reassuringly on the arm and turned away disappearing back in the direction of which they had arrived.

Nathaniel was alone once again, and as he looked in front of him towards the street of cobblestones and the rickety buildings with its sparse street lighting and suggestion of hidden danger, he knew that he'd have to muster up all of his courage to put one foot in front of the other and enter this theatre of the unknown.

As he walked forward, just as he'd done not so long ago on the edge of the cliff, he thought, 'I've been here before… does this actually ever end?'

But there was no answer forthcoming, and he knew that in all honesty, there wouldn't ever be one.

•

Artichoke retreated back into the woods with Nelly in the backpack, kicking loose Lego bricks off the path and into the undergrowth. He found a safe place and then he rolled up his jacket sleeve to reveal a watch-like piece of equipment that basically consisted of a leather strap and a small circular screen. He manoeuvred his wrist around in all directions until, using the light from the three moons above, he finally located the signal from the camera obscura and observed Nathaniel wandering up the path towards The Village.

Chapter 19

Nathaniel moved cautiously but with purpose. He knew that he had to get through The Village in order to get to The Point. He was aware of the strange three moons that hung in the sky above him that added extra illumination to the ominous environment that he found himself in… although their presence gave little comfort to his predicament.

He guessed that he must be walking down the High Street and soon came to the first two side roads leading off from it. They both had street signs, the one to his right said PENNYDRAGON LANE which seemed to disappear down into darkness, and the one to his left said CRAB APPLE STREET which took a sharp decline but was lit by tall gas lamps. Although he was curious to see what might be down both of them, he resisted the temptation to explore as the urge to actually get out of The Village was greater, so he pressed on. He'd become aware of how deserted the place was, even though there were a few lights on inside some of the buildings that he was passing, there was no sign of life until someone stepped out of the shadows and blocked his path.

Nathaniel stopped walking.

In front of him was a tall, well-dressed man who looked like a gentleman dandy from Georgian times back in the *real* world. His facial features were sharp and chiselled, a bit like a squashed weasel's face might look, and he was wearing a silver coloured top hat. He was also carrying a silver topped cane. The man smiled and raised his hat in a well-intentioned greeting.

"Ahh," he said, "I knew you were coming this way, someone had already informed me. News travels fast around these parts. Some people get tipped off beforehand, but some people don't. No matter, there's always a way to find out information… there's always a snake in the grass, it's amazing what some people will tell you for the promise of a penny… a pretty penny that is."

It was then that Nathaniel felt the presence of someone else behind him, and looking around, sure enough there was another man… shorter in stature and wearing a bowler hat. The man was smiling and, as he looked Nathaniel up and down, he started to circle around him like a hyena inspecting its intended prey.

"Please excuse me, I haven't even introduced myself or my well intentioned partner. My name is Horatio Lambert and this is my assistant, Mr Kraken T Butler."

Mr Butler nodded towards Nathaniel in a gesture of greeting.

Nathaniel did not return the gesture and said nothing in response to Lambert's introduction.

"Very well then," continued Lambert as he took a step forward, leaning on his cane and looking Nathaniel directly in the eyes. "Like I have said, news travels fast around these parts and it has come to my attention that you have gained the possession of a penny from heaven…

am I correct?" Lambert's tone had become assertive and intimidating.

Nathaniel wanted no part of this conversation and so decided to become assertive himself. "Excuse me, gentlemen, but we have nothing to discuss, so I'll be on my way."

He took a step forward in order to bypass Lambert but the top-hatted gent quickly raised his cane up and blocked the exit route. Nathaniel tried to side step in order to get past but immediately felt someone grab him by the elbow. It was Butler, grinning with excitement, his breath smelling like a thousand filthy ashtrays.

"Now, now, let's not be hasty. Would you like one of these?" said Lambert, holding out an open packet of cigarettes.

Nathaniel was very tempted, very tempted indeed, but his gut instincts told him that it was a trap so he didn't take the bait.

"Alright then, it's quite simple. You just give me the coin and then you can be on your way." Lambert stretched his palm out towards Nathaniel. Nothing happened, there was a moment's silence and then Lambert roared into Nathaniel's face, raising his cane.

"GIVE ME THE COIN, YOU BLOODY IMBECILE!" he screamed.

Nathaniel took a step backwards and tried to escape from Butler's grip, but to no avail.

Kraken T Butler was obviously no stranger to these situations and immediately restrained Nathaniel by both arms.

"You can't have it. *I'm* keeping it," Nathaniel shouted, as he'd already realised the importance of the gift from up above earlier on and although he didn't understand it at the moment, he knew that it must be worth much more than just the face value of an old penny or a cigarette.

"Well, if that's the way you want to play it," said Lambert, "I need to introduce you to a few of my friends, who are no gentlemen and who, unlike me, haven't got the patience to waste time! Summon them!" Lambert ordered, striking his sidekick on the arm with his cane, but instead of obeying, Butler released Nathaniel and started to back off. The man in the bowler hat looked terrified, whimpering and pointed over Lambert's shoulder

Lambert spun around to see what Butler was already staring at… standing at the corner of the next street about thirty feet away was the undeniable silhouette of the Shadow Stalker.

"Quick, Butler! Run away! That's the other side of *you*, Phischermann… the part that you've disconnected from. It only joins you when you're in the light and then only when you choose to capture it again. We want nothing to do with it, but mark my words, we'll be back for you." Lambert pushed Nathaniel to the floor, and then he and Butler sprinted off down the High Street and disappeared into the darkness.

Nathaniel looked up towards the Shadow Stalker and stood up.

"WHO ARE YOU?" he shouted out again.

The shadow didn't answer, merely turned and melted away around the corner of the street.

Nathaniel jumped up and sprinted off to pursue the mysterious character, determined to reveal its identity once and for all.

Chapter 20

When he reached and turned the corner, he paused. He was looking down another dim street. It was lit by a few sparse old-fashioned gas lamps, and, as he peered on, he couldn't make out any movement or shadow that would indicate the presence of the Shadow Stalker. The only thing that caught his eye was the light cast onto the cobblestones about halfway down to his left, there were buildings either side of the street but this was the only one that had light emanating from within. He proceeded with caution, aware that Lambert and Butler could ambush him at any point.

As he approached the building, he saw a sign hanging from the outside wall above the front door. More to the point, he could hear the sound of merriment and laughter coming from within. When he was close enough he saw the sign that proclaimed the establishment was called, The First and Last, and it was obviously a public house.

He peered through one of the windows and observed a scene of happiness… everyone inside seemed to be enjoying each other's company, at some of the tables it could even have been described as riotous laughter. He walked on a few steps and looked at the flyer in one of the windows…

TONIGHT IS COMEDY NIGHT
FEATURING:
FLOTSAM AND JETSAM
BENSON AND HEDGES
Phloem and Xylem
Brahms and Liszt
AND OF COURSE OUR RESIDENT BAND
THE SEA CREATURES
Plus Late Night Heavy Metal:
Bentley Nevada Wobulator

Nathaniel looked up at the metal plaque that was displayed above the front door and it read:

Mr Stanley Blumenthal
Licensed to sell all intoxicating liquor for consumption on these premises.

He looked around and deciding that he had nothing to lose, he took a deep breath and entered The First and Last.

He went nervously through the door as he was expecting everything to stop like in one of those old Western movies when even the piano player ceased playing, but that didn't happen. Nobody actually acknowledged him, they were all so engrossed within their own social situations, so he edged his way through the crowd towards the bar area. It was only a small pub – olde world, if you like – it was certainly no modern day Wetherspoons.

The one thing that instantly struck him was the fog of tobacco smoke that hung in the air. He observed people stubbing cigarettes out into ashtrays and even a few older men and women smoking clay pipes. At the far end of the bar was a small stage.

He was now very dubious about whether or not to actually approach the bar and order a drink as he had no money on him… then he laughed to himself… 'What is the currency in the Land of Khartoonz anyway?' he thought. 'Mickey Mouse money, probably.'

Well, there was only one way to find out. He had nothing to lose and patiently waited until he managed to force himself into a space at the bar.

"What will you be having, old boy?" asked the old gentlemen behind the bar.

"Just a pint of lager, please… whatever it is you do," Nathaniel answered.

"Ahh, so you come from over there, do you? I was warned that you were coming. Well, we don't have anything like that over on this side, you're going to have to pick something else… so what will it be?"

"Fair enough. What do you have?" Nathaniel asked.

"There's only two choices of ale available here, one's called The Way Forward and the other one's called The Way Backwards. So what will it be?"

He was about to ask which one that the landlord would suggest when he noticed that the people around him had become a lot quieter in their conversation, as if in anticipation of his answer. Indeed, as he looked from side to side, it was apparent that some of them were even staring at him. It was obvious that in this environment the only answer should be a positive one.

"I'll have a pint of The Way Forward, please," he said.

The landlord nodded in agreement and began to pour a pint, and immediately the people around him resumed their amiable chatter.

"Get down!" shouted the landlord at something that was obviously bothering him at his feet. "Henry, get down! You'll have to excuse him, he gets so excited when someone new comes into The Village."

Nathaniel made the assumption that Henry must be the landlord's pet dog.

"No problem. How much do I owe you?" he asked as the man placed the drink in front of him.

"Well, I normally charge a penny but the word is out that you only have one, so I'll set up a tab for you... we'll square it up later on, you know, further on up the road." The landlord then turned his attention to the next customer as The Sea Creatures took to the stage.

Chapter 21

He'd been there a while, having taken up a position at the bar near the front of the stage. The band had been good and he'd enjoyed listening to the songs. They were a strange pair of women… a singer who played electric violin, and a drummer who certainly knew her way around a drum kit.

And you could have knocked him off his feet at the next song that they played.

"This one is for our friend at the bar," the singer said, looking in his direction. "This song was written by Nathaniel Phischermann, who has graced us with his presence tonight." She looked in his direction, pointed her bow at him and winked.

He was gobsmacked at what was happening as most of the audience turned and smiled at him, some of the closer members even patted him on the shoulders.

"This is a ballad and it's called *Back to the Lunar Module*, which is all about someone who has lost his way and realises that he really needs to go home. And it goes something like this… in fact, it goes exactly like this…"

She began to play her violin and then started to sing…

All alone tonight,
Where has the feeling gone?
Where has the meaning gone?
All alone tonight,
The sky's from blue to grey,
I could not wait today.
All communications lost,
I'm running back to the Lunar Module.

All alone tonight,
I tried to field the pain,
But I was wrong again.
All alone with you,
I could not see the worth,
I wanna come down to earth.
All communications lost,
I'm running back to the Lunar Module.

I suddenly find a way I can break it,
It's the only way I can take it,
I've only got myself to blame,
And now I'm freedom fighting.
To go it alone and flow with the violent,
But no man is an island.
I only hope I'm not too far,
And you're still in my orbit.

All alone tonight,
"Come on you," I could say,
"And save my life today."

All across this space,
Throw me your smile so fine,
And be my lifeline.
All communications lost,
I'm running back to the Lunar Module.

All alone, alone tonight,
Alone, tonight, tonight, tonight,
All alone, alone tonight.
Alone, tonight, tonight, tonight, tonight, tonight…

Nathaniel was dumbstruck and, for a moment, the crowd just looked on in stunned silence, but then the band left the stage to rapturous applause and the bar was flooded with eager punters waiting to order their next round of refreshments.

Having eavesdropped on the bar chatter in between songs, it seemed like the support act – who were called Benson and Hedges – had already been on and done their turn, and the headlining act of Flotsam and Jetsam were up next, topping the bill.

He'd been slowly sipping his pint of beer, which actually tasted quite good. And he was fully aware that he only had a penny in his pocket and he couldn't afford any more, but more than that, he knew that the penny in his possession had a deeper special meaning than just the price of a pint of beer. He had no intention of parting with it, however dishonest that might be.

Even in the crowded pub, Nathaniel was very aware of the landlord's constant suspicious glancing at him, even when he was more than occupied with serving the other customers.

He needed to keep a hold of the penny, the one that the bird had dropped on him, the one that was engraved with a cryptic message. He needed to leave the bar for a moment,.

"Excuse me," he said, turning to the person on his left, "where are the toilets in here?"

"Just over there, of course," the obviously intoxicated individual – who was bizarrely dressed like a court jester – laughed out loud and pointed to everywhere, flailing his arms in all directions. "Good luck, hope you find 'em, and by the way that was a bloody good song what you wrote, you should keep it up. You know that Rome wasn't built in a teacup, don't ya? Don't give in, you jest don't know what's around the corner! Maybe even the loos, if you're lucky, jest don't run around like a blue-arsed, headless chicken." The Jester burst out laughing. "My name's Lester and I'm very pleased to meet ya."

"Yes, likewise," Nathaniel replied, putting his glass down on the bar before standing up and politely headed for the door through which he'd entered the building, moving through the throng of the crowd, smiling all the way. He eventually reached the exit and opened the door, the fresh air immediately hit him and it was such a welcome change from the atmosphere he was leaving. And then a hand landed heavily upon his shoulder.

"Going to spend a penny, are we?"

It was the landlord.

Nathaniel froze, unsure of what to do.

"You've got a tab to settle with me," said the landlord.

"Can we sort it out tomorrow?" Was Nathaniel's quick and quite pathetic response.

The landlord's eyes widened threateningly in a serious mood of intimidation, but then after a few seconds, he burst out into guffaws of laughter, releasing his grip on Nathaniel's shoulder.

"If you come back, you'll be the first one that ever has. You're all the same you lot from over there… full of promises. Although you might appreciate this," he said, handing Nathaniel a business card. "You might want to stay there tonight, instead of aimlessly wandering around."

Nathaniel looked at the card. It had the address of 121 Crab Apple Street printed on it.

"Go on your way, then," the landlord said. "And hopefully I'll see you tomorrow… but I won't hold my breath."

Nathaniel took the card and walked out into the road… although the street he was now walking along was a totally different street from the one that he'd entered the pub from.

Chapter 22

"I'm a bit concerned about all of these Lego bricks that we keep finding scattered about," Artichoke said to Nelly.

They were sat around a small campfire in the middle of the woods, Artichoke chewing on berries and Nelly gnawing on the carcass of a small, wild Brown Trout.

"Do you think that he's falling apart again?" Artichoke asked.

Nelly cleared his throat and said, "Well, it wouldn't be the first time, would it? Hmm? I mean he tries his best but if it wasn't for the Wood Lobsters picking up the pieces, he'd never get a second chance… or a twenty-second chance… I think that's the count so far." Nelly put his head down and continued nibbling on the trout meat, waiting for Artichokes response.

"He means well," said Artichoke.

"We all mean well," replied Nelly.

"Not everybody does," said Artichoke.

Nelly looked up. "Yes that's true," he said, "but what *you* have to remember is that *you* have a very important job to do and the buck stops *with you*. Regardless of the efforts of the helpers, at the end of the day it's down to you to guide the lost souls, and at this point in time our latest one is indeed lost and running wild in The Village."

"So what do *you* suggest?" Artichoke asked, as he trusted the wisdom of his old feline friend.

Nelly continued eating and then with a start he spat something out onto the floor. "Yak, you've got to pick the bones out of these things sometimes, you know," choked Nelly.

"What? The fish?"

"No, no, no," Nelly responded shaking his head and clearing his throat. "The situation… the situation of the man. Think about it and tell me what you know so far."

"Well, I know that he's found himself here in the Land of Khartoonz through no choice of his own."

"Go on," said Nelly. "Keep thinking it through."

"Although I suppose that at the time he made the decision to jump that was his choice, it's just this isn't where he thought he was going to be… he thought he was going nowhere… that it was all over. But now he knows that it isn't finished, and, whether he likes it or not, he still has to get to the point of it all, you know, what it's all about, that thing that they call 'life'. He's being forced into doing it, to keep on the journey until he finds the answer."

"Very good," acknowledged Nelly. "And what else do *we* know so far?"

"We know that Albie is on his side and is watching over him. And also that he's been dropped the lucky penny, but whether it carries good luck or bad luck for him remains to be seen… I guess it depends on what he decides to do with it," Artichoke offered.

"Yes, exactly. Now let's finish off here and make our way

around The Village and wait for him on the other side for when he emerges. And also don't forget that Grimaldi and his troop of skunk apes have acknowledged his presence here… and so have a few other undesirable individuals. Nathaniel Phischermann is in a very vulnerable position and although this is his own personal journey, we must do everything we can to help and protect him. It's why we're here, it's why we exist."

Artichoke agreed and, as the campfire waned and the trout and berries were consumed, the two of them prepared to make their way around the outskirts of The Village to the other side in order to greet their charge when he hopefully emerged unscathed from his trip through it.

And if that didn't happen, then it wouldn't be the first time that a soul had been lost forever… and they both knew that it wouldn't be the last.

Chapter 23

Nathaniel wandered down the road, hoping that it was Crab Apple Street, clutching the business card and peering at the house numbers. He was looking for 121.

The houses were large and terraced, so he assumed that the odd numbers would be on one side and the even numbers would be on the other. However, this was not the case.

Everything was jumbled up… there was no rhyme nor reason to the numbering of the buildings in this street, although in theory it should have been a simple task when the architects and builders had constructed the place. He moved onwards, steadily looking at each doorway. It was like a game of bingo or a lottery, there was just no way of guessing what number would be next, so he weaved his way from one side of the street to the other… realising that it was totally absent of parked cars or any other form of transportation. Just like the rest of The Village.

It was a long street that kept heading downhill, and even though he was trying hard, he wasn't managing to find number 121… every number but that one. He'd even passed a door number plate that read 3.146, if only it was *that* easy! It was as if he was being taunted and made a fool out of.

He continued on, determined to find the address, but then he heard a curious sound coming from the bottom end of the street. It sounded like a slow-paced tapping on the cobblestone road, but magnified many times, as if there were a herd of horses slowly making their way up the hill. But the sound wasn't hooves, it sounded more wooden-like. He wondered if it was the Wood Lobsters returning to greet him but the sound was more thicker and heavier and not as frenetic as the Wood Lobsters. He stopped and waited for whatever was making the sound to come into view… and it wasn't long before the most bizarre sight began to emerge from the light of the street gas lamps.

It took a few seconds to register but as the sound came closer, so did the entities that it belonged to. He could never have dreamed or imagined such a spectacle, but coming toward him were what only could be described as a group of large hedgehogs… and not your common or garden type, these were the size of cows, and even more disturbing than that… they were walking on stilts.

'I've gone crazy… I realise that now,' Nathaniel thought to himself. 'I've thought it before, but now I know for sure, so I'll just stand here and see what happens. Maybe they'll just walk right past me, but then again, I guess they probably won't.'

It wasn't long before they'd reached him and, no, they didn't walk right past him. They stopped and stared at him. For a while, time stood still and strangely enough there was an embarrassed silence. Nathaniel didn't know whether to say hello or run away.

"Are you looking for number one two one?" asked the hedgehog at the front of the herd.

Nathaniel peered up at the creature, which must have stood at least twelve feet off the ground, teetering on its stilts. After a few seconds, he gathered his thoughts and replied. "Yes, that's right. It's the number on the card that the landlord gave me."

"Ahh, yes," replied the Head Hedgehog. "It's the place that they all try to find."

"Who are *they all*?" enquired Nathaniel.

"The people like you. The lost souls. We knew that you were coming, we were told. So here we are, and we are going to help you find number one two one. Oh, and by the way, we are the Stilt Walking Hedgehogs from Crab Apple Street and this is what we do. We try to locate the house numbers, a bit like your postmen, if you like... you know, trying to find the right letterbox and all that. Sometimes we get it right but sometimes we get it wrong. You'll be pleased to know that most of the time we get it right."

Nathaniel just stood there transfixed by what he was seeing and being told.

The gigantic hedgehog turned around on its stilts. "Okay you lot, we're looking for number one two one, so away you go and shout out when you find it, this gentleman needs a bed for the night."

The rest of the Stilt Walking Hedgehogs moved away in different directions, some back down the hill and some continuing back the way that Nathaniel had come, all of them eagerly looking at the door numbers as they went.

He stood there, the business card in his hand, observing the scene unfold in front of him as a group of overgrown hedgehogs balancing on stilts attempted to locate his lodgings for the night.

Nathaniel watched on as the enthusiastic searchers strode up and down, and as the minutes passed by, and as the search was obviously revealing no quick results, he turned around and looked at the house in front of him, the one that he had his back to whilst all the chaos was unfolding.

Beyond the old iron gate of the small garden there were half a dozen steps leading up to the front door. His eyes followed the staircase upwards and then he saw it: the number plate by the side of the door… 121… one two one.

His eyes widened and he was about to shout out that he'd found it, but then like a reluctant recipient of a surprise lottery win, he immediately kept his mouth shut. He felt that this was a personal experience and selfish though it may have seemed, he decided to edge his way off the street, so, opening the gate he slowly, he climbed the steps and left his dedicated helpers behind him, still searching for something that they might never find.

Chapter 24

The house was in darkness apart from a poorly illuminated window in the apex of the roof. As he ascended the well-worn stone steps he noticed that there was also a nameplate on the wall underneath the door number. As he reached the top step he could clearly read it: 'Hiraeth' was the word but it meant nothing to him. However, standing in front of the door, he immediately got an uncanny feeling of déjà vu… this was the place of his childhood dream, a dream that had recurred again and again throughout his entire life. He felt a spiritual longing for this home which he'd never had the chance to experience; it was a feeling of nostalgia for an ancient place that he hadn't been allowed to return to. It was like an echo of a lost place of his soul's past and he was overcome with grief. He felt that the emotion he was experiencing was strangely somewhere in the wind, the trees, the rocks and the waves, and that the feeling was nowhere… *but it was everywhere.*

The door had an old fashioned doorbell and he felt compelled to ring it. Would anyone answer his call? And if so, who? He could hear the clacking of the Stilt Walking Hedgehogs continuing to search up and down the street. He knew that he'd have to go on without any interference so he reached bravely out and pressed the button. He heard no sound, but waited patiently with his heart in his mouth. The seconds passed by, but there was no indication of movement from within the building. He pressed it again… and waited… he counted to twenty… there was no response. Dare he try the doorknob? Maybe it was unlocked? He knew that he'd to give it a go, so he reached out and tentatively twisted it. It turned all the way, so he gently pushed it and the door slowly opened. There was no creaking of hinges and he peered around it into the darkness of the hallway. There was no movement from within, so, feeling like a thief in the night, he took the decision to carefully and quietly enter the house. He stepped inside and took a few slow paces forward into the carpeted hallway.

The place smelled musty and even though it was dark he could see that the décor and furnishings were reminiscent of the Victorian age. In front of him was a staircase, it was *the* staircase that he already knew was going to be there, and the one that he'd nervously gone up a thousand times before in his dreams. He stood there contemplating his next move, but what was the choice? Turn around and go… or press on and finally see what had never been revealed to him in the past? Obviously a no-brainer, so he steeled himself then walked forward, putting his hand on the banister. Looking up into the gloom, he placed his foot on the first step and slowly – one by one – he forced himself to keep going.

Every movement he made felt like swimming through treacle, like his legs were made of lead. The further up he got, the more frightened he became. If he was right and this *was* the house in his dreams, then he knew what would be at the top of the stairs. Nevertheless, he kept on going.

He reached the top and turned left. As he stood on the landing his premonition came true. In front of him was a doorway that was slightly ajar. He knew that it was a doorway to a small bedroom. Although his subconscious anxiety was screaming at him to turn around and go back downstairs, he had an overwhelming urge to carry on and to go and have a look at what was inside the room. Would it be the same as before? Would it be different? He inched forward until he was directly in front of the door. He knew that this one creaked. He could see through the crack between the door and its frame… and he saw that the room was in darkness, as it had been many times in the past. And so, with his heart going ten to the dozen, he reached out and gently pushed the door open.

The creaking noise was deafening in the silence and so unnerving that goosebumps immediately appeared on his skin and the hackles on the back of his neck stood up to attention.

The door opened and Nathaniel peered inside.

The contents of the room were just as they always had been: a small single bed to the left and a small set of drawers underneath the window in front. The curtains were open and the streetlight cast ominous shadows onto the walls. But it was the thing in the right hand corner of the room that caused his blood to freeze in terror. It was the thing that had haunted his dreams all of his life, turning this part of it into a nightmare.

Was it a monster? Well maybe it was a monster in disguise, or maybe there was a monster hiding behind it… the thing that he was looking at was another door, and it oozed pure evil. It beckoned to him and he felt so drawn toward it that once again he had no choice but to move forward. He stood in front of it and he could not resist the familiar overpowering sense of macabre curiosity that overcame him. His hand reached out to the door handle, he gripped it, then paused for a second before slowly pressing it down and gently pushing… nothing happened.

The door didn't open.

Like a thousand times before, the door didn't open.

He rattled the handle up and down, again and again, applying more pressure to the door itself with his other hand, determined to get it open. He needed to know what was on the other side. Surely now that he was here for real the door should open?

But it wasn't budging so he rattled the handle harder and put his shoulder and full weight against it, increasing the force, relentlessly thumping against it… determined to get it open.

Whatever was on the other side had haunted him for all of his life and now he was ready to reveal what it was, but it was just like banging his head against a brick wall. He wanted to scream out, "Just let me in, you bloody bastard thing!" But he didn't, he kept it all in because he didn't want to disturb any malevolent forces that might be observing him, and as he realised that his efforts were going to come to nothing, he began to cry.

At this time, my friend, it's only fair to point out that as I'm diligently trying to write this manuscript, some lunatic is trying to break down the door to my writing room. Not to worry, it's not the first time it's happened and it probably won't be the last. Oh and by the way! One of the spiders has just scuttled across the table… how distracting!

As if I haven't got enough to deal with.

Chapter 25

Nathaniel gathered his emotions and once again came to the conclusion that this was a door that could never be opened. Well, not by him anyway. At this point in the past his dream would break and he would either wake up or find himself in another dream, but this time that wasn't the case. So he resigned himself to acknowledge that he was in a state of reality, which felt worse… as there was no quick means of escape. It was pointless staying here so he made his way out of the small bedroom, down the staircase, through the hall and down the steps and onto the pavement. The first thing that he noticed was the absence of the Stilt Walking Hedgehogs, there was neither sight nor sound of them. The strange thing was that it had apparently been raining. The road was wet, as were the roofs of the houses reflecting the moonlight of the many moons hanging in the otherwise clear sky. He'd obviously missed the passing of the rainclouds when he'd been inside the house.

He was now faced with another choice: down the hill of Crab Apple Street or up the hill of Crab Apple Street? As he was pondering his decision, he noticed something on the pavement at his feet… it was something small and yellow. He stooped down and, recognising what it was, picked it up.

It was a Lego brick.

He immediately looked around in all directions but there was no movement… nothing. And absolutely no sign of Tiny Toppings. Nevertheless he put the plastic brick into his pocket and as he did so he felt it rub against the old penny, which reminded him of the apparent importance of the coin. He felt the need to move on and so chose to go to his right… up Crab Apple Street.

He came to the junction with the High Street and, looking to his right, he recognised the way that he'd entered The Village, the only difference being that the road was now totally overgrown with what looked like years of vegetation growth… bushes, trees and other plants that were now totally blocking the route, making it impossible for him to go back from the direction that he'd come in from.

So now he had two choices: either to go back up the High Street and attempt to reach the opposite end of The Village, where Artichoke and Nelly said that they would wait for him, or forwards into the side street called Pennydragon Lane. He paused for a while in thought, and although he knew that he would eventually have to make it to the other side of town, at this moment in time something was drawing his attention to whatever was down Pennydragon Lane. So far he'd found the High Street quite a threatening place to be and so with nothing to lose, he walked forward and made his way into Pennydragon Lane.

Just like Crab Apple Street, the top of the lane headed downward and Nathaniel soon found himself walking downhill into a place that wasn't as well illuminated as the rest of The Village. There were terraced houses on the left hand side, but on the right there were no buildings, just an iron railing fence that provided a barrier to the ominous pervading woodland that seemed intent on invading the space that was beyond it.

He walked down to the bottom of the lane and turned left, as it was the only direction to go. It wasn't long before he noticed a glow of light that was being projected into the otherwise desolate darkness of the street about a hundred yards down. He continued walking forward, eager to find the source of the light.

When he neared it, he could see that it was coming from the large open doors of a workshop, which resembled either a garage or maybe a disused stable. Cautiously he approached and then peered into the building. Inside, beyond the immediate area of what was obviously a place of work, he could see a solitary man in a leather apron stood at a workbench. He was in the process of carving something out of wood and seemed quite happy in his business as he was quietly singing to himself. Nathaniel stood there observing him, and then without even turning his head or missing a stroke from the job in hand, the man said, "Hello. Can I help you with something?"

Nathaniel was shocked… was the man talking to him or someone else? He stayed silent.

The man sighed, put his chisel down on the workbench and turned to face Nathaniel. "Yes, I'm talking to you. Once again, can I help you with something?" the man gently asked.

There was no doubt about it, the man was staring at him directly in the eyes. Nathaniel had no choice but to respond, so he walked out of the shadows and into the workshop, noticing an overpowering aroma of pinewood. He was unsure of exactly what to say.

"You look lost," the man said.

"I am," replied Nathaniel. After all, it was the truth. He was also slightly surprised at how easy it had been to admit it to this stranger.

"You have nothing to worry about. Come on in," the man beckoned for him to come and join him at the workbench.

Nathaniel didn't hesitate and walked forward to join him.

"It's good to meet you at last," said the man. "I was told that you were coming. My name is Zhackery Thackery and I'm the carpenter, joiner, woodworker and chief wood butcher in this village." Zhackery paused, staring at Nathaniel waiting for a response. When there was none, he just burst out laughing. "You need to relax, my friend, you need to chill out. Why are you so uptight?"

"I think you know," said Nathaniel. "I think you all know. You don't have to patronise me. Yes, I'm lost... and yes, you're right about that. I don't know where the hell I am, where the hell I'm going or where the hell I've been." Nathaniel stopped and inhaled deeply. "I'm sorry, I'm just confused that's all."

"That's fine, the worlds that we all live in are very confusing and all of our worlds are different. Take, for instance, my world. Look around you. What do you see?"

Nathaniel looked around at the workshop and instantly saw something he hadn't noticed before. Hanging from the walls on what could only be described as small meat hooks were lots of Wood Lobsters. Some were nearly complete, some had legs missing, a few only had one claw and some consisted of just a body with no tail.

"So, what *do* you see?" Zhackery asked him again.

Nathaniel thought before he answered. "I see creation. I see things in the making. You are the creator of these things… so does that make you some kind of god? Actually, thinking about it, *are* you God?"

Zhackery didn't answer that question, but instead he said, "I need to show you something else." He clicked his fingers and from an adjacent room a smaller figure wearing a flat cap came shuffling in. "This, by the way, is Harry's Son. I call him that because he *is* the son of Harry, and he's my apprentice."

Nathaniel nodded to the smaller man.

Zhackery continued, "And he has something to give to you, think of it as a talisman, a good luck charm." Harry's Son held out his hand, which was empty.

Nathaniel looked confused. He turned to Zhackery.

"What?" said Nathaniel. "There's nothing in his hand! So what are you talking about? What good luck charm?"

"Can't you see it? He's offering you his hand. Does he have to be holding anything of material value? Can't you see that what he is offering is worth much more than gold? He is offering a *helping* hand, *his* helping hand."

Nathaniel instantly realised what was transpiring and in

his embarrassment he wished that the earth beneath his feet would swallow him up.

"I'm so sorry," he said to Harry's Son, who was still extending his hand.

Nathaniel reached out and gladly took the small man's hand.

Harry's Son instantly beamed out a smile brighter than the two suns of Khartoonz… and then, once again, everything changed.

Chapter 26

Nathaniel was now walking on a path at the side of a duck pond. It must have been springtime because all of the surrounding trees were in full bloom, the pink cherry blossom being very prominent. He still felt the grip from Harry's Son's hand, but, as he glanced down, it wasn't the small man that he was looking at… it was a young boy, a toddler perhaps two years old.

"Will you be my daddy… *please*?' the boy said. "I really want *you* to be my daddy."

Nathaniel was once again shocked at the new situation he was now in, but he felt the need to immediately respond to the child. "But you've already got a dad… haven't you?" he asked.

"No, not yet, but I will have… I think so anyway!" was the child's confused response.

"So where's your mam? And who is she?" Nathaniel asked, looking nervously around, checking to see if anyone was observing this strange man walking and talking hand-in-hand with a child that he'd never met before in his life.

"I don't know. I haven't really met her. I'm still inside her… I haven't come out of her tummy yet."

They both stopped walking and the boy looked up at Nathaniel with a sorrowful expression on his face.

"Please will you be my daddy? *Please*," he pleaded.

•

At the same time that Nathaniel was having his vision, unbeknownst to him, Judy was talking to her mother.

"Why did you leave him then, Judith?" Judy's mother was washing up the pots at the sink in her bungalow.

"Because it's been going on for too long and nothing ever changes with him. He can't see the wood for the trees," replied Judy as she sat at the table nursing her cup of coffee.

"In what way?" her mother asked.

"Because he's always been full of promises and we never get any further forward. He's bloody useless, and he's always playing that sodding guitar and he smokes like a trooper." Judy sighed and took a sip.

Judy's mother also sighed and dried her hands on the tea towel. She took a seat at the table beside her daughter. "Judith, do you love him?"

Judy closed her eyes and put the cup down. She began to tremble and tears ran down her face. "Yes," she blurted out. "Yes I do, but I can't trust him. I mean he's so irresponsible. It's like he's living in another world. It's bad enough as it is now, but how's he going to be when…" and then she pulled *herself* up short and immediately stopped crying, quickly glancing sideways at her mother.

"I thought so," said her mam quietly. "When's it due, Judith? When's it due?"

•

There was a brilliant flash of light and Nathaniel found himself back in the Land of Khartoonz, totally unaware of the conversation between Judy and her mam, but still holding the hand of Harry's Son who was beaming with happiness, and they were once again back in the woodworking shop.

"Was he of any help to you, then?" asked Zhackery, nodding towards Harry's Son.

The small man in the flat cap let go of Nathaniel's hand and retreated back into the room that he'd initially emerged from.

"I'm not quite sure… I don't really know," was Nathaniel's confused response.

Zhackery turned to address Nathaniel. "You're not the first one to pass by here, and you won't be the last one either, but I can tell you this much… none of them have ever come back to say hello, thank you or *kiss my arse*! So when you continue on your journey, which you're about to do, remember this, 'No good deed goes unpunished'. In other words, don't trust anyone, certainly not in this village. And keep your hands on your penny. So, where are you heading next?"

"I need to get to the other side of The Village," replied Nathaniel.

"Then my suggestion is to avoid the High Street at all costs. The individuals who frequent that place will have the shirt off your back in no time at all. If you stick to this street and keep on going forward you'll bypass the High Street and soon find yourself near to the other side of The Village. Oh and by the way, before you go, I found this on my workbench this morning and I believe it was intended for you."

Zhackery picked something up and offered it to Nathaniel… the object was a red Lego brick. Nathaniel took it.

"The road isn't always straightforward," said Zhackery, "and sometimes you need guiding, guides, help, assistance, call it what you will, but I know that no man can make it on his own. So you can go now, and thank you for stopping by… and goodbye… and good luck."

Zhackery Thackery turned back to his workbench, picked up his chisel and continued with his labour of love, carving the life into his magical wooden creations.

Nathaniel silently turned and headed out of the warmth of the workshop into the darkness of the night. Humbled by the carpenter's words of wisdom, he put the red Lego brick into his pocket with the other one, which was nestled beside the penny.

Chapter 27

He'd turned left out of the workshop and now found himself walking along the street with houses on the left hand side and the fenced off woodland to his right. He looked up and marvelled at the sight of the moons in the clear sky above him. He counted three, all of different sizes and pastel shades of colour; all in different stages of their individual Lunar cycles.

The largest of the moons was amazingly close and filled up nearly a quarter of the sky. One of them was encircled by rings, just like Saturn. They were all framed within the bible black backdrop of the infinite universe they inhabited, and, as he looked on, he observed the silhouette of a large bird – like the one he'd seen earlier on – slowly gliding past in front of it. For some reason, Nathaniel felt a strange sense of reassurance from the presence of the bird, but also a feeling of desperate loneliness… a dislocation from reality as he looked at the vacuum of the darkness between the moons and the barren emptiness of the moon's surfaces. There were no stars in the sky, just the void of cold silent eternity. The bird soon drifted out of sight, so he concentrated his efforts back onto the route that he was taking.

The street was dark and sparsely lit. Once again there was a lack of vehicles and the windows of the buildings were all in darkness. As he journeyed on, Nathaniel passed several streets to his left that led upwards, obviously leading to the High Street, but he decided to ignore them all, instead heeding Zhackery's advice.

It only took a few minutes and then he found himself at the end of the street and near to a turn in the road that headed up to the left. It was a blind corner but the most encouraging thing was a signpost, which read:

THE OTHER SIDE OF THE VILLAGE

There was even an arrow pointing him in the correct direction. For the first time in a long time he actually felt encouraged and confident that the he was doing the right thing. So, with a spring in his step and buoyed up with the thought of a reunion with Artichoke and Nelly, he advanced.

He turned the corner and looked up the street, walking confidently and determined to make it through The Village, with the hope of reuniting with the people that he now thought of as friends… even though one of them was a cat and so not technically a person! But that didn't matter.

He walked forward… and then stopped dead in his tracks.

He smelled them before he heard them and before he saw them.

A long way up ahead there was quite a commotion going on, the sounds of running and shouting, as well as a disturbing grunting and snarling noise.

"There he is," a voice shouted out. "Go and seize him."

It wasn't long before they came into view and immediately Nathaniel realised what was happening... Horatio Lambert leading the charge down the hill, waving his cane and whipping the Grimpanzees into shape. The stench of the sewers and the noisy drone was all the proof that Nathaniel needed, and so, without hesitation, he quickly realised that it was the time for him to turn on his heels and run for his life.

Chapter 28

He was no Olympic athlete, especially with the hindrance of his smoking habit, but the speed that he ran back down the road would surely have broken the 100-metre sprint world record (in any world that is, even the Land of Khartoonz). Behind him the hooting, howling and hollering of the Grimpanzees and the clattering of long finger and toenails on the cobblestones filled him with terror. It was like being chased by a pack of demented wolves. His one hope of escape was to dive back into Zhackery's workshop, which wasn't far up the road, where hopefully he could gain sanctuary from his evil pursuers. And, thinking about it, at least there were sharp instruments in there... chisels and the like that he could use as weapons.

But as he got closer to the woodworking shop, his heart sank. The shutters were down, the lights were off and there was a big sign hung outside which simply said, 'SORRY, CLOSED FOR THE NIGHT'. He didn't stop running but he was becoming more and more exhausted. He could hear the beasts behind him getting closer by the second... they would surely turn the corner shortly and spot him. His only option was to keep going but he knew that soon, with an uphill run in order to reach the High Street, in all honesty he didn't think that he had it in him to make it all the way, so maybe he should just resign himself to the fact that he was going to get ripped to pieces… just give in and stop running… but it was then that he heard it…

"PSSST!" The voice was coming from directly in front of him, to his left, out of the woods. "PSSST, get over here. Get in… jump in, quickly," it said.

Nathaniel didn't even think about it, or the consequences, he just followed the voice, leapfrogged the fence and crashed into the undergrowth.

As soon as he landed, sprawled out on his front on the ground, someone dived onto his back, put their hand over his mouth and applied their forearm to the back of his neck.

"Don't move," the person whispered in a voice that sounded strangely familiar… *just like his own.* Which was weird. "Don't even breathe!"

Nathaniel felt the weight of the person who was holding him down and he was totally happy to be compliant with his rescuer's (or his kidnapper's) demands. It wasn't long before he heard the stampede of the Grimpanzees running past his hiding place. They sounded like a pack of hounds baying for the blood of a helpless victim and they stank like a thousand rotting corpses, probably like the ones that must have met their end after crossing their path before.

"Find him, you imbeciles! I *want* that penny, I *need* that penny." Horatio Lambert was running alongside them and, although Nathaniel couldn't see it from where he was, Lambert was beating the animals with his cane in order to instil a feeling of urgency into them. Even Butler, who was dragging behind them with the stragglers, was kicking them into shape as he desperately held onto his bowler hat.

Nathaniel listened as the rampaging mob headed up Pennydragon Lane, baying, hooting and screaming with excitement with Lambert shouting out orders all the way. Eventually the sound became more distant until they must have disappeared somewhere into the High Street and moved on until they were no longer audible.

His breathing was shallow and laboured and he awaited the next move from the person who was restraining him when the weight on his back vanished, as did the hand on his mouth and the arm on the back of his neck. He thankfully inhaled a massive breath of air and then quickly turned onto his side.

There was nobody there, but the only movement was a shadow, one that was becoming familiar. It disappeared into the undergrowth and there was no sound to its retreat, only silence.

He was alone, in the dark, in the bushes, wondering once again what the hell was going on?

Chapter 29

He lay there for a while, contemplating his options. He felt quite safe in the place where he was for the moment and so felt no need for any knee jerk reactions that might break his cover. He was on his back and he stared up at one of the moons through a gap in the branches of the trees. It looked like an alien eye observing his pathetic situation, silent, non-judgemental for now, but just hanging there watching everything unfold, gathering its own evidence and awaiting the time when it would be called upon to deliver its probably damning verdict on him. A member of the celestial jury in the sky. A spy in the sky?

'Stop it, you fool,' he silently shouted to himself. 'Stop it with those thoughts.' He shook his head, ejecting the negativity from his mind.

He knew that he had to get to the other side of The Village above everything else at the moment, and he trusted Artichoke and Nelly as he was convinced that they were trying their best to lead him to some kind of conclusion, so he had to regain contact with them. He knew what to do. He just had to do it, and more to the point, he knew which way to go… after all, he'd seen the signpost.

So, without further ado, he gathered his courage, stood

up and, with caution, he left his temporary sanctuary. He crawled gently over the fence and proceeded on his way down Pennydragon Lane, following his original route before he'd been rudely interrupted by the crazed mob of what he could only describe as being a total bunch of unhinged psychos.

He edged his way along the road, looking left and looking right but all was still and quiet. He got to the turning in the road and once again found himself in front of the sign that declared that THE OTHER SIDE OF THE VILLAGE was indeed in the direction he was travelling. He stopped and peered around the corner. There were no obvious signs of lunatics, and even if there was going to be an ambush, and although he felt frightened, he decided to go ahead and walk up the road anyway. He eventually got to the top uninterrupted by any attempt or threat of anything that might hinder his way.

He reached the junction of the High Street and decided that caution would be his best strategy. He crouched down at the corner of a brick wall and slowly peered out, first left and then right. There were no visible signs of movement and no audible sound. To his right, he noticed that the High Street, which was sparsely illuminated anyway, led very quickly into a path of darkness.

'That's the other side of The Village,' Nathaniel thought. 'That's where I have to go.'

It didn't take long. In less than a heartbeat, he made the decision to stand upright and he sprinted into the black uncertainty of the woods beyond. Unchallenged, he carried on forward into the forest, darkness engulfing him, as the path had soon changed from cobblestones and back to mud and pine needles. After a while he stopped running. He didn't feel threatened. He felt quite safe, but, nevertheless, he took the precaution of having a breather so he crouched down at the roots of a large tree… whereupon his hand touched something on the ground that seemed strangely familiar. He picked it up and looked at it… the object was, of course, another Lego brick. Duty bound, he put the brick into his pocket and just sat there, contemplating.

It had been a long night and, as the adrenaline wore off, his eyes started to close. It didn't take long for him to give in… and very soon he fell into a deep sleep.

Hello, my friend. I'm whispering because I don't want to wake him up. Just to let you know that I have written a thousand stories in the past and my ideas are like a multitude of butterflies trapped inside the washing machine of my mind, not all of them will make it out clean and alive. In fact, most of them will die in the process, but this time I'm confident that our butterfly will have a clean escape, because I have a good idea of how the story will end. It's just that I haven't written it all yet! And by the way, the spiders are crawling all over my hands, which doesn't make things any easier.

So let's just be quiet for now and let him sleep… shhh!

Chapter 30

Horatio Lambert and Kraken T Butler were sat in a private booth inside The First and Last, both of them exhausted from their failed pursuit. The stench of the Grimpanzees hung heavy on their clothes, which suited them to a tee because, even though the place was packed, nobody made a move to join them.

"Here, take one of these," said Lambert, offering Butler an open pack of cigarettes.

Butler took one out of the packet without hesitation, as did Lambert. Butler in turn took a box of matches out of his pocket and immediately struck one and offered the flame to Horatio, who, without acknowledgement, allowed Butler to light the cigarette that was already between his lips. Butler lit his own and awaited for his boss to speak.

"This is how it works… we have him in the palm of our hands if we can only convince him to part with the penny and take another breath of smoke. He's gone a long time now without a drag of a fag, so he must be feeling it. He must have the craving. The longer it goes on the more desperate he'll get, and there will come a time when he *will* cave in. And that's when we get the penny off him. I think it's going to be difficult to do it by force, although we'll keep trying that tactic, but, in the meantime, we just have to stay calm and bide our time. The opportunity will arise. At all costs we have to keep him here in the Land of Khartoonz, that's our job, that's what we do. Agreed?"

"Yes, boss, that's agreed," replied Butler, through a hasty exhalation of smoke.

"We can't allow him to go back to where he came from, that's why *we* need that penny… and if I get my hands on it, then that's *my* ticket out of this shithole. Agreed?"

"Yes, boss," said Butler, whose attention had turned to the stage. He was trying not to choke on his own sycophantic words as Bentley Nevada Wobulator finished tuning up.

"You are taking me seriously, aren't you?" Lambert asked him.

Without turning his gaze from the musicians, Butler merely mumbled the words, "Yes, boss."

"Well, I don't think you are," Lambert informed him.

And as the band struck up the first deafening chord of their heavy metal music, Lambert took his half smoked burning cigarette and crushed it into the back of Butler's hand.

Butler screamed, knocking over his pint glass as he recoiled in pain and horror.

Nobody in the pub either heard or saw this incident, everyone's attention being glued to the band, all sounds being drowned out by the unforgiving maelstrom of guitars and drums.

Unfortunately for Butler, it wasn't the first time that this had happened and judging by the way things were… it wasn't going to be the last.

Chapter 31

Nathaniel woke up with a start from his dreamless sleep and the first thing that he noticed was that the darkness had given way to the strange light of the Khartoonz dawn.

The other thing that immediately struck him was that the birds were singing again. It wasn't exactly a dawn chorus but the ones that were joining in sounded quite happy to be alive. He didn't move but instead concentrated on recalling the events from the night before.

One by one they came tumbling into his mind: the meeting with Lambert and Butler, the appearance of the Shadow Stalker, The First and Last, the band actually playing one of his songs, Crab Apple Street, the Stilt Walking Hedgehogs, Zhackery, Harry's Son, the Grimpanzees, the stranger on his back. He shook his head, so much had happened but here he was sat in the woods where he'd slept in peace. He took some time to gather his thoughts… and yes, he *was* gagging for a cigarette.

After a short period of quiet contemplation, he slowly rose to his feet. He was as stiff as a board but nevertheless he moved away from his resting place at the roots of the tree and walked back onto the path. He knew which direction he was travelling in and he knew that he had to get to The Point in order to try and make sense of everything. And hadn't he been told by Artichoke and Nelly that they would join him again? He looked around… there was no sign of them. Nevertheless, he put his best foot forward and continued onwards, positively encouraged by the morning light and birdsong.

•

Artichoke was tapping on his wristwatch camera obscura; he'd struggled throughout the night to get a decent signal because of the limited illumination of the lunar light. But now with the sun's rays starting to have an impact on the day, he was hoping to receive a clearer image.

"Ahh, there he is!" said Artichoke.

"Let me see," said Nelly, jumping enthusiastically up onto his shoulder. They both looked upon the image of Nathaniel walking on the path through the woods.

"He's survived the night!" exclaimed Artichoke with a grateful sense of relief.

"Yes, and it looks like he's heading in the right direction. Let's go and find him before somebody, or *something*, else does," suggested Nelly.

Without hesitation, they set off to rendezvous with Nathaniel. There were several ways that he could have exited The Village, but judging by the lay of the land and the foliage that was present in the image on the camera obscura, Artichoke had a good idea of where they should go, so he aimed to head him off at the pass.

•

Buoyed up by surviving his journey through The Village last night and his determination to get to The Point, the rhythmical pace of his footsteps triggered a memory of another one of his songs and it wasn't long before Nathaniel began to sing it to himself, at first quietly but when he realised that his voice was sounding pretty cool and in tune, he raised the volume and sang out confidently to his passing surroundings and whatever inhabitants lived within them.

The song was called *Rough Sea, Smooth Stone...*

Let me talk to you,
About what I've been through,
Welcome through my door.
So good of you,
To find where I've been to,
Between the deep blue and the shore.

It's where I live,
It's where I find my home,
Where the rollers are a-breaking,
And the rocks turn into stone.
Where the days seem to drag,
But the weeks fly by,
And the years turn into blurs,
Don't ask me why.

Rough sea, smooth stone.
It's just the way I'm feeling when I'm standing on my own.
Rough sea, smooth stone.

It's just the way I'm feeling,
It's just the way I feel.

Sitting in smoke rings,
Staring at the floor,
Everybody's thinking,
"Come on, is there any more?"
And you can only dream,
The places I have been,
Underneath the white horses,
I'm way above the law.

Rough sea, smooth stone.
It's just the way I'm feeling when I'm standing on my own.
Rough sea, smooth stone.
It's just the way I'm feeling,
It's just the way I feel.

Natural imperfection's what I'm guilty of,
And when I'm courting Miss Direction,
The breakers fire above.
She says, "Are you alright?"
And I say, "No because I'm all that's left."
To be a beacon in the night,
I surf upon the wave's high crest.

Rough sea, smooth stone.
It's just the way I'm feeling when I'm standing on my own.
Rough sea, smooth stone.
It's just the way I'm feeling,
It's just the way I feel…

He'd barely finished the last word when something from the undergrowth at the side of the path grabbed him by the ankle. It wrenched him off balance and instantly dragged him into the depths of the ferns and bushes. Crashing downwards through the plants on his back at speed, Nathaniel had no time to react although the shock and pain of his unexpected abduction caused him to scream out in panic.

Artichoke and Nelly heard the noise in the distance.

"Oh no, they've got him. We're too late," shouted Artichoke.

"Quick, run, go, go, go," Nelly screamed out, springing up from the backpack.

Artichoke sprinted off in the direction of the cry for help with Nelly clinging onto his neck for dear life.

Chapter 32

Nathaniel's unwelcome descent through the woods ended when he was released and deposited on a shore of rocks and boulders. He blinked and realised that he was near a sea, with waves gently breaking upon the pebbles. The place smelled strongly of salt and seaweed, and, as he gathered his senses, he almost lost his mind when he gradually looked up and tried to take in the sight of the abomination of a creature that was standing in front of him.

It was a hideous mutation of a crustacean. It was on its hind legs and stood about ten feet tall, red in colour, one claw bigger than the other, its two eyes on stalks and focused directly into his.

"I heard you singing. I was curious. I liked it. So I just had to invite you down. This is where *we* live," explained the monster.

Nathaniel said nothing, paralysed as he was with fear.

"Let's get to the point… actually, let's *not* get to the point. The thing is, you have something of mine, something that belongs to me. Oh and please excuse me, my name is Cruschtov and I am the King of the Crabs. Let me introduce you to my loyal family of followers," he said.

The creature raised its big claw and clicked it together

three times. Gradually there was movement from the rocks, the boulders and the ledges of the gulley walls.

Nathaniel watched on in horror as all kinds of crustaceans began to emerge from their hiding places, summoned by their leader. Crabs and lobsters of all species… spider crabs, velvet swimming crabs, edible crabs, peeler crabs, even hermit crabs dragging their shell homes along with them in order to appease Cruschtov.

Nathaniel was soon surrounded by the creatures from the sea. When they had all settled down, Cruschtov addressed his assembled audience.

He pointed a claw at Nathaniel. "Look at him," Cruschtov ordered, and they all did. "He comes from a different place, but he doesn't know what he's got. He thinks that he does, but he's wrong. He thinks that he has freedom, but he hasn't. He thinks that he has freedom of choice, but he hasn't. He thinks that he has freedom of speech, but he doesn't know what to say… because he has nothing to say. He doesn't know where he's going because he doesn't even know where he's come from. He is pathetic, he is a wretch, and he is a progressive rake as Hogarth would certainly testify to."

Nathaniel thought that for a gigantic mutated crab-like creature, Cruschtov actually spoke very intelligently… although he didn't like the way that his rhetoric was swaying the surrounding stinking audience against him. After all, he'd done nothing wrong… had he? And even so, why was he being singled out like this?

"The problem with him," Cruschtov was still pointing at Nathaniel… and all of the eyes were now upon him, "is that he thinks he knows better. He thinks that he has a mind of his own. And we all know what happens to people like him, don't we?"

They all agreed.

Cruschtov continued, "United we stand or divided we fall. We have to weed out individuals like him and get rid of them, never to be heard of or seen of again."

All the creatures cheered, most by just clacking their claws together.

"Look at me closely now," Cruschtov – with his weird googly eyes – addressed Nathaniel, "and watch this... WHEN I SAY JUMP WHAT DO *YOU ALL SAY*?"

The congregation of crustaceans suddenly burst into life as if awoken from a hypnotic sleep, and as one they all shouted out "HOW HIGH, YOUR MAJESTY?" as if it was an actual question... but they didn't wait for an answer, they instantly all just launched themselves into the air without waiting. Well, actually not all of them did.

The ones that enthusiastically jumped up soon landed with a clatter on the surrounding rocks, but picked each other up quickly and arranged themselves, standing in front of Cruschtov.

Nathaniel watched on, observing the strange chaos, but what caught his eye was a lone crab who wasn't quite as red in colour as the others. It was standing right in front of Cruschtov... but it hadn't jumped. it had refused to jump.

The Crab King was on the situation in an instant. "You again. I've warned you in the past, but how dare you try to show me up when we have a very special guest looking on… ENOUGH IS ENOUGH."

One of Cruschtov's claws sprang forward and grabbed the poor crab. The monster started shaking it around and smashing it against the rocks, side to side, up and down. The crab screeched horribly as shards of its shell flew like shrapnel through the air, bits of lungs and legs were scattered around, and when it was all finished with, the shattered corpse of what was left of the brave revolutionary lay twitching, smashed to pieces at the feet of the tyrant Cruschtov.

A lot of the audience had backed off, some even retreating back into their dark shelters in the rocks.

The gaze of the dictator quickly fell back to Nathaniel.

"You see," he said, "this is what happens when people don't do what they're supposed to do… what they're *told* to do. He's been PUT IN his place. Order has to be established and maintained. And so you're probably wondering what all this has got to do with you? Well, I'll tell you *exactly* what it's got to do with you… in order for me to expand my empire, which *is* going to happen by the way, I have to invade the place where you've come from. But the admission price is something that I haven't yet got. However, you have it. You have the penny, it's the price of admission… my admission to a greater world, a greater life, so just give it to me NOW!"

He slowly extended one of his claws towards Nathaniel until it was just inches away from his face. The creatures that had shied away began to once again emerge from their boltholes and safe places and soon surrounded

Nathaniel as they awaited his next move. Which, one way or another, would prove to be decisive.

Chapter 33

"Down there," shouted Nelly. "He's got to be down there!"

Artichoke looked at the broken foliage that led off the pathway.

"Yeah, I think you're right," he agreed and stopped running. Then he went cautiously down the incline, following the trail of trampled bushes and undergrowth. It was so steep that he had to make most of the way down on his backside.

As they began to near the end of the temporary pathway, Artichoke could smell the salty seawater and he began to hear the distinctive crashing of waves on the pebbles.

"I thought so," he said to Nelly. "It's The Sea of No Return and, from what I can hear, it sounds like they've already got him."

"Oh crap!" exclaimed Nelly as he made a slow tactical retreat back into the darkness of the backpack.

"Mmmm, thanks, pal," said Artichoke, edging his way closer to the action.

"Don't worry, I'm still in here," Nelly's muted voice informed him from the safety of his sanctuary.

"I'm so happy to hear it," Artichoke whispered. He could now see Nathaniel standing in front of Cruschtov, the King of the Crabs. His claw was extended towards Nathaniel and, apart from the sound and motion of the waves, the moment appeared to be frozen in some kind of traumatic tension.

"What's it going to be, then? Are you going to do what you're told or do you want to end up like that pathetic wreck?" Cruschtov asked Nathaniel, indicating the still twitching corpse of the brave, free-thinking crab.

Nathaniel didn't respond, he just stood his ground. There was no way that he was going to voluntarily give up the coin.

"Very well then, it's your choice. If that's the way you want it, then that's the way you're going to get it."

Cruschtov started to move slowly forward, but it was Artichoke who saw it first… in the sky behind the so-called King of the Crabs, he noticed a fast moving shadow. It was close to the surface of the water and it was closing in just like an Exocet missile. It didn't take long for Artichoke to recognise that it was Albie coming to the rescue.

Cruschtov, unaware of the threat behind his back, stopped his advance and opened his claw and moved it towards Nathaniel's neck.

"This will be the last lesson you'll ever learn and it's quite simple… you are just a number, a pawn in the game, just another brick in the wall. You are a pleb and you are expendable. So let *me* give *you* the pleasure of ending your worthless existence."

Just at that moment there was an almighty crash as Cruschtov was dramatically launched forward at such a pace he was jettisoned into the woods beyond the foreshore and smashed into the tree trunks. Feathers and bits of shell fell down around him.

Nathaniel could only stand there paralysed in amazement at how the large crustacean had managed to clear the distance over his head without colliding into him. All of the other cowardly creatures immediately scuttled away back to their hiding places.

Artichoke seized the moment. He dashed forward and grabbed hold of Nathaniel. "Come on," he said, "don't say a word. Let's go."

Nathaniel didn't argue and, without hesitation, they both started to scramble back up the track that they had descended on.

When they finally reached the top, Nathaniel and Artichoke both collapsed to the ground gasping for breath.

After a few seconds, Nelly popped his head out. "Is everything alright?" asked the cat.

The two men looked at each other in disbelief and, although there were many answers and expletives to that question, after a few seconds of thought they were unanimous in their answer…

"Everything's fine," they replied in unison.

"Good," said Nelly, "then we need to start moving, just in case they *all* decide to come looking for us. Which, by the way, is highly likely. We need to distance ourselves from this place."

So they got to their feet and, like obedient clockwork toys on an endless journey, propelled by cogs that seemed that would never stop turning, the two started to walk. One leading the way with the cat on his back, and one tagging obediently along behind with no idea, once again, where he was going to end up.

Chapter 34

The weather in the Land of Khartoonz, with its binary star system and its many satellite moons, could obviously be very unpredictable. As they trudged along, the pair noticed that the light was fading and Nathaniel saw that clouds were gathering. They looked very dynamic; the wind picked up and the branches of the trees began to dance to the rhythm of the cool breeze. It wasn't long before the precipitation began to fall, but it wasn't rain, it was snow. Small flakes at first, but soon the size of the aerial avalanche began to thicken and it started to have an immediate impact on the dry floor of the forest and its surroundings.

"This isn't looking too good, is it?" Nathaniel shouted forward to Artichoke.

"Just keep going," he responded. "We're not that far away now."

"Far away from what?" Asked Nathaniel.

"The Point… don't you remember? You want to know what The Point is, don't you?"

"Yes, I do," replied Nathaniel, feeling slightly embarrassed at his question.

They pressed on up the path and the snow came down accordingly. Soon everything was covered in a thick white blanket of the stuff… the pine trees, the path *and* the pilgrims all receiving their fair share of the unwelcome wintry offering.

•

They crunched forward... it was that kind of dry snow, you know the type that you can make igloo bricks out of? The heavy kind of snow, you know what I mean? Maybe not.

Anyway, hello again, my friend, and I hope that you are managing to keep pace with our adventurous trio.

As they say in the army, 'If you're not marching then you're fighting' and for now they're marching... but what lies ahead?

Let's stick with them and find out!

And just to keep you updated, some of the spiders are now even crawling through my hair. Lovely... I'm so happy... NOT!

•

The heavy snowstorm had darkened the day but nevertheless Nathaniel dutifully followed his guide, placing his feet in the footprints of the man in front of him. The man whose feathered hat was now comically festooned with about six inches of snow on the top of it.

As they rounded the corner of the path, a strange strobe light effect began to flash between the silhouettes of the trees. It was weird but compelling, and, as they carried on, the light became brighter. It was rhythmical and consistent, and strangely frightening to Nathaniel but it didn't seem to faze Artichoke, who just carried on putting one foot in front of the other.

Nathaniel pondered on the fact that the guy of small stature was leading the way, bravely and with purpose, and he was doing it on his behalf. Why? They had never met before… or had they? In a previous life or something?

So, as they trudged along, these thoughts triggered a memory of a song he'd written not so long ago, and he began to sing it in his head, it was called, *Don't Like These Sad Goodbyes.*

Ten years I have sat here,
And watched the sun rise up and down.
For ten years I have waited,
And watched the world turning around.
Today I feel a reason,
Not to sit here anymore.
And today I'm asking questions like,
"What the hell am I here for?"

"Think," said he,
"Why don't you come?"
"Will you still be thinking, when I am on the run?"
Don't like these sad goodbyes!

Ten years I have stood here,
And watched the sun rise up and fall,
For ten years I have suffered,
And seen no reason to it all.
Today I feel a reason,
Not to stand here anymore,
And today I'm asking questions,
And today I'll kick down the door.

"Think," said he,
"Why don't you come?"
"Will you still be thinking, when I am on the run?"
Don't like these sad goodbyes!

Ten years I have travelled,
And chased the sun across the sky.
For ten years I have lost myself,
I began to wonder why,
That the answers to my questions,
Are all starting to come true,
And the answers lie within me,
And the questions start with you.

"Think," said he,
"Why don't you come?"
"Will you still be thinking, when I am on the run?"
Don't like these sad goodbyes!

He liked that one and he thought that it was quite poignant, and it had also taken his mind off the trek he was on. The illumination of the strobe light had become stronger, the contrast between the darkness of the forest and the brilliance of the white snow was now quite hypnotic. Black then white, black then white… and repeat.

Chapter 35

When they finally emerged from the forest they were met with a view of a majestic structure. They stopped walking and observed the wonder in front of them. It was a lighthouse and it was massive. The light on the top was slowly rotating, which instantly explained the strobe light effect in the trees.

As he stood there taking it in, Nathaniel noticed that there were many windows with people looking out of them. They didn't look very happy… some had their hands pressed against the glass, some even had their faces pressed against it. And even though it was a lighthouse – a beacon of security and a helpful warning of danger ahead to those who had lost their way – Nathaniel sensed a feeling of morbid foreboding associated with the building. He also seemed to recognise the shape of the thing, although he couldn't recall from where.

"Follow me," Artichoke beckoned to Nathaniel.

Without questioning, they both walked towards the base of the structure until they stood in front of its stone foundations.

"Look around and tell me what you can see," Artichoke asked.

"Well, I can see a lot of rocks and boulders but not much else," Nathaniel replied.

Nelly popped his head out. "That's because you're not looking hard enough. Look again… closer," said the cat.

Nathaniel walked towards to the stonework and then he realised that the rocks and boulders were all covered with sculptural graffiti. There were names and dates carved into the stones… like epitaphs. It was weird.

He read a few of them and then he turned back towards Artichoke.

"What is this place? Why've you brought me here?" he asked.

"Because this is The Point. You asked what it was. Well, here it is! But you haven't looked hard enough yet. Look over there." Artichoke pointed to a rock that was close by.

Nathaniel turned and walked slowly to what he was being directed to. He peered down and read the freshly chiselled inscription.

NATHANIEL PHISCHERMANN
RIP?

He immediately spun around.

"Are you kidding me? Is this some kind of sick joke? Did *you* do this? Have you both brought me all the way here for *this*?" Nathaniel was confused and angry, but both Artichoke and Nelly were not fazed by his reaction.

"You need to calm down," said Nelly. "You asked what's The Point. Well here you are at The Point, and The Point is this. You have a choice in your life, whether to go forward or to go backward. So we have given you a choice right here and right now. You can enter the lighthouse and the door will close behind you. You will be in there for eternity and there will be no exit from your voluntary internment, which is fine if that's what you want. Or you can change the path you're on and turn around, retrace your steps and try to find your way home. Either way, we wish you well. We do care about you, about *all of you*, but at the end of the day, it's *your* life and the choice is yours, and we do respect that. We'll respect your decision. It's entirely up to you."

Nathaniel turned back to face the lighthouse and took his time. What was the lighthouse? What was in there? What future was in there? The people inside didn't look too happy with *their* predicament. And what about turning around and going back? Back to what? Back to face the music and back to exactly the same mess that he'd left behind? Neither of the two options seemed to be enticing, so he stood and pondered for a while… for a long while… in fact, for a very long while…

Chapter 36

Judy and her mam, Joanne, who was known as Johnny – a nickname from her childhood that had stuck – were watching the early morning local news on the TV. It was the usual stuff… cost of living crisis, dog poo on the streets, pollution in the sea, etc., etc., etc.

Neither of them had slept very well, Johnny got up off the sofa and went into the kitchen.

"What d'ya fancy for breakfast?" she shouted through.

Judy thought for a second. "Have we got any of that bacon left?"

The fridge door opened. "Yes… what about bacon and beans… with buns?"

"Ooh, yes please!"

"Alright then. But if you get up off your arse and help me, it'll happen a lot faster."

Judy didn't get up straight away but continued watching the news. Some breaking news had started to happen.

"Do you want tea with this? Or coffee?" Johnny shouted from the kitchen.

Judy ignored her as she listened intently to the reporter on the TV.

"The emergency services were contacted earlier on this morning at Saltburn and it was the coastguard who were the first on the scene. No details have been released yet, but it is believed that a body was discovered at the foot of the cliff by dog walkers. The police believe that the incident may be connected to an abandoned car that was found in the car park close to The Ship Inn." The camera closed in on a Mini that was surrounded by blue and white police tape, and Judy recognised the registration number plate straight away.

"Mam! Quick! You need to look at this, now!" shouted Judy.

Johnny reacted immediately and ran into the room.

Judy was pointing at the TV screen. "It's his car! And there's a body been found!"

"Whose car?" asked Johnny.

"Nathaniel's," Judy replied.

"Oh my God… whereabouts?"

"Ship Inn car park," said Judy.

"What? The body?" Johnny was confused.

"No, the car… the body's on the beach." Judy informed her.

All thoughts of breakfast forgotten, they grabbed their coats and headed out of the front door.

Chapter 37

"What's he doing?" Lambert asked Butler, who was looking through the binoculars.

"He's just standing there. He's not doing anything. He's just staring at the lighthouse," replied Butler.

"I know what he's doing," said Lambert. "He's making his mind up. He's making his choice. Let's just hope he makes the right one for my sake… I mean, for *our* sake, of course."

Butler didn't flinch, he just kept on observing.

Nathaniel had been staring at the scene before him for a long time. The importance of his decision had obviously not been lost on him. He turned his head… Artichoke was still stood there with Nelly on his shoulder. Neither of them spoke nor indicated what he should do.

Nathaniel returned his gaze to the windows of the lighthouse. The situation hadn't changed, the people inside still looked lost and abandoned, staring back at him with sad, hopeless eyes. It wasn't good, it wasn't a place where he wanted to be, he was in no rush to join them, and so his decision was made.

He turned around.

"I don't want to go in there," he told Artichoke and Nelly. "So what do I do now?"

"Well, you have to go back to where you came from,"

Artichoke informed him, gesturing towards the snow covered path that had brought them here.

"Okay then, let's go." Nathaniel walked past them, then, turning his head, asked, "Are you coming?"

Artichoke just stood there. "Sorry, not this time," he said. "Now you're on your own. It's just the way it is. It's just the way it has to be."

Nelly disappeared into the backpack and Artichoke walked towards the lighthouse. Nathaniel watched on as Artichoke knocked on the old wooden door, which slowly opened. His friendly escorts entered the building and the door closed behind them.

Nathaniel felt a deep sense of sadness at this, but nevertheless he turned and began to retrace his footsteps in the snow.

"He's coming back!" said Butler.

"Excellent," replied Lambert. "Quick, let me see."

He snatched the binoculars from Butler, almost breaking his helper's nose in the process, then focused the lenses and watched as Nathaniel walked back into the woods.

"Oh no! Oh no!" exclaimed Lambert

Butler didn't dare ask.

Nathaniel had the sense that he was being followed by something familiar and spun around. It was the Shadow Stalker. He turned back and immediately saw something different, something that he hadn't noticed before. In front of him, on the snow covered path, every time the strobe light from the lighthouse illuminated the area, a shadow appeared on the floor in front of him. It was *his* shadow and the realisation that *his* shadow had been absent throughout his journey hit him like a ton of bricks

"Oh my god, so it *was* me all along… just like Lambert said. It *was* me trying to find myself. I'm the Shadow Stalker, and I've been following myself, waiting for the decision to be made, waiting for *me* to make my own decision."

And although his two friends had left him, he didn't feel so alone anymore. And buoyed up, as he now was, with a new found confidence, he strode forward… back down the path that he'd come in on… just him and his shadow.

"Bollocks! He's reconnected with himself," shouted Lambert in frustration.

He struck Butler around the back of the head, knocking his bowler hat off into the snow… just for the hell of it.

Chapter 38

"Don't grab it, you fool, he's coming. Just stay hidden and see what happens. We'll use it as bait, it'll stand out against the snow," explained Lambert as he restrained Butler by the arm, forcefully digging his fingers in.

Nathaniel was hoping to retrace the footsteps in the snow that had brought him to the point of reckoning, which he now understood. The path was a long and straight one, however the footprints had disappeared covered by another layer of snow. It was now just a white walkway, apart from a small black object that lay upon it in the distance that looked strangely out of place.

It was then that the second sun rose in the sky, and it rose quickly. The temperature increased at an amazing pace. Nathaniel stopped walking as he observed the snow turn back to water. The trees started dripping and the birds started singing. The retreating snow then revealed various options of minor pathways that led off the main one that he was currently traversing. He was wide open to suggestion because he was in no rush to go back to The Village, and, to be honest, he had absolutely no idea where he was supposed to go.

It was then that he heard it, coming from the distance on his right hand side, down below… a sound of merriment… or was it a scream of torture? He decided to follow the noise.

"Dammit!" shouted Lambert. "Damn this place. I try my best to get me, I mean *us*, out of here and it's always the weather that stops me, every time. Now go and grab your hat, we've got work to do."

Lambert pushed Butler out of their hiding place, sending him stumbling and crashing onto the path. Then Lambert eased himself carefully out of the foliage and stood beside Butler, who was scrabbling around trying to retrieve his battered bowler hat.

"Can't you go any faster, you bloody imbecile? My future's at stake here," Lambert shouted.

And so, with all the care and duty of a responsible adult, not only did Lambert kick Butler in the ribs whilst he was on the floor, he thought he'd do it twice. Just for good measure… you know, just to get the point across.

Chapter 39

Nathaniel looked down at the thawed ground in front of one of the paths to his right and noticed something small and bright yellow. He bent down and picked it up.

Of course, it was a Lego brick.

He shook his head, wiped the brick on the side of his trousers and placed it into his pocket with the others, and then he descended in the direction of the strange noises.

When he reached the bottom of the path and emerged from the woods, he was met with the most amazing sight: in front of him was a windmill, and its sails were turning… although, strangely, there was no wind. And it was here that he realised this was where the sounds were coming from.

The wooden sails were creaking in a uniform rhythm, and as he approached he saw that the surroundings of the windmill looked more synthetic, like cloth, felt and sponge. Totally different to the other seemingly real life vegetation. He closed in on the strange area and stood in front of the windmill. The scene before him looked somehow hauntingly familiar, a memory from deep back in his childhood.

"Wooooo hooooo!" an excited voice screamed out at him.

He looked up to where it was coming from, and as he

turned his gaze in the direction of the sails, he focused upon the source of the voice. It was Lester the Jester and he was strapped to one of the four sails, and it seemed that he was having the time of his life.

"Whay haay! This is the best ride I've ever been on! You know you'd pay good money for this at the fairground but this is for freeeeee! Wooooo hooooo!"

Nathaniel looked on totally gobsmacked as the Jester came around time and time again and now and then he got snippets of conversation.

"There's somebody here who's got something for youuuu!" Lester announced as he reached the bottom of his rotation. He went up and then came back around again.

"I think it's something to do with… ahhhhh!" He was whisked back up.

"I said, I think it's something importaaaant!"

Nathaniel just stood there perplexed at the scene in front of him and he waited for the next important announcement of information, but when the Jester came around again all he got was a resounding, "Wooooo hooooo! This is brilliaaaant!"

It was then that the door at the foot of the windmill slowly opened. Out of the darkness within, a figure emerged. It walked slowly forward to stand in front of Nathaniel. The character was wearing a hat and a smock made of felt and sponge… as disturbingly was the person's face, which had no mouth. It was clutching a small, hessian sack in its mitten-like hands. It offered the sack to the confused Nathaniel.

"You have to take it. It's importaaant!" shouted Lester on his way round.

Nathaniel looked at the sack that was being offered to him and he noticed that the word FLOUR was inscribed upon it, although the U and the R had attempted to be crudely erased.

"Will you just take it, please? I know this is fun but I can't go on foreeeeeeeeeeever!"

Nathaniel took the sack. It was sealed by string stitching and was lighter in weight than he thought that it would be. The strange figure in front of him said nothing, how could it with no mouth? The character simply turned around and skilfully entered the windmill back through the doorway, avoiding the rotating sails without even breaking its pace.

Nathaniel stood there in a daze until Lester awoke him from his confused thoughts.

"You have to go now, keep going!" cried Lester. "You know that Rome wasn't built in a teeeeeacuuuup, wooooo hooooo!"

The sails kept turning and Nathaniel turned away, he clutched the sack and put one foot in front of the other and continued along the path.

"By the way," the Jester called from behind, "I hope that you know, you've now just accepted to become the Postman of the Postmortems." His demented laughter chased Nathaniel up the path until thankfully he could finally hear it no more.

So, he and his newly found shadow continued onwards.

Although he was still willing to honour his choice of

going back to where he'd come from by walking forwards and not entering the lighthouse, his mood felt like he was about to embark on a cold, long, wet weekend in Whitby… not *too* good!

And with that thought, just like a total solar eclipse, the day instantly turned to night as if he'd prompted it to happen, as if someone had just turned the lights out. Such was life on a planet that belonged to a binary star system.

Chapter 40

Nathaniel trudged on and rounded a corner to the left where the path inclined. The forest on either side became thicker and the noises from within became more sinister and disturbing. There were rustlings, the snapping of twigs, whisperings and clacking. He knew that he was a wanted man, and that he was on the run, so in order to distract himself from the menace that was surrounding him, he began to summon up the magic of music that was within his head.

And so, like an old vinyl record that had been long buried in a cardboard box… in a dark inaccessible place, in an unmarked grave, in a cemetery of attic-like remembrance, once loved but now forgotten… he managed to pull something out of the back of his mind, and again it was one of his own songs.

It was a strange one, but he'd written it at the time when Judy's mam had been diagnosed with cancer. Johnny was a poet and a writer, her daughter was a very talented artist, but the eternal conflict was: what is actually the monetary value of art? It got him to thinking about the use of animal images on coins and bank notes, and then the value of the lives of actual animals, as in the many different species of lifeforms that live on the same planet as the arrogant, ignorant species called homo sapiens, who seem to think that they own the place, and who, with their selfish and greedy behaviour, are eventually destined to destroy themselves and the planet Earth itself.

They both thought that they were going to lose Johnny at one point as they sat beside her hospital bed, and, in a not very helpful twist, Judy took an overdose because she couldn't bear the thought of life without her mam.

He felt so helpless, so had written a song in order to express his feelings. He called it *Animal Value* and it went like this:

Johnny is about to die,
She looks around with open eyes,
Never one to lay to rest,
Johnny is the very best.
She takes her pen for one last time,
Writing down a final line,
Full stops the page with a poet's tear,
And says, "Get the hell right out of here."
Johnny is my poet friend,
She gave me words right till the end,
But Johnny is much closer, see,
That woman's just like me.

So look into their faces,
They've cornered off my aces,
And liberated zoo,
There's nothing here for you.
Just if I could see them,

It'd justify my freedom,
But they haven't got a clue,
Of animal value.

Judy, she is fading fast,
We try to make the moment last,
Pastel shades and autumn scenes,
Painting pictures of my dreams.
The brush she holds is old and worn,
The canvas image ripped and torn,
Judy has no time to wait,
She desecrates her self-portrait!

"Why I do this," Judy says,
"Is to show it's crime not art that pays,
For money's no object to me,
I've never had it so how can it be?"

A pound of flesh,
A lionheart,
A banker's draft,
A work of art,
Artistic licence,
Heads and tails,
Find them in the summer sales.

Crime and season,
Rhyme and reason.

Thankfully, Judy recovered from her panic and desperation, and Johnny, her mam, had also managed to make a full recovery from the unwelcome invasive enemy… for now.

Chapter 41

The song had helped him to focus, and he finally reached the top of the incline. In front of him was The Village. Without hesitation, he stepped forward onto the cobbled street and kept moving forward. It wasn't long before he was in the middle of the High Street where he felt a lot safer than he'd felt back in the woods, although he knew that he was still being pursued by negative forces.

Eventually he reached the front door of The First and Last and dived inside. It was a lot quieter than the last time that he'd visited. Stanley, the landlord, who was stood behind the bar polishing a beer glass, clocked him straight away. Henry the dog barked.

"Be quiet," said Stanley.

Nathaniel approached the bar.

"Same again?" asked Stanley.

"That would be really good, but I haven't paid you for the last one."

"Plenty of time for that. Making a delivery are you?" asked Stanley, staring at the hessian sack Nathaniel was holding as he pulled the pint of beer.

"Yes, I think that's what's happening," Nathaniel replied, unsure even of his own motives. "So how do you organise your opening hours, if you don't mind me asking? I mean night and day and all that?"

"Pretty simple," answered Stanley. "We just never close. People come and go as they please, there's always something going on any time of the days or the nights, and the bits in-between."

Stanley finished pulling the pint and offered it to Nathaniel.

"Well, anyway, if I were you I'd hide around there," Stanley said, gesturing with a nod of his head towards a dark corner at the side of the bar.

Nathaniel accepted the pint of beer with a grateful nod and retreated around the corner.

"So why is it so quiet tonight… or today?" he enquired in a whisper.

"Well, it's poetry night, isn't it! I mean who comes out on poetry night?" And without waiting for an answer Stanley walked away while Nathaniel tried to blend back into the shadows. He thought about it and agreed with the question… I mean who the hell does come out on poetry night? And he immediately got the answer back from his own subconsciousness… *Well, you do, Nathaniel Phischermann… because you're bloody standing here, aren't you?*

He turned away, faced the wall and sheepishly took a few sips of beer. He put his glass down on the shelf. So far, so good. And as far as he could tell, nobody had followed him into the pub… well, not yet anyway.

Somebody took to the stage, he was dressed a bit like William Shakespeare might have been, and he had the pointed grey beard to complement the outfit.

"Good evening, my poetry loving people. I am The

Bard and I am your host for tonight's exquisite festival of literary excellence."

'Oh God,' thought Nathaniel. 'Beam me up, Scotty!'

"I'm going to kickstart this evening's performances with one of my own compositions that I have entitled *Mr Korpseley's Funeral.* I hope that all four of you enjoy it."

One of the audience tittered in appreciation of The Bard's introduction and his acknowledgment of the lack of attendance.

The Bard cleared his throat and began:

Mr Korpseley's funeral was such a grim affair,
As I took him by the ankles and
I dragged him down the stairs.
I put him at the table and I sat him on a chair,
I offered him some buffet,
But he respondeth not,
So I kicked the chair from under him,
And I ate the bloody lot.

Mr Korpseley's funeral was still a grim affair,
So we strapped him to the armrests upon his wheelchair.
We sent him coursing down the hill,
Into the funeral pyre,
Maybe we should've checked at first
to see that he'd expired.

Mr Korpesley's funeral just kept on getting worse,
We nailed him in the coffin,
Then we chucked him in the hearse.

The weather was abysmal,
And the vicar was appalled.
When he asked us for his surname,
We'd forgot what he was called.

Mr Korpseley's funeral was held before he died,
Because on his death certificate,
Mr Korpseley, he'd lied.
He'd lied about his birthday,
And he'd lied about his age,
However, Mr Korpseley's funeral is still happening today.

The sparse audience sat in silence until one of them decided to clap and then the other three reluctantly followed suit.

Nathaniel was only halfway down his pint when the front door of the pub opened.

The landlord looked up and then quickly glanced at him. "Go that way," he said without pointing a finger, but instead gestured with a nod of his head.

Nathaniel didn't wait to see who was coming in through the door, but immediately turned and headed to the back of the building where the landlord had indicated. He entered a corridor that led to a kitchen area, walking quickly through it and soon finding the back door. He tried the handle and the door opened. He stepped out into the street and quietly closed the door behind him, before promptly trotting off… trying to put as much distance between himself and the pub and whoever had just entered it as he could.

This time he recognised where he was. Once again he was back on Crab Apple Street and he was walking downhill. It looked slightly different, but he had a good idea of where number 121 was… and he felt compelled to go there.

He didn't bother ringing the doorbell this time, just tried the door and it opened without resistance. He entered the house. Nothing had changed, everything was the same as always… the musty smell, the Victorian decor. He closed the door behind him and advanced slowly towards the foot of the staircase. He gathered his courage, took a deep breath and then one step at a time, still clutching the sack, he ascended the steps, as he'd done a thousand times before in his lost dreams of a thousand yesterdays and yesternights.

He cautiously entered the small bedroom, as always, and made his way to the mysterious door of secrets, the one that never opened. He had an overwhelming feeling that this time though, it just might. The thought filled him with terror, but he reached forward anyway and tried the handle… it didn't budge. He tried harder with more force, twisting, pushing and pulling… nothing, the door was locked. It was stuck fast.

•

Hello again, my friend. Surprise, surprise, it's happening again. I'm covered from head to toe in spider webs and there's someone trying to get into my room, my office, my headspace! The door is being rattled with eager intent and here I am trying to write a story. It's such a distraction. I don't know… should I let the person in? Just to get it over with? Well, what do you think?

I'll tell you what I think… if I manage to untangle myself from these spider webs, and make my way down to the door and let him in, then it would be like smashing a two way mirror, a lose-lose situation. I never get to finish the story and he never gets to know the truth. So even though he is trying to break the door down, I am going to calmly keep on scribbling away. And despite the fact that the spiders are trying to truss me up like a Christmas turkey, and I am resisting their efforts to prevent my hand from writing, I will continue. So please, my friend, read on! Thank you.

Chapter 42

Horatio Lambert made his way to the empty bar with Butler limping closely behind him, and addressed the landlord. "Have you had any strangers in here tonight?" he asked as he scoured the basically deserted pub.

"No," replied Stanley abruptly. He'd never liked these two.

Lambert looked Stanley straight in the eyes. "Are you sure?" he enquired with positive intent, his cigarette breath betraying his dirty habit.

"Yes, I'm sure." Stanley fixed his stare.

Lambert waited for the landlord to ask him what he would like to drink, but the offer never came.

"You don't like me, do you?" asked Lambert.

"No, sir, I don't actually, now you come to mention it." Stanley never blinked.

There was a pause… a long one… Henry barked… and eventually Lambert gave in and, with a string of expletives, he turned, kicked Butler then headed out of the front door. Butler scuttled behind him like an injured puppy, battered bowler hat in hand.

Before they left Lambert turned around. "It's nice to know who your friends are, we'll be back for you!" he said, pointing at Stanley with a threatening look. "And by the way, can't you do something about this bloody Lego?

It's everywhere, it's really starting to piss me off!" He kicked away at the various Lego bricks that were scattered on the floor. "It's worse than walking in dogshit!"

The front door slammed behind them and the performer on stage, who hadn't been fazed at all by Lambert's outburst, finished his rendition of *The Rime of the Ancient Mariner* by Samuel Taylor Coleridge. He went back to his seat to stark but approving applause from the four members of the poetry club.

Stanley turned away and looked down to his feet. "How the hell did *we* end up in here?"

Henry the dog replied by whimpering sympathetically, he didn't know either… but here they were, nevertheless.

Chapter 43

"So how's he doing?" asked the lighthouse keeper, pouring another drop of Pusser's Rum into Artichoke's glass and another drop into Nelly's saucer.

"It's hard to tell," replied Artichoke as he tried to get a signal on his camera obscura wristwatch. "I think he made it to The Village, but then the image broke up."

"What's your gut feeling?" asked the lighthouse keeper, sitting down at the table clutching the bottle of rum. He was an old man with white hair and a long white beard, although his weathered face framed his sparkling blue eyes, which were bright, alert and youthful. He always wore a sou'wester and a pair of wellington boots turned down at the top even when he was indoors, and he might have been around for a long, long time but he still felt that he had a long, long way to go. He had a job to do, he was the Guardian of the Last Hope, just like Artichoke was the Guide to the Lost Souls, the place where they came to when they were convinced that there was no going back. It was a thankless task, although he didn't actually feel the need to be thanked.

The lighthouse keeper, whose name was Alexander, glugged a wee swallow from the bottle and set it down on the table.

Artichoke sipped a dram from his glass and Nelly lapped a few licks from his saucer.

"You're looking a bit distant, son. What's on your mind?" said Alexander.

Artichoke thought for a few seconds and then replied, "The thing is, I know that he's made up his mind and that he's making his way back but he's not safe, is he? I mean most of them do end up here in the lighthouse, this mausoleum, but the chance of those who want to go home getting back safely to where they've come from is quite slim, and most of them come to a really bad ending. It's just I think that me and Nelly should be doing more to help them back if that's what they want and not just leave them to their own devices."

"This is really good by the way," piped up Nelly, looking up from his *empty* saucer. "The rum, I mean… not the conversation. We've done our job, he's made up his mind. Any chance of a refill, please?" he asked, doing his best cat smile.

Alexander nodded and glugged another small splash into the saucer. Nelly started lapping it up with all the enthusiasm of a very happy feline.

"Come on," said Artichoke, standing up. "We're not finished yet. Let's go… besides we have to get home anyway. Thanks for the drink, but I think that we've still got a role to play in this one."

Nelly greedily slurped the last dregs down.

"Well, it was great to see you again, and good luck," said Alexander.

Nelly crawled into the backpack, and Nathaniel put it on then headed for the door.

"Likewise," replied Nathaniel. "And keep those lights shining! It's important." He gestured upwards.

"I know, son. I will. And stay safe," Alexander told them.

"I'll try," replied Artichoke.

"*We'll* try, he meant!" Nelly shouted out from the inside of the backpack.

Chapter 44

Nathaniel closed the front door of number 121 behind him, feeling despondent that once again he hadn't managed to gain entry to the room. He walked down the path and back onto Crab Apple Street, this time he turned left and headed down the hill, clutching the sack as he went on his way.

He was nearing the bottom of the street when he came across a book that had been abandoned on the pavement. He bent down and picked it up. The title on the front was spelt with a strange kind of font in gold leaf, which made him frown, it said:

THE BIg Book of LiEs

It was a black leather-bound tome with a brass clasp that secured it shut. He looked around and there was nobody else to be seen. He had no intention of carrying anything else other than the sack, so he placed the book on the wall of a front garden, hoping that the owner would come back to claim it. Then he began walking forward again.

He hadn't gone very far when he heard a door open. He stopped and turned around. Somebody was picking up the book.

"Thank the Lord, you've come back to me," the voice said.

The person holding the book was dressed like a missionary preacher from years gone by and he seemed overwhelmed with the rediscovery of the book.

"I'm so so sorry, I'll never deny your words again, please forgive me," the strange character announced, clutching the book to his chest. "Who brought you back to me? Who was it?"

The preacher was looking wildly around, his black smock twirling in unison with his movements, and Nathaniel stood stock-still hoping that he wouldn't clock him. His previous encounters with organised religion and their representatives hadn't been good and this was the last thing that he needed. He couldn't deal with any more interruption to his own mission… as to where that destination was exactly at this point in time, he had absolutely no idea.

The preacher, who bore a startling resemblance to his old teacher Mr. Hardcastle, stopped, stared straight at Nathaniel then pointed a finger, "You. It was you, wasn't it?" The preacher's face lit up.

'Oh shit,' Nathaniel thought. He didn't respond.

The preacher began to advance towards him and although he was quite a distance away, Nathaniel turned on his heels and ran down the hill as fast as he could.

"No, don't run away, my child," the manic preacher shouted out as he pursued Nathaniel down the street, waving the strange book in the air. "It's not too late… if you repent, all your sins will be forgiven."

"Jesus Christ!" Nathaniel shouted out. "This is all I need." He reached the bottom of Crab Apple Street and took a left turning and ran as fast as he could. It wasn't long before his lungs began to complain. He could hear the footsteps of the religious maniac in hot pursuit behind him.

"Stop, my child! 'Suffer the little children' is what *he* said, *our* Lord, and if you don't stop, my little child, then I will make *you* suffer… beyond your wildest dreams so… STOP NOW!!"

Nathaniel didn't stop and he had no intention of doing so.

"All I ask for is a small contribution to the church funds, a penny will suffice. Think of it as the widow's mite and remember that it's easier for a camel to go through the eye of a needle than it is for a rich man to enter through the gates of the kingdom of Heaven."

The preacher was screaming at him now. And it was then that ironically Nathaniel started praying for a miracle, and strangely enough it actually happened.

He heard an almighty clatter behind him and the sound of bodies crashing to the ground accompanied by angry shouts and cries of help and mercy from the preacher, along with the dull thuds and thumps of a savage beating that was being mercilessly dispatched.

"That's *my* penny, you bible bashing fool!" A voice shouted out, as the beating continued. "Hit him harder… HARDER!"

Nathaniel recognised the voice and he stopped, and turned around… it was Lambert.

The preacher was crouched on the floor and Butler, who had the book in both of his hands, was beating the defenceless man continuously over the head.

"Please! In the name of God," the preacher pleaded, which prompted Lambert to squarely boot him in the face.

Nathaniel turned quickly around, sickened by the scene, and miraculously found his second wind. He continued painfully sprinting forward without questioning as to what was happening behind him.

He reached the end of the road, the houses thinned out and the cobblestones turned to grass, which led him to a dry stone wall with a small wooden gate in it. The sounds of violence behind him were more distant now as he opened the gate and stumbled into the woodland beyond it.

Chapter 45

He'd been walking for a while, not willing to stop even though he was short of breath. It was still dark but he followed the narrow, wild looking pathway. He just kept going with no idea, once again, where he might end up. One foot in front of the other, clutching the sack, anything to put distance between him and his pursuers.

One of the suns came up – or rose… or set… whichever way you'd choose to explain it, Nathaniel wasn't sure anymore – and the lights came on again. The light was welcome and as he emerged from the forest into a large area of grassland, he felt like he'd stepped into an arena… perfect grass surrounded by a circular wall of trees. The temperature went from cold to warm and instead of wandering on across the meadow, his attention was drawn to a break in the foliage on the left side of the green.

He decided to walk around the perimeter edge in order to reach what looked like another path. This place didn't feel right, it felt like a killing zone. So he set off carefully and eventually he got to the opening. He glanced back but there was nobody there. He walked through it and back into the cover of the woods.

This place seemed strangely familiar, there were

beautiful flowers and butterflies, he even disturbed a deer and it wasn't long before he found himself in front of a wall, with a wooden door which had a pile of envelopes at the foot of it.

It was the other side of the door that he'd originally been confronted with, the one that he'd peered through the letterbox of… and the letterbox was still there, it was just that this was the other side of it. A different angle, the other side of the letterbox.

He walked forward, eager to take a look at the pile of letters. When he reached the door he looked down at the envelopes, some had been opened and some were still sealed. The ones on top looked relatively new but they seemed to become older and more weathered towards the bottom of the pile, the ones that he could see anyway. It was a large stack of obviously handwritten correspondence and whoever had written the letters had taken the trouble to post them, but the strange thing was as far as he could see there were no stamps on the envelopes. There were no postmarks, nothing to do with the normal post office delivery system. In fact, most of them didn't even have an address on. Lots of them were blank, a few said 'To Whom It May Concern', some said 'I'm sorry', and a couple stood out as being addressed 'To Mam'.

He stood there staring and then he decided to pick one up to read it, but as he did, there was a thrashing sound to his left hand side in the undergrowth. He recoiled backwards. Was it Lambert? If it was, then he was going to stand his ground and, if necessary, he was prepared to attempt to kick the shit out of the cowardly bastard. He stood there poised and ready for an attack.

The thrashing of the undergrowth grew louder until the perpetrator finally appeared.

A young woman dressed in a white smock, with eyes closed and waving a white stick from side to side emerged. She stopped in front of Nathaniel. She smiled, he didn't. She could tell, even though she couldn't see, not through her eyes anyway.

"Why are you here?" she asked.

It was a simple enough question but Nathaniel was stumped for an honest answer… why the hell *was* he here? He dodged the psychology and merely answered, "Because I am!"

The woman sighed. "Okay, fair enough, if you don't want to talk, that's fine." She turned around and with a thrashing of her stick, she began to make her way back to where she'd appeared from.

Nathaniel was immediately embarrassed by his response and he kicked himself big style.

"I'm sorry, I was so rude. It's just I'm so confused with everything… please come back," he pleaded.

The woman stopped and turned around, then she walked back to him, "Well, that's your first and last warning. It's just that *I* do know why you're here, if you're interested." She waited for a response.

"I'm very interested… thank you." He smiled, although he thought it was probably a ridiculous thing to do, as she was obviously blind. But it wasn't… because, to his amazement, she smiled back at him.

"Things aren't always what they seem, you know. People can feel things without actually seeing them… I felt you smile and it felt nice," she said.

"I *saw* you smile!" he replied. "I was lucky I guess, in that respect, I suppose." He felt like he was putting his foot in his mouth again but thankfully she laughed.

"Have you read any of the letters yet?" she asked.

"No, I've just got here," he answered. "I haven't had the chance yet."

"Why don't you try this one?" she said, tapping at one of the envelopes near the top of the pile with her white stick.

He looked down and picked it up. Instantly he recognised it as the envelope that he'd discovered in his dream of years ago, at the top of the crab apple tree. He stared at it in amazement… it had his name on it and it was still sealed. He took a deep breath and he prepared to open it.

"By the way, I think that sack's a delivery for me," she said, pointing to what he was holding onto. "Just put it down by the door."

He did so, saying, "How do you know it's for you? And what's in it?"

"More letters and notes unfortunately, from people who have been up the creek and through the mill. And I know it's for me because it's got my name on it… Has the penny dropped yet?" she asked.

He was dumbfounded. "No, it hasn't. Who *are* you?"

"The clue's on the sack… it's my name!" she said.

He glanced back down at the sack of letters. His head jerked back and he addressed the woman. "You're Flo, aren't you?"

"Yes, and I think you've got something for me… besides the sack… haven't you?" she prompted him.

"Oh yes, yes, I think I have," he said, fumbling around in his pocket amidst the Lego bricks. And then he found it. He pulled out the old penny and held it up in front of her. Although he knew that she couldn't see it, she smiled anyway. She could obviously feel its aura.

"I think it's from your mam! At least that's what it says on it."

And as she reached out in the direction of where she thought the coin was, an almighty crashing noise came from the far side of the clearing.

Nathaniel spun around and as a result Flo didn't receive the coin.

He ran forward to the edge of the clearing and on the other side, crashing out of the treeline, came Cruschtov and his red army of subservient cronies. Nathaniel stuffed the unopened envelope into one of his pockets as he observed the bizarre scene unfolding in front of him.

The giant crab walked defiantly on its two hind legs to the centre of the clearing, limping slightly from an obvious recent injury, and his soldier crabs marched sideways and took up position on either flank of their leader. When they were all in position and formed up, Cruschtov spoke. "Give me the penny and I will spare your lives. Resist and I will kill you and take the coin anyway. Quite simple really."

"Please don't do it," said Flo, who had joined Nathaniel.

"Don't worry," Nathaniel replied. "I have no intention of doing that." And as he spoke the words, he smelled the distinctive aroma of tobacco smoke. There was movement to his right, and emerging from the path that he'd entered on came Lambert, swaggering with a cigarette dangling in the corner of his mouth. He was dragging the preacher by his ear. The preacher's hat was missing and he was now sporting a black eye and badly cut lip. Butler was enthusiastically still beating him with the now battered book. They stopped twenty yards in front of Cruschtov and they paid him no respect. Lambert let go of the preacher, who collapsed whimpering to the ground.

"Do you see this? This pathetic wretch of a man?" Lambert was directly addressing Nathaniel. "Well, this'll be you next, unless you give me the penny."

Nathaniel didn't respond, but Cruschtov did. He clacked his claws with vigour, his googly eyes on stalks aimed with anger at the ignorant Lambert. The first row of crab infantry began to march sideways, closing the gap between themselves and Lambert, Butler and the preacher.

Lambert turned around and reacted quickly. "NOW!" he screamed. "NOW! CHAAARGE!!" He directed his cane from his left side and pointed straight towards the red army.

The treeline burst apart as a hundred Grimpanzees, led by Grimaldi, smashed their way out of their hiding place in the woods. They sprinted forward hooting and hollering and crashed into the crab army.

The fight was furious and bloody. Fur flew, as did crab legs. Shells cracked and Grimpanzees were tossed through the air, crustaceans were being dismantled like unwanted furniture. The noise was horrific and the image was one of unforgettable carnage.

Using the distraction of the battle, Lambert turned back and moved towards Nathaniel, who stood his ground unperturbed. And then an amazing thing happened… from the right hand side of the clearing, uninvited but more than welcome, dozens and dozens of Stilt Walking Hedgehogs emerged from the woodland and quickly advanced to form a defensive line in front of Nathaniel, cutting him off from Lambert's aggressive movements.

Nathaniel peered between the stilts and saw that Lambert was still coming forward, his face contorted with rage.

"Sod your bloody hedgehogs. I'm going to get my penny," shouted Lambert. He started sprinting, but as he did so, from the left hand side, like a professional rugby player, Lester the Jester totally took him out with a brilliant tackle. Lambert's silver top hat flew away like a champagne cork from a newly opened bottle.

One of the hedgehogs dismounted from his stilts, and grasping one of them like a jousting pole he ran forward on his hind legs, charging towards Lambert who was wrestling on the ground with Lester.

Butler saw what was happening and released the preacher, his attention focused on the quickly developing situation. The preacher seized his chance and began to crawl away to the edge of the clearing. The cavalier hedgehog stopped when he reached Lambert.

Lester saw him, immediately stopped fighting and rolled away as the hedgehog pointed his stilt at Lambert, who'd realised what was happening. The hedgehog looked at Butler who was still clutching the battered book, then it gestured towards Lambert in a manner that said, "Let him have it then because he's had it anyway, you might as well have your pound of flesh."

The hedgehog paused with its weapon just inches away from Lambert's throat.

Butler understood what he was silently being told and that he could now do whatever he wanted to do with his domineering master because in a few moments there would be no possibility of any kind of repercussions towards him… because Lambert was about to be executed by the point of a hedgehog's stilt.

Butler grinned and moved forward raising the book in the air. "This has been a long time coming, you bastard," he cried. "Every dog has its day and this is mine." He took off his bowler hat and tossed it away like a Frisbee, then laid into the screaming Lambert with all the fury of an unleashed animal that had been subordinated for all of its life, existing only to serve the selfish will of its cruel owner. He beat Lambert so hard around the head with the black book that teeth and flesh were ripped away without mercy… when one of his eyes popped out of its socket, the hedgehog decided that enough was enough, so he leant forward with all of his weight and pushed the sharp point of the stilt slowly but firmly through the neck of the squirming idiot Lambert on the ground. The sound from the murder victim's throat sounded like a million scalded cats and Butler danced around with glee like an excited elf on Christmas Day morning.

Nathaniel winced as he watched the grotesque scene and then he turned around… Flo was still there, she was standing by the doorway. He turned back to witness the ensuing battle.

The line of Stilt Walking Hedgehogs began to advance towards the violent skirmish between the crabs and the Grimpanzees.

Cruschtov was holding Grimaldi in the air by his ankle. Grimaldi, in turn, was slashing at the huge crustacean's googly eyes. When the hedgehogs crashed into the maelstrom, it was like watching a bomb go off… stilts, hedgehogs, crabs and apes thrown into the air like confetti that had been caught up in a freak whirlwind.

"What now?" Nathaniel asked, turning back to Flo in desperation.

She grabbed his arm and led him back to the door.

"I never knew my mam," she said calmly.

He was surprised by her air of serenity and her detachment from the violence of the battle.

"And she never knew me," she continued. "I was taken away from her when I was a baby. She was too young and unmarried and I was partially blind from birth. What chance did we have? But I do remember something, and you might think I'm stupid… but even though I was just a baby, I can still hear her saying, through her tears, that she loved me, that she would never leave me and that one day we would see each other again."

"I think you need to have this now," Nathaniel said, giving her the old penny.

"Thank you so much… I can feel the words on it."

She began to cry as she rubbed the coin with her fingers. "And so, in return you need to have this," she replied, producing a key. "Take it and open the door. And when you get through, make sure that you lock it and post the key back through the letterbox."

Nathaniel took the key and he turned it in the lock. He looked back. "Will you be all right?" he asked her.

"I'll be fine, just get out of here. I know how to use *this*!" she told him, brandishing the white stick in front of her like a sword.

Nathaniel pushed the door open and stumbled out onto a pathway that he recognised from not too long ago. He quickly shut the door, locked it and posted the key back through the letterbox, as instructed. The noise of the battle was instantly muted.

"Thank God for that," he said to himself, collapsing onto his backside and starting to cry into his hands, shaking with adrenaline and confusion.

Chapter 46

"I know who's car that is," Judy told the police officer, pointing at the Mini that was now crawling with forensic detectives dressed in white paper overalls.

"Oh, okay, ma'am, and so do we now. We've run the plates through the system. Would you like to tell me something?" he asked.

"Yeah, it's my boyfriend… Nathaniel. We broke up yesterday. Is it him… over there?" She nodded towards the activity of the emergency services on the beach.

"I don't know and I really couldn't tell you even if I did. Is it okay to take a statement off you?"

Judy began to weep and nodded.

•

Nathaniel felt a tap on his foot. He opened his fingers and through blurred watery eyes he saw that it was one of the Wood Lobsters… Mr Slater. He clicked and clacked away with his wooden pincers and Nathaniel managed a smile. He had no idea what the strange creature was trying to communicate but when he pointed one of his claws, Nathaniel heard a welcome creaking sound that he hadn't heard in a while and he looked up in the direction Mr Slater was pointing. The bushes parted and Tiny Toppings strode out onto the path. Tiny walked towards him and scores of Wood Lobsters scuttled around the plastic giant's feet, skilfully managing to avoid being trampled on, as if they had done it a thousand times before.

The Lego man stopped in front of him. "I'm sorry I lost you, I tried to find you but I couldn't," he explained in his low booming voice. "But I haven't been myself lately. I've been losing parts of me as well, you see. I think that *you've* got some things that belong to *me*." Tiny bent down and put one of his hands out towards Nathaniel.

It was instantly obvious that one of Tiny's fingers was missing.

Mr Slater began tapping again enthusiastically on Nathaniel's foot and so he searched in his pocket and retrieved the Lego bricks that he'd picked up on his journey. He reached out with an open palm and offered them to the Wood Lobster, who took them one by one, and began to reassemble Tiny's missing finger. When the job was complete, Tiny stood up straight.

"Let's try again. You've made your choice so follow me one more time and let's get you out of here," the giant offered.

Without hesitation, Nathaniel stood up. "Okay, let's go," he agreed.

And off they went, walking back down the path that he'd arrived on, when he'd first entered the strange Land of Khartoonz… where nothing had seemed to be real, but everything actually had been… so far.

Chapter 47

"So where are we going?" asked Nathaniel as they walked back down the familiar path of pine needles and pine cones, some that were as big as pineapples.

"I'm going to take you home," replied Tiny. "Look up and who do you see?"

Nathaniel looked upwards and through the gaps of the tree's canopy he saw the large bird gliding along with them leading the way.

"I told you that Albie was looking down on you, didn't I ?" said Tiny.

"Yes you did and I know that he's been there all along," Nathaniel agreed.

They carried on walking for a long time, the Wood Lobsters scurrying around in and out of the forest and generally making a nuisance of themselves. Tiny stopped walking just before a bend in the path and Nathaniel stopped too.

"Why have we stopped?" he asked.

"Because this is where you came in, and so this is where you have to go out."

Around the bend, out of sight Nathaniel heard someone – or some*thing* – crashing through the undergrowth. Was it Lambert and Butler… or Grimaldi… or Cruschtov… or all of them?

It turned out that it was actually none of them, the small man with the feathered hat came running around the corner and stopped in front of the leaving party.

"Artichoke!" exclaimed Nathaniel.

"Yes, we knew of a shortcut back to here. We don't normally do this," said Artichoke, "but there's something that we need to share with you." Nelly popped up from the backpack.

"This wasn't totally my idea by the way," said the cat. "Because we feel that you may have something more to give to your world than just your mere existence, Artichoke has something that he wants to give to you. Go ahead, do it." Nelly prompted.

Artichoke removed one of the long white feathers from his hat and presented it to Nathaniel.

"Use it wisely, and write great things with it... song lyrics, poems and stories, and never forget the Land of Khartoonz, everyone you met here and everything you experienced here."

"I won't forget... I promise," replied Nathaniel, overwhelmed by the unexpected gift.

"Now, you have to turn around, take three steps backwards and your journey here will end," instructed Artichoke.

Nathaniel paused and sighed, he knew what he had to do because he'd already made his decision at the lighthouse. It was time to go back and face the future... *his* future.

He turned to Tiny Toppings and said, "Goodbye to you all and thank you for your help."

"Goodbye and good luck," boomed Tiny as the Wood Lobsters clacked their own version of farewell.

Nathaniel started walking backwards… one, two, three… and back in the room.

Miraculously he found himself on the top of the cliff where he'd originally been… how many days ago? He had no idea. The sun had risen but it still hadn't reached a high point in the sky. Behind him there was a rustle of feathers and then a large seabird ran past him and launched itself from the cliff edge. He watched on as the now familiar bird glided gracefully away from him toward the horizon and eventually disappeared from view.

"Goodbye," he whispered under his breath. "Thank you for being there for me."

Nathaniel looked at the feather in his hand and took a few paces backwards onto the cliff path. He then turned and began to walk back along Huntcliff towards Saltburn. As he ventured forward he became aware of a dramatic scene below him on the beach. There were a lot of people crowded around a particular spot, the Coastguard Land Rover was parked up there with its emergency lights flashing. He could make out paramedics and police officers milling around and even the inshore lifeboat was in attendance. Whatever had happened had obviously been very serious.

Chapter 48

Judy had given her brief statement and was stood alongside Johnny and the policeman, who had introduced himself as PC Pease, watching the small group of other officers wandering down the steps from the cliff.

"Did you find anything?" PC Pease shouted out.

"Nothing suspicious, there's no people up there," replied a policewoman as they made it down to The Ship Inn car park. "Strange thing was though," she said as she approached them, "there was a large seabird, like an Albatross, but it didn't move. It wasn't fazed at all by us being up there. It was if it was waiting for something to happen! Weird, but that was all."

It was then that they heard the voices of the stretcher-bearers walking up the slipway heading for the ambulance that was parked at the top. Judy saw the body bag they were carrying and immediately ran towards it.

"NO!" she screamed out. "Is it him? Is it my Nathaniel?"

"Come on, Miss, calm down now," said one of the attending paramedics, managing to restrain her before she reached the ambulance.

Johnny soon caught up and flung her arms around her daughter, although she too was crying.

"I only wanted to scare you, to give you a nudge, you idiot. You didn't have to do *this*," Judy bawled at the corpse in the bag on the stretcher. "You selfish bas…" Before she could finish the sentence, a familiar voice shouted out from behind her.

"What's going on?" it asked.

Judy managed to turn around and her jaw dropped… was she looking at a ghost? She couldn't speak.

Nathaniel was stood there, a white feather in his hand.

Judy broke free and ran to him, and embraced him with tremendous force. "You stupid bastard, don't ever scare me like that again," she sobbed into his chest.

After a few moments, she turned her head and looked back at the ambulance, its doors now shut.

"I'm sorry," Judy whispered to the unfortunate soul inside. "I didn't mean to shout at *you*… whoever you are… or were."

"Come on," said Johnny. "I think we should all go home, back to my place."

Chapter 49

"Where did you get the feather from?" Judy asked Nathaniel as they sat in her mother's front room watching the local news on TV. They were on the sofa and Johnny was sat in the armchair. The three of them were drinking mugs of tea and helping themselves from a plate of biscuits.

"Oh, a good friend of mine gave it to me," he answered cautiously.

"So why did you have it with you?" she enquired, frowning.

He paused for too long.

"Are you hiding something from me?" she said. "Is there somebody else? Why were you there? I thought you'd killed yourself, for God's sake!"

"No, no, nothing like that." He put his mug down on the coffee table. "To tell you the truth, it was *your letter*. I couldn't handle it. I know I'm not perfect but I am who I am. And yeah, I love you… there I've said it. You broke my heart, Judy, you broke my heart." He turned his head away and made his best attempt to stifle the emotional outpouring that was attempting to erupt from the depths of his very soul.

At that point, the news presenter on the TV began to talk about a new story, and everyone in the room focused in with concerned intent.

"Early this morning, a body was found at the foot of the cliffs at Saltburn-by-the-Sea. The incident was attended by local emergency services, including the Coastguard. So far the police have yet to issue a statement but it is believed that the victim was a local resident." There was a pause as the presenter moved onto the next story… it was something to do with river pollution in the area. The three of them soon lost concentration, but then the next piece caught Nathaniel's attention.

"The family of a missing woman are appealing to anyone who may have seen her over the last few days as they are desperate to get her back home safe. She was last seen leaving her place of work in Loftus on Saturday night." The image of a young woman's face was briefly shown on the screen.

A massive penny dropped.

"That's her!" Nathaniel shouted out. "It's her!"

The face of the woman had triggered a memory… when he'd been walking along the cliff top to his place of chosen self-execution, she'd walked past him and smiled. He recognised her face and he also remembered not returning the gesture, consumed as he was with his own self-pity.

He was convinced that it was she who had committed suicide, for whatever reason he didn't know. So what might have happened if he had smiled back? Would that have changed things? Would that have changed her state of mind at that crucial point in her life? Had he pushed her over the edge without meaning to do so?

"What do you mean 'it's her'?" Johnny asked, snapping Nathaniel back into reality.

"That girl, on the tele. She walked past me on the cliff. I think it was her on the beach, on the stretcher, in the body bag."

"Then we need to call the police."

"I think they'll put two and two together, if they haven't already. But more importantly…" he said turning to Judy, pausing for quite a while, "like I said, I know I'm not perfect, but, then again, who is? What I'm trying to say in a roundabout way is…" He grasped her hand and looked her straight in the eyes, "Will you marry me?"

In shock, Johnny instantly spat out a swig of tea she'd just taken.

Judy stared at him perplexed, like the proverbial rabbit trapped in the headlights. The pair of them didn't blinked and it was in that instant that Judy knew that he meant it… and much more than that too. She felt that somehow he'd had an epiphany, an awakening, a kick up the arse, if you like, and he was being true and honest.

"Yes," she softly replied. "Yes, I will. And there's something else you have to know… you're going to be a dad!"

Chapter 50

Hello, my friend, it's good to talk to you again, and even though our hero has decided to leave the Land of Khartoonz, I am still here unfortunately… no lucky penny for me, I'm afraid. So here I am in the attic of 121 Crab Apple Street, scribbling away amidst the arachnids and the damned webs they weave, those invisible threads they use as pathways and highways. I am currently on my fourth candle – yes, I did say 'fourth candle' and not 'fork handles' – for the benefit of you comedians out there! Although I'm writing this story, I can't for the life of me think what is written on the letter inside the envelope that is addressed to him.

Can you…?

Chapter 51

Nine months later…

Nathaniel was sat on a hard plastic chair by the side of the hospital bed that Judy was laid upon. In her arms, swaddled in small white cotton sheets was a newborn baby boy. Nathaniel was ecstatic, Judy looked knackered. They had agreed to call him Albie, in respect of Nathaniel's grandad… even though Judy knew nothing about the Albatross or the Land of Khartoonz.

It was exactly twenty-one minutes past one o'clock in the morning. Nathaniel was tightly holding Judy's hand and the tears he'd been crying were still stinging his eyes. Witnessing the birth had been both traumatic and fantastic. God only knew how Judy was feeling right now! The baby was asleep, the little boy was beautiful and Nathaniel had noticed a distinctive birthmark on his arm. It was blurred but it looked a bit like a series of numbers. He gently let go of Judy's hand and quietly stood up.

Judy had moved back in with him shortly after the incident on the cliff. He'd managed to pack in smoking, the last one that he'd lit up had been during the night when he'd tried to sleep in the Mini. They had managed to have a small wedding at the local register office, which Johnny helped to pay for.

He was now playing his music at gigs in various local

establishments and had managed to get himself a part time job in one of the pubs as a bartender. Life was a 100% better now than when he'd climbed up the steps to the top of the cliff all those months ago.

He walked out into the corridor and passed the duty nurse, who was typing on a computer keyboard. She looked up and smiled and he made a point of smiling back. He pushed the green exit button on the side of the doors and they opened. He then made his way to the coffee machine, a journey that he seemed to have made a thousand times during the course of the day.

He put the coins into the slot and reflected on the fact that a year ago he would have been gagging to go outside and have a fag, but nowadays – thanks to his strange encounters in the Land of Khartoonz – he no longer felt the craving. He took the hot plastic cup from the machine and sat down at a table in the small café area, the chairs here were so much softer and comfortable than the ones in the ward. He'd already texted Johnny with the good news and she'd replied with her congratulations. It was a something that he'd been happy to do.

He stared at the wall in front of him and the clock still said 1.21am. The wallpaper was decorated with images of forests, trees and woodlands. He took a sip of coffee and his mind drifted away… after all, it had been a long, long day.

Chapter 52

"Do you remember him?" asked Nelly.

"Who?" Artichoke replied.

"You know, the one who got the penny, the one with the bird?"

"Bird, penny? What the hell are you talking about?" said Artichoke.

Artichoke Underwood and Nelly the cat were in their treehouse, sat at the table in front of the stove, it was night time and they were preparing to go to bed. Artichoke racked his brains and then it came to him.

"That was months ago, but yes, I do… I remember *him*. Nathaniel the fisherman. Yes, I remember he went back, didn't enter the lighthouse. He went back again, it caused quite a stir."

"You can say that again, it was the biggest battle that the Land of Khartoonz has seen since the Man on the Moon tried to claim political asylum on the other side of nowhere, and that didn't end too well, did it? In fact, he was crucified by the Martian elitist movement on a massive paper cut-out of Woody Woodpecker."

"What the hell are you talking about? How many of those mushrooms have you eaten by the way?" he asked, gesturing towards the bowl of freshly foraged funghi. "I've told you to leave off the orange ones."

"That's by the by, think nothing of it, you'll understand one day, but for now," purred the cat, "it's time to engage in stage two of his future, the fisherman that is… he has no idea!"

"Oh my God, you're serious, aren't you?" Artichoke questioned.

"Yes, I am, so let's get on with it," he said, staring at Artichoke through his massively dilated pupils. "Let's just get on with it," the cat reinforced.

"Okay, so I have to go and run a few messages," Artichoke responded. "And yeah, you scare the shit out of me sometimes. Just keep off the orange ones!"

"Just go!" Nelly commanded. "It's this one last thing, and then it's all done with… well, for *him* anyway. And don't forget to take the letter, the one that dropped out of his pocket before he went back. You're playing the role of postman now."

"Yeah and I guess my nickname's Pat, and you're my black and white… oh forget it!"

"Jess get on with it," Nelly grinned his feline smile, his whiskers bristling with mischief.

Artichoke stood up without smiling and grabbed the backpack, though this time Nelly didn't jump in.

The small man with the feathered hat left the comfort of the treehouse on his own, and with a dark sense of foreboding, descended to the floor of the forest via the wooden elevator contraption.

Chapter 53

I wasn't expecting it, so when it happened I was quite surprised and I even had to put my quill down in order to respond. There'd been a shuffling sound underneath the door, the one at the bottom of the attic steps. I rose from my desk and brushed off the spiders and all of their entrapments.

When I reached the bottom of the stairs, I saw it… a creased envelope that had been pushed underneath the door. So I picked it up and to my surprise it had my name and address on it. Well, my dear friend, you could've knocked me down with a feather… not for the first time in this story. And, the way things are going, it probably won't be the last. I guess we just live our lives and get on with it, what else can we do?

Chapter 54

"Wake up, Mister Phischermann." The nurse was shaking him gently by the shoulder.

He awoke with a start.

Shocked at his sudden awakening from his dream state, it took a few seconds for him to realise where he was, and then he noticed that he was still in the café at the hospital. The clock on the wall must have run out of batteries because still it displayed twenty-one minutes past one. He'd obviously slept, but he still felt exhausted and his neck was stiff from the uncomfortable position his body had been in.

"Is everything alright?" he asked the nurse. She looked vaguely familiar and was squinting at him through thick-lensed spectacles.

"Would anyone like any refreshments?" another friendly voice enquired, as the porter wheeled a squeaky trolley laden with drinks and pastries into the room. The man also looked familiar, his clothes underneath his white porter's jacket were bright and jovial. "Miss Nightingale, would you like something?" he asked the nurse.

"Not just now, thank you. Maybe later," she replied.

"Do I know you two?" Nathaniel was confused, he was sure that he'd met these people before.

"You probably know us better than you know yourself," the porter grinned. "After all, Rome wasn't built in a teacup, was it?" He winked as he wheeled the squeaking trolley out of the room and then laughed like a demented mental patient, staring back over his shoulder looking Nathaniel squarely in the eyes.

"What's going on?" Nathaniel turned back to look at the nurse, but she'd disappeared. He was alone in the café. Whatever had just happened was weird and he didn't like it.

It seemed like he was having some kind of an episode of reliving the trauma of when he was in the Land of Khartoonz. His first thoughts were of his wife and newborn child.

He got up and walked towards the double doors that would gain him entrance to the maternity ward. He noticed that the duty nurse had left her station. He pressed the button on the intercom, but there was no reply. He gently tapped on the glass door with his knuckles. He waited but nobody came. He tried again with more force, but there was still no response.

Panic descended upon him and when he looked around for a solution to his predicament, he couldn't believe where he actually was.

Chapter 55

"Same again, sir?" asked Stanley the landlord.

Nathaniel just stared at him dumbfounded. No longer was he in the hospital, he was back in The First and Last, and he was standing at the bar. He was holding an empty pint glass and the place was packed. It was buzzing. He looked into Stanley's eyes and there was only one answer to the question. "Yes, please," he said slowly, offering the glass to Stanley.

"Clean glass, sir?" Stanley asked as he took the used glass.

"Yes, please," Nathaniel quietly responded.

"What was it again, sir? It's so busy in here tonight that I honestly can't remember. Was it a pint of The Way Forward or a pint of The Way Backwards?"

Nathaniel was bemused and in his confusion he simply said, "You know what, I think I'll just have a half of each… and please just put them in the same glass, thanks."

"My pleasure," the landlord grinned and made his way to the beer pumps. He soon returned and placed the pint of ale on the bar in front of Nathaniel. "I'll just put it on the slate with everything else, sir! And I think I'll name this cocktail the Neither Here Nor There."

"Thank you. I appreciate it," Nathaniel replied as he

raised the glass and took a sip of the strange concoction. "And by the way, why *is* it so busy tonight?"

"Well, it's the ninth Tuesday in the fifth month before the first season of the last Spring, which of course means that it's Magic Night," Stanley told him, putting a flyer in front of Nathaniel on top of the bar. "Everybody around here knows that! You've got to try and keep up, old boy! Oh and please try to behave yourself this time around because the last time you were here you caused quite an unwelcome stir."

With that, he walked away to serve another thirsty customer.

"Of course, it's so obvious… it's magic night," mumbled Nathaniel as he looked at the flyer and read the acts that were performing.

TONIGHT, or today, at THE FIRST AND LAST

IT'S MAGIC NIGHT

featuring:

HERE TODAY, GONE TOMORROW

•

NOW YOU SEE IT, NOW YOU DON'T

And headlining the show:

NATHANIEL PHISCHERMANN

as

THE GUY WHO THOUGHT HE WAS HAPPY!

(The one who thought he'd escaped)

IT'S MAGIC!

And as always… supported by our magical house band,

THE SEA CREATURES

The last time he'd been in here, he'd had to run through the kitchen and out of the back door in fear for his life, but this time it felt different. He couldn't believe he was here again, he'd thought all of this nonsense was long behind him. It was then that he felt a firm hand upon his shoulder.

"Would you like to join us for tonight's performance?" the voice whispered in his ear.

Nathaniel spun around. "Oh my God, I thought that you were dead!" he exclaimed.

The scarred face of Horatio Lambert, now sporting an eye patch, was grimacing back at him.

Lambert laughed out loud. "Hahaha… what is death? I'll tell you what it is… it's just another door opening when the one behind you closes. So are you going to join us for tonight's performance or what? Oh and would you like a cigarette or a cigar? I hear that you're celebrating."

Chapter 56

Nathaniel came back down to earth with an almighty crash when he fell off his chair.

"Are you alright, mate?" The security guard offered him a helping hand to get up off the floor.

"Where am I?" asked Nathaniel.

"You're in the hospital. I've been watching you for a while. You've being talking to yourself in your sleep," replied the security guard.

"Oh my god, this is the second time that I've woken up here. Can I go back in *there*?" He gestured to the double doors that led to the ward, as the quietly piped music of the Beatles singing their arrangement of Please Mister Postman came through the speakers.

"Of course, just go back in," answered the guard.

So once again Nathaniel pressed the intercom button, and once again he noticed that the duty nurse was absent. But when a voice did reply, it chilled him to the bone.

"What a beautiful child you have, I'm sure that he'll be so welcome in the Land of Khartoonz. Look on the bright side, he'll never have to grow up and go through the pains that you have… a penny for your thoughts?"

The smiling voice then broke out into a piercing scream of hysterical laughter and Nathaniel instantly knew that it was Lambert. As if to qualify his recognition, a disgusting blast of cigarette smoke came from the intercom speaker. Nathaniel nearly choked on the vile fumes and his head started to spin with the information that he'd just received. He turned quickly around to ask for the security guard's help but he too had disappeared… and when Nathaniel looked at the clock on the wall it still said 21 minutes past 1.

Chapter 57

Artichoke had managed to navigate a safe passage to the lighthouse. He knew of a lot of shortcuts and had used them to his advantage. He knocked on the door. At first there was no response, and as he tried again using more force than was probably necessary the door was opened and he nearly struck the lighthouse keeper squarely in the face.

Alexander quickly took a step backwards in surprise. "Is everything alright?" he asked.

"Yes, but I need talk to you," Artichoke replied.

"Come on in," Alexander said.

Nathaniel went inside and once again they sat at the table, two glasses immediately being placed upon it and the man wearing the sou'wester and wellies once again opened the bottle of Pusser's Rum and poured them both a tot… albeit a large one. They both took a sip.

"You look troubled," said Alexander.

Artichoke placed the glass gently down on the table. "You believe in life after death, don't you?" he enquired.

"Of course, I wouldn't be here if I didn't? Some people get it, some people don't. The ones who don't choose to stay here, and the ones who choose to go home simply go back home. You know all of this and you have done for a long time, so why are you asking me now?" Alexander looked puzzled.

"It's just something that Nelly said to me a bit earlier on, you know… Nelly the cat?" Artichoke said.

"Of course I do, I've known him for years. I'm the one who found him when he was an abandoned kitten. What did he say to you?" asked Alexander.

"He said that sometimes people who go back get a wobble on! They falter and, although they've made a big decision in their lives, sometimes they become weak again. You know, when the pressure builds up and all that," explained Artichoke.

"So what's your point?" Alexander pressed him.

"Well, it's that Nathaniel is doing really good at the moment, but I've just got a bad feeling that things could fall apart for him," Artichoke looked concerned.

"So what are you saying? What have you done?" Alexander stared at him.

Artichoke didn't respond immediately, he just looked at his glass.

"Aren't you going to tell me? Hang on… judging by your response, I think I know exactly what you've done. Oh my God, what *have* you done? You've sent someone over to the other side, haven't you? THE OTHER SIDE OF THE BLOODY LETTERBOX!" said Alexander, raising his voice.

"I thought it was the right thing to do. I'm sorry," Artichoke said.

"Who did you send? Tell me now," demanded Alexander. "It was the blind girl, wasn't it?"

Artichoke just nodded his head. He couldn't look into in the eyes of his accuser.

"I thought so. But she wasn't alone, was she? Please, please don't tell me that you've sent that lunatic with her... the bloody village idiot," Alexander implored.

Artichoke didn't respond.

Alexander jumped up out of his seat. "You have, haven't you? God damn it, this is all anybody needs. You're here to do a job, that's all, not to take control. When they go, they go... when they stay, they stay... it's that bloody simple."

"His heart's in the right place," Artichoke fought back.

"But his head's in the wrong one," Alexander ranted. "You're going to have to sort this one out and quickly, or else people are going to get hurt. I just hope that they're the only ones who've managed to escape out of the back door, for all of our sakes. I hope that you realise what you've done. You have to go, right now."

Alexander pointed to the lighthouse door.

Artichoke rose from the table and without saying a word he left the building, his head bowed in shame. He'd gone there for help and advice, but he went away feeling that he'd been rebuked and charged with a mission that he never would have wished upon himself in a hundred and twenty one million years.

What on earth had he done? And where or what was Earth anyway? He'd heard of the place from the people that he'd helped, but he'd no appetite to physically visit it.

Chapter 58

It took Artichoke another few hours to get back home to the treehouse, time enough to formulate a plan. He knew that he had to go somewhere that he'd never been before, but he wasn't going to go alone, he was going to take some muscle with him, some protection.

When he entered the room he found Nelly curled up at the bottom of the bed, sound asleep. He looked at the bowl of mushrooms on the table and thankfully it seemed that the cat hadn't eaten any more since earlier. Artichoke was confused and unsure of what to do next, but he was also exhausted and in need of sleep. He had no intention of waking the cat, hoping that a few hours of sleep would cure him of his hallucinogenic state, so instead he undressed and climbed into the bed, pulling the covers over himself.

Outside, somewhere deep in the forest, the wolves howled once more… and inside, somewhere deep in his heart, he silently joined in with them.

Never a good deed goes unpunished!

Chapter 59

Nathaniel searched his pockets for his mobile phone and when he couldn't find it, he remembered that he'd left it on the bedside cabinet next to Judy's bed. He walked out of the café with a sense of urgency, in search of someone who could be of assistance.

He wandered down corridors and entered rooms and offices but the place was deserted. He kept going, then he realised that he was lost in the labyrinth of the hospital, the seemingly *empty* hospital, the one that had been bustling earlier on in the day. He stopped when he came across a large sign on a wall. It was covered in ward names, directions and arrows in all different colours, it was more difficult to decipher than a London Underground map. He desperately began to read it, in order to find his way back to the maternity ward, but after a few seconds he shook his head and spoke out loud, pleading, "Oh no, for God's sake, don't do this to me! Please don't do *this*."

It hadn't taken him long to realise that the names on the board were all related to the Land of Khartoonz. There were some he recognised... Razorfish Falls, Grim Valley Mires, The Path Of Least Resistance, The Point, The Pharos At Alexandria, Crab Apple Street, Pennydragon Lane, The First and Last, and some he didn't... The White Feathers, The Rainbows, The Robins.

There were many more but, in his confusion, he just turned away. To his amazement, in front of him stood the nurse with the thick glasses.

"It's you, isn't it? Flo, it's you," he asked.

"Yes it is," she innocently replied.

"What on earth are you doing here? And what's going on?" Nathaniel enquired desperately.

"Do you remember the battle? When you gave me the penny and I gave you the key and you escaped?" He nodded his head and she continued. "You locked the door and posted the key back to me through the letterbox, I picked it up and put it back in my pocket. The battle raged on for quite a while, but when everything fell silent I felt it was my duty to wander forward and see if I could help any of the casualties, regardless of their political motives. I'm only partially sighted by the way, it's difficult but I can find my way around. Everything was blurred to me, of course, but the stench of crabs and sewers was horrible. The sounds of the injured and dying were hard to stomach as well. The first person I came across was barely recognisable apart from the way that he was dressed… like an Edwardian Dandy, if you like. He was battered and bloodied but still breathing. So I knelt down to take a closer inspection. I asked how he was, he opened his one good eye and it seemed like he recognised me, his eye lit up. He sat up and grabbed the walking stick that was by his side and then he swiped me across the head with it. I fell backwards in a daze, but I remember him rifling through my pockets. I passed out, but when I came around I realised that he'd taken the key, you know the one that I'd given to you because you had paid me that special penny?"

Nathaniel nodded and she continued. "So I made my way back to the door and when I got there, it was open, but the key was still in the back of it. He'd obviously just unlocked it and darted out in a panic."

"What happened then?" Nathaniel asked, rivetted by her story.

"I immediately closed it and locked it. Then I took the key and put it back in my pocket, but I knew that I had to tell someone straight away." Flo rolled up the arm of one of her blouse sleeves. "Have you got one of these?" she asked, pointing to the camera obscura wristwatch that she was wearing.

"No, what is it?" asked Nathaniel, frowning.

"It's a way of communication. Artichoke invented it. Very advanced and it works well… when the weather's right that is. But anyway, I managed to get in touch with him and by using the sign language and lip reading that I had taught him, he soon got the message," she explained.

"So what was his response?" Nathaniel was intrigued.

"He told me to grab the first person at hand and go out of the door and enter your land… this land, the place where we are now," Flo explained.

"Who did you bring with you, then?" Nathaniel earnestly asked her.

Before she could answer, the squeaky wheels of the trolley betrayed the entrance of the porter as he rounded the corner. Grinning from ear to ear, his jovial appearance betrayed him straight away.

"I knew it was you from the first time around," Nathaniel said, shaking his head in mock disbelief.

"Well, aren't you happy to see me?" asked Lester.

"Actually I am, I could do with a laugh… but then again, this isn't a laughing matter. I need to get back to the maternity ward. Lambert's in there with Judy and our baby, and I'm totally lost in this labyrinth, the signs don't help and there's nobody here," Nathaniel told him.

"Don't worry," said Lester. "Just follow me. And trust me, I know where we are. After all, I do work here."

"By the way," said Flo, "you did lock the door behind us, didn't you?"

"Door? Which… oh shit!" was Lester's apologetic response.

"Hang on a second," Nathaniel interrupted. "You guys are saying that this has just happened, but to me it was about, I don't know, nine months ago or even more."

"Well, it's all about parallel universes, wormholes, time travel, the speed of light, different dimensions… you know, all of the boring stuff," Lester began to explain, smiling as he wheeled the trolley around the next corner.

Nathaniel and Flo both followed the annoying squeaky wheels, and, as if by magic, they found themselves back in the small café area.

"Through there," pointed Nathaniel. "I have to get in there, but there's nobody here and the doors are locked. How am I going to get in?"

"I can get us in. After all nothing's impossible, everything's possible," announced Lester, letting go of the trolley – which was quite apt as he'd always been off his trolley anyway – and he advanced towards the doors. He simply pulled one open, walked through and closed it behind him with a click. He sat down at the duty nurse's desk and pressed the intercom button, then spoke, "It's very simple," said the voice from the intercom. "Just tell me your name and I can let you in."

Nathaniel was looking dumbfounded through the door's window.

"Just humour him," encouraged Flo, who was behind him.

"I'm Nathaniel. Can I come in, please?" he said, feeling rather embarrassed.

"Of course," laughed the Jester, pushing the button under the desk that released the locking mechanism.

Nathaniel opened the door and walked through, closely followed by Flo.

"Why the hell didn't you just let us in with *you*?" Nathaniel shouted… but his rant ended when he smelled cigarette smoke, and then Lester stopped smiling because even he knew that things were about to get serious.

Chapter 60

Nathaniel led the way, the other two following close behind, Lester leading Flo by the hand. Nathaniel knew which room that he was heading for.

When he reached it, he had no hesitation of entering.

There were four beds but only one was occupied. Judy was still asleep in one of them close to the door… at least Nathaniel hoped she was just asleep, it was hard to tell.

In the shadows in one of the back corners, he could clearly see Horatio Lambert standing there. He was recognisable by his battered, silver top hat and his equally battered face.

In his left arm he cradled baby Albie, in his right hand he held a lit cigarette between his fingers. He raised the cigarette to his lips, took a deep breath and then exhaled the fumes directly into the face of the baby.

"YOU BASTARD!" screamed Nathaniel, darting forward.

"Not so fast," shouted Lambert, swiftly taking the cigarette and holding it inches away from the face of the baby. "You know I'll do it."

Nathaniel stopped dead in his tracks.

"You don't want him to end up blind like that one, do you?" Lambert said casually, gesturing towards Flo. "Because I can easily arrange it, and anyway it pays to teach them young, doesn't it? You know, to get the smoke in their lungs, to give them the taste, to give them the best start in life. It gives me strength, it empowers me, so go on… empower me." Lambert nodded at one of the beds.

Nathaniel looked at to where he was indicating and saw that there was an open packet of cigarettes and a disposable lighter.

"Go on then, do yourself a big favour. Take one, light it and inhale the beautiful smoke. You know you want to. Don't worry, it's free," Lambert informed him.

"Put him down, you bastard," Nathaniel told Lambert. "Leave him alone."

"No, no way, you smoke a whole cigarette and I might consider it, but until then I'll hold him hostage with the promise of serious physical damage unless you do what I tell you to."

It had been a good nine months since Nathaniel had smoked his last cigarette and he was really proud of himself for achieving that, it was something that he never thought that he would be able to do. It was something he'd promised himself that he'd never go back to, but at this point in time, the stakes were too high… he had no choice.

Reluctantly, he reached out and slowly took the packet from the bed, along with the lighter. He took one out and sighed as he placed it between his lips.

Lambert was eagerly moving his bodyweight from side to side, eyes wide open, his mouth contorted in a horrific grimace of evil pleasure.

Nathaniel flicked the lighter, which immediately sparked

a flame. He made contact between the tip of the cigarette and the point of ignition, but before he'd the chance to light it properly and take a lungful, everything in the room paused… because outside in the corridor came the sound of running feet and desperately shouting voices.

"They'll be in here," shouted one of them.

"No, they'll be down there," shouted another.

Lambert – who, judging by his startled reaction, clearly recognised the voices – and he immediately panicked.

It was a good job that Nathaniel was taking notice because Lambert just chucked the baby away before trying to escape out of the room. Nathaniel dived like a rugby player in slow motion and grabbed the bundle of swaddling clothes, landing safely on one of the empty beds.

Lambert ran to the door and violently pushed Flo out of the way. She fell backwards onto the floor, banging the back of her head in the process and her glasses flew off. She screamed out in pain.

Lester was having none of it, charging forward he shoulder barged into Lambert's stomach, which instantly knocked the wind out of him. They both crashed to the deck.

Nathaniel got off the bed and quickly put Albie into Judy's bed with her – strangely, both her and the baby were still sound asleep despite all of the commotion – then he turned his attention back to the action.

Lester was on top of Lambert, who was writhing around desperately trying to free himself from the Jester's grip. Lambert let out a roar of defiance and managed to push Lester away with incredible force. Lester flew through the air and crashed into a filing cabinet near the door, and then he slumped to the ground, dazed and in pain.

Lambert was getting to his feet.

"NO, YOU DON'T, YOU BASTARD!" screamed Nathaniel. He ran forward, knocking Lambert back to the floor and then jumped on top of him.

"Get off me, you bloody imbecile," shouted Lambert as they wrestled with each other.

Nathaniel grabbed both of Lambert's ears and tried to bang his head on the floor, but Lambert resisted and succeeded in turning Nathaniel over so that he was now on top.

"Let's see how you like it," Lambert grimaced. He grabbed Nathaniel's ears and successfully started the head banging process.

Nathaniel wasn't strong enough to resist.

"Once, twice, thrice…" Lambert threw his head back and laughed with uncontrollable glee.

Nathaniel started to see stars, but he managed to get one of his legs in between Lambert's and, mustering all of his strength, he managed to knee Lambert directly in the crotch.

Lambert let out an ear-piercing scream and, clutching his groin, immediately rolled off Nathaniel.

Nathaniel was so dizzy that he struggled to stand up and when he did, he collapsed sideways onto one of the beds. He felt like the room was spinning and all of his energy was spent. He could only look on as Lambert managed to painfully struggle to his feet.

Seizing his chance to flee the room, Lambert hobbled

quickly forward towards the door, whereby Lester, who was still on the floor, stuck his leg out, tripping Lambert up and sending him crashing out into the corridor. He landed face down onto the ground and immediately three people jumped onto his back.

"Put the handcuffs on him," ordered Artichoke.

Harry's Son did as he was told and, with the aid of Zhackery Thackery, they managed to restrain the tyrannical monster, who was screaming and complaining like the pathetic wimp he was.

"Stand up, you're coming back with us. You don't belong here," said Artichoke. "You've caused enough damage in the past."

The posse managed to get the captured criminal to his feet.

"And you two have to come with us as well," he told Lester and Flo. "By the way, good work… you did a good job," he added, helping Flo to her feet and retrieving her glasses.

Lester managed to get to his feet with the help of Harry's Son, while Zachary Thackery continued to restrain Lambert.

Before they left, Artichoke turned back and looked at Nathaniel, who was still lying on the bed. "Once again, you've had a lucky escape," Artichoke told him. "We're all going now, the rest is up to you."

"And don't forget… Rome wasn't built in a teacup," Lester reminded him, poking his head back round the door.

Nathaniel managed a smile and watched as the

entourage disappeared and he heard the door of the ward opened and closed. He stared in silence at the clock and observed with relief as it turned from 1:21 to 1:22.

Judy instantly woke up. "What's going on?" she asked, blurry eyed. "I was having a really weird dream."

"Nothing, everything's fine," whispered Nathaniel. "Go back to sleep."

And so without hesitation, noticing that their baby was safe and sound, she closed her eyes and was soon sleeping again.

Chapter 61

It was five years later on a Saturday and Judy was at the sink washing up the breakfast dishes. Nathaniel, who was stood next to her, was staring vacantly out of the window at the pier below and the horizon of the North Sea.

Judy looked at him. "A penny for them!" she said.

He snapped out of his thoughts. "Sorry," he said. "What did you say?"

"You've been stood there for ages just staring. What's on your mind? And while you're just standing there doing nothing, make yourself useful and put those pots away," she told him.

He smiled and turned and picked up a bowl. He took a couple of steps towards the cupboard but then stopped and turned his face towards the back of Judy's head.

"Go on then, say it," she said, without missing a stroke, her female intuition on overdrive. "I'm all ears."

He placed the bowl down on top of the worktop and took a deep breath. "Do you remember the time when…" he started to say, but then he was interrupted.

"Dad, Dad, come and look at this. Come now, come on," the desperate voice of a young child was summoning him from the living room.

"You'd better go," Judy said. "There'll be no peace if you don't."

Without speaking but instead with the reluctance of a devoted parent, he abandoned the conversation with his wife and headed for the living room.

"What is it, Albie?" Nathaniel asked as he walked into the room, grinning with false enthusiasm, as he'd done a thousand times before.

His son was surrounded by Lego bricks scattered all over the floor, but he'd built an impressively huge tower.

"Dad, you have to hold it so I can put some more on," Albie instructed.

"Okay, I'll hold it like this." Nathaniel grasped the wobbling structure with both hands as Albie continued to place the bricks on top of each other until he could reach no higher.

"Dad, *you're* gonna have to do it," said Albie.

"Okay, you pass them to me and I'll put them on," Nathaniel told him.

So one by one, very carefully, the structure was completed because eventually it was impossible to build it any higher.

Albie was ecstatic. "It's the biggest tower in the world," he announced, leaping around the place like some kind of lunatic, before he stopped and said, "But no, it's a robot, not a tower… it's the biggest robot in the world."

"Then we'll have to give him a name," said his dad.

"I know!" Albie replied.

"Go on, then," Nathaniel encouraged.

"It's Tiny Toppings," Albie screeched with glee, continuing his dance of jubilation.

The hairs stood up on the back of Nathaniel's neck…

it was a name that he hadn't heard for many years, and how the hell did his son know of it? He froze in deep thought and his lack of concentration caused the structure to crash to the ground.

"Dad, you let it fall," Albie chastised him.

"Sorry, son, it just got a wobble on… sometimes things fall to pieces like that, nothing lasts forever, you know. You build another one and I'll go and see your Mam."

"Okay, but first I need the toilet," Albie announced as he ran out of the room.

Nathaniel walked back into the kitchen as Judy was drying her hands on a tea towel.

"By the way, did you see that letter that came for you?" she said, nodding towards a pile of junk post that had accumulated on the kitchen worktop.

"No," he replied as he began rifling through the marketing rubbish, but then he came across it. Once again, he froze as he picked it up. It was *the* letter.

"How on earth it got delivered here with that address on it, God only knows. And where the hell's Crab Apple Street anyway?" she enquired. "What is it? Some kind of a chain letter or scam or something?"

"Maaam," came the shout from the bathroom. "I need you to wipe my bottom."

"Oh, the joys of Motherhood!" she exclaimed as she went to perform her maternal duties.

Nathaniel just stood there holding the envelope, staring at it like it was some kind of cursed icon, as if it had found him out and had come back to haunt him. The first time that he'd seen it was at the top of the crab apple tree when he was a kid when it was in pristine condition, which it wasn't anymore, and the last time that he'd seen it was when Flo had pointed it out to him many years ago on the pile of other letters and he'd clumsily stuffed it into his pocket before equally as clumsily losing it shortly afterward. Why the hell had it turned back up again now? There was trouble brewing, he could feel it, and he didn't like it.

However, alone in the kitchen, with nobody looking, he took a deep breath and ran his forefinger underneath the lip of the sealed envelope. He then tentatively removed the note and slowly unfolded it, afraid of the contents.

But, when he did unfold it, he couldn't believe what he was looking at. He quickly turned the single page and looked at the other side in disbelief… the sheet was totally blank on both sides… there was nothing written on it.

'What the hell?' Nathaniel thought to himself. 'After all this time… nothing… absolutely nothing.'

He felt both cheated and taken aback by the apparent sick joke that had run for many years at his expense. But what did it really mean?

He looked up from the blank piece of paper and stared out of the window for a few seconds at the expanse of the sea, which was beyond the reach of the pier head… the unreachable horizon… the mysterious lands that, as a child, had been beyond his grasp. Somewhere in the back of his mind, he both felt and heard a penny drop, and realised he had a bone to pick with himself.

Chapter 62

Hello, my friend. It's only fair that I should keep you in the loop. When that letter was delivered underneath my door, I took it in with a strong sense of concern. I propped it up in front of one of the spent candles on my writing desk, but as I kept scribbling throughout the long years, I never felt compelled to open it. You see, that letter wasn't addressed to me, but it was always there, staring at me, daring me. Until I couldn't take it anymore. I made the decision that it was time to deliver it to its rightful recipient. So I took the envelope and left the sanctuary of the attic and made my way out of the house and out of Crab Apple Street. It was a long trek for me, but eventually I managed to locate Flo, the gatekeeper to the other side. When I explained the predicament that I had found myself in, she allowed me to go through on the condition I was as quick as possible and came back straight away.

I agreed, and so she let me through.

I found myself in front of an outside door. I looked around… it was an impressive building… behind me was the sea, a promenade and a pier. I had no idea where I was, but I knew that I had to gain access. So I reached forward and, to my surprise, the door just opened and I walked inside. I found myself stood in a hallway, a staircase right in front of me. I instinctively knew where I had to go, so I began to ascend the steps. The place had the feeling of a hotel, probably long converted into flats and apartments, an old hotel… probably Victorian or Edwardian.

I reached the top and turned left onto a landing, I walked forward and found the door that was numbered 121. I stopped and posted the envelope through the letterbox. And I couldn't help myself… I lifted the flap and peeked through, whereby I witnessed a scene of apparent domestic bliss. A mother, a father and a small child just being happy… as a family.

I quickly made my exit, the mission completed, and found my way back to the Land of Khartoonz.

Chapter 63

Nathaniel took the blank sheet of paper and the envelope and went into the bedroom where his writing desk was situated in the corner and he closed the door behind him.

"What're you up to?" Judy shouted through from the other side of the door.

"I've just got a bit of writing to do. I won't be long," he replied.

"Well, make sure you're not, we're taking Albie to his friend's birthday party this morning at the Back Alex, remember?" she said.

"Yeah, that's fine, I won't be long," Nathaniel replied.

He placed the envelope and the blank letter on the top of the writing desk. He sat down in his writing chair and after a couple of minutes of getting his composure and some deep thinking, he took the quill that Artichoke had given him a long time ago and gently dipped it into the inkwell and then he put pen to paper…

A NOTE TO MYSELF,

We haven't always seen eye-to-eye over the years, you and me, but here I am now talking to you one-to-one. If I could write a letter and send it back in time to you then it would go something like this… and I'll try my best…

There will be times when the world will make you feel worthless, there will be times when you will feel alone, there will be times when you will wish that you had never been born and there will be times when you just want to end it all.

But it's at those times when you have to be the strongest, it's at those times when you have to be brave, it's at those times that you have to realise that you don't know what's around the corner and that the next few minutes could be the best life changing experience that you could ever have wished for. But if you weren't here anymore then you would never have found out. So it's worth just hanging on in there, just hang onto that crab apple tree branch, kid… just hang on. And even if you fall off, you can still climb back up again. Believe me, because I know.

Signed,

Me

Nathaniel put the quill back into the inkwell and dabbed the note with a sheet of blotting paper, blew on it to dry it out – just for good luck – then folded it and placed it back into its original envelope. He took a roll of Sellotape and sealed the torn edge, making sure that it was in a good state for delivery.

"Come on, get a move on," Judy shouted from outside of the bedroom. "We're going to be late."

"I'm coming," Nathaniel shouted back.

He propped the letter up on the side of the inkwell and rose from his chair. Then he left the room, bracing himself for the upcoming wonderful experience of the kids' party, he could hardly contain his excitement… but then again, how lucky he was to have the chance to experience it!

One day in the future, he knew he'd be glad that he'd made the effort.

Chapter 64

It had been a long day. The kids' party was as exhausting as he thought it was going to be and then afterwards Judy had suggested a walk down on the beach. Nathaniel had reluctantly agreed with a smile on his face, they'd spent a fortune on fish 'n' chips, and the rest of the day had been taken up with the usual havoc of family life at home with a young child. Sometimes you can just have more than enough of Paw Patrol repeats on the TV.

They were all in bed now. Albie was already asleep, the lights were off and Judy was snoring. Nathaniel was on the brink of grateful oblivion himself and he thankfully gave into it. He didn't take much rocking. Then he dreamt…

He found himself back in the Land of Khartoonz. It was night time, *their night time*, and everything was quiet and still. He was stood on Crab Apple Street outside the front door of number 121. In his hand he was holding the letter, the one that he'd written earlier on in the day, the one that had been passed from pillar to post throughout the years. He didn't bother to ring the bell or knock on the door… he just knew that he would be granted access… and he was.

He entered the familiar hallway. He ascended the staircase and then turned left onto the landing. Once again he walked forward and made his way cautiously into the small bedroom. Everything was the same, even the foreboding atmosphere. He paused and turned his head towards *the* door, the one that never opened, the door of secrets, fear and mystery.

He approached it with the familiar knot in his stomach, the one that he'd felt from childhood. He stood there, his heart was racing. He was clutching the letter and his breath was coming in sharp intakes. He felt that it was now or never. So, regardless of what had happened in the past, he reached out, gripped the handle and turned it as he'd done a thousand times before… only this time something different happened.

The door opened.

At first he couldn't believe it. He firmly held the handle and slowly pushed the door open inch by inch. It creaked like a long forgotten soul crying out for help, it was quite unnerving. All was dark on the inside and, as it opened wider and his eyes adjusted, he noticed that there was a set of stairs immediately leading upwards. He glanced up toward the top of the small stairway and saw that there was an open plan type of room with old wooden beams spanning the roof space… well, after all it was an attic, he supposed.

After all of these years this was finally it, his chance to find out what was behind the door. For whatever reason, he'd been allowed to enter and he was about to find out why. So he walked forward and one by one climbed the stairs until he reached the top.

In the gloom, he could just make out, by flickering candlelight, a table halfway down the room with a person sat at it. Whoever was sat there didn't respond to his presence, but Nathaniel noticed that he was scribbling away with a quill like the one that Artichoke had given him. Nathaniel didn't feel the need to speak or introduce himself, it was as if this moment in time was meant to be, it was just waiting for the right time for the door to open… and it had opened and here he was.

Slowly but confidently, Nathaniel walked forward and stood at the side of the table.

The person stopped writing and turned to look at him.

Nathaniel thought that he was looking in a mirror, because the person at the table was himself.

"Have you got something for me?" I asked.

"Yes," Nathaniel replied in disbelief and held out the envelope.

"Thank you," I said and took it from him. "Did it take you long to write it?"

"Just all of my life," Nathaniel replied.

"Okay, you can go now and enjoy the rest of your life." I smiled and gestured back toward the staircase with my quill.

It was then that Nathaniel's dream started to fall apart. It fractured and disappeared and he awoke with a start.

"Are you okay?" asked Judy, still half asleep herself.

"Hmm, yeah, I think so," he replied.

"It's just like you were talking to yourself in your sleep. It sounded weird," she mumbled.

"I'm fine. Night, night," he reassured her.

"Night," she replied.

They cuddled in, but it took quite a while for Nathaniel to go back over, although eventually he did.

When he awoke the next morning, the broken dreams of last night began to filter into his mind. As he lay there, he lifted his head and looked towards the writing desk. The letter that he'd put at the side of the inkwell had disappeared.

He sat up. It wasn't there.

He got out of bed for a closer inspection… it definitely wasn't there.

He sat back down on the edge of the bed. He'd awoken Judy.

"Are you sure you're alright?" she asked.

"I don't know to tell you the truth," he replied.

She sighed in response, which wasn't for the first time and she knew that it probably wouldn't be the last.

Then she pulled the duvet back over her head in the vain hope that maybe she could get another few minutes of sleep.

Chapter 65

So my friend, my loyal reader… the secret's out. It was good to see me again. I'd been waiting for so long to reconnect. It gets so lonely up here, just scratching and scribbling away all by myself… or should I say the half of myself that cares… the half that sees things that the other half misses. It hurts when he ignores me, it always has, but there's a time and a place for everything… for a reckoning, for a realisation and an acknowledgement towards the truth. And I'm glad that it's happened, eventually, the reconnection of the real with the unreal, the so-called normal existence that we feel compelled and obliged to have to continually bow down to… day after day after day… which goes on and on… and is just a charade. It's simple… and that's a fact.

I… he… me… have had an awakening and my eyes are wide open. I'm going to sign off for now and then blow out the candle.

Thank you for reading my story so far… because, after all, everything's real. Isn't it?

Yours sincerely,
Nathaniel Phischermann

PS: And yes, the spiders are still hanging around… and listening.

ISBN 9981-09-012-3
D.L 2004/0737
Rue Essanaani, ex.Angle rues Daguerre et Chevreuil
-Bourgogne- Casablanca

Slim

les femmes, la mort...

Bahaa Trabelsi

Slim
les femmes, la mort...

Roman

M.Y.B Retnani
EDDIF

DU MÊME AUTEUR

Une Femme tout simplement, Eddif
Troisième édition

Une vie à trois, Eddif
Deuxième édition

Slim et les femmes

I

Slim a des réveils de plus en plus difficiles. En réalité, il ne dort pas, il " comate ". Il a inventé le verbe " comater ", le jour où il s'est rendu compte que, pour trouver le sommeil, il doit s'enivrer à mort, pour sombrer dans une sorte de coma éthylique. Nuit après nuit, de bar en bar, de boîte en boîte, il a augmenté la dose pour vaincre ses insomnies récalcitrantes, jusqu'à ce qu'il ait cette sensation vertigineuse de vivre définitivement dans le flou. Et, quand il en parle à ses amis, ceux-ci qualifient son flou de flou artistique, car, pour eux, Slim est un artiste. " Pourquoi pas ? riposterait Slim avec son sourire qui n'en est plus un à quiconque qui lui demanderait son avis, si artiste signifie pochard. " Lui, il se définirait plutôt comme l'ami des artistes, avec des velléités avortées de création et une immense tendresse pour le genre humain dont il considère qu'il ne fait plus partie. D'un poète déchu la dégaine.

Et, à force de paraître poète déchu, les vrais poètes ont fini par croire qu'il a toujours fait partie de leur corporation !

Pourtant, Bouthaïna, elle croit en lui. Bouthaïna, mon amour, mon cœur, ma vie ! Je ne suis pas Jamiiil. Je ne suis que Slim.

> Ne me grandis pas.
> Arrête de m'aimer pour ce que je ne suis pas.
> Arrête de m'aimer tout court.
> Bouthaïna, un poème !

Un mélange étonnant de candeur et de lucidité. Mais… la lucidité des imbéciles. Episodique. Inutile. Slim pense que ce qui l'a de prime abord attiré en elle, c'est son prénom. Un prénom rare et désuet. Un prénom d'héroïne de tragédie avec un parfum d'amour absolu, interdit. Sa sœur s'appelle aussi Bouthaïna. Le seul prénom original dans sa famille, composée pourtant de dix enfants. Un prénom de bourge. Il n'y a que les bourges et sa mère, dans un éclair d'inspiration, pour trouver des prénoms pareils à leur progéniture.

Un prénom, un destin. " Le mien était tout tracé ", vous dirait Slim. Slim, cela ressemble à un diminutif. Celui de Salim peut-être. Diminué déjà, au départ. Salim : sain. Pourquoi pas saint tant qu'on y est ? " Le saint dessein qui est le mien. " Errer jusqu'à épuisement, ressentir jusqu'à l'écorchure, porter la croix. Pour un musulman, cela signifie s'alourdir d'un fardeau qui n'est pas le sien.

" Bouthaïna, ma belle, réveille-toi ! J'ai besoin d'être seul pour me refaire la gueule. Tu n'as rien à voir là-dedans. Ce n'est pas toi que je ne veux plus voir, c'est ma gueule défaite dans ton regard surfait. Mais ouiii, je t'aime ! Je ne te le dis pas assez ? Arrête de me poser la question ! Je me sens minable. Encore plus que d'habitude. Pitié ! Barre-toi ! "

" Aimer ! En suis-je encore capable ? " se demande Slim. " Et puis tel que Bouthaïna le conçoit, l'amour n'est qu'un ramassis de clichés comme on en voit dans des magazines féminins et des romans à l'eau de rose. Elle s'est mise en tête de m'épouser, cette conne ! Elle est complètement givrée. Et, il n'y a pas que ça quelle a en commun avec la bouteille de vodka que j'ingurgite chaque jour ; elle me saoule, elle me nargue, elle me racole, elle m'attache à elle comme à une bouée de sauvetage. "

" Mon salut est ailleurs. Dans la mort. Mais elle que je désire plus que toute autre, elle, la star de mes nuits de cauchemar, elle, elle ne veut pas de moi. Il faut me mériter, semble-t-elle me dire chaque fois que j'essaie de l'approcher. Je ne suis pas une de tes pétasses faciles à impressionner et qui passent dans ton existence comme des ombres fugitives. Moi, c'est pour la vie ! "

“ Mais où est Dieu ? ”, ai-je envie de lui répondre. “ Où est ton père ? Et le mien voit-il pas que je suis perdu pour lui ? Ne voit-il pas que je ne le rencontre plus que dans les yeux de Ihsane ? Des yeux immenses, illuminés, beaux comme la démence. Ailleurs. ”

Ihsane, un autre prénom, un autre destin. Ihsane, fascinante et incompréhensible. Un autre amour de Slim.

Slim l’a rencontrée dans un bar. Un de ces bars glauques de Casablanca qu’il affectionne et où il lui arrive de dénicher une déchéance encore plus grande que la sienne. Ça le rassure. Disons que dans ce genre d’endroit, il consomme sans culpabiliser l’élixir de son sommeil.

S’accouder à un de ces comptoirs signifie pour lui partager une complicité unique en son genre avec d’autres vétérans de la dive bouteille. Sans contraintes. En verres en rouges et contre tout. À la gloire de l’oubli. À la mémoire des amnistiés.

Toujours est-il que c’est dans un bar qu’il a rencontré Ihsane. Elle y occupe, la nuit seulement, et avec une dextérité touchante, les fonctions de serveuse. D’autant plus touchante que Le matin, elle se réincarne en l’une des étudiantes voilées de la faculté des sciences. Ihsane lui fait penser à l’héroïne d’un vieux film, un classique du cinéma : la femme aux deux visages. À la fois ange et démon. Un ange corrompu à cause des vicissitudes de la vie et un démon séraphique par la grâce de sa foi.

Une foi totalitaire qu'elle impose autour d'elle à coups de tracts et de racolage volubile auprès de ses sœurs musulmanes. Foi qu'elle tente de promouvoir au moyen d'une rhétorique ingurgitée à la va-vite. Verbiage insipide pour des esprits éclairés, inculqué dans des cellules de formation d'un groupe politique aux mêmes méthodes surannées — mais oh combien efficaces ! — de certains groupuscules gauchistes d'avant la chute du mur de Berlin. Groupe qui porte à peu de choses près, le même nom faussement prometteur que Ihsane.

Dieu merci pour Slim, les recommandations que la virginale enfant prêche à ses acolytes ne sont pas toujours valables pour elle.

Ihsane n'est pas vierge.

Quand Slim lui fait l'amour dans les vapeurs de ses ivresses, il s'imagine qu'il est le Christ et Ihsane, Marie-Madeleine, sa dernière tentation, la pécheresse pardonnée à la faveur de sa résurrection. Car, il faut que vous le sachiez, Slim a été éduqué chez les cathos, en bon chrétien qu'il n'est pas. Son père, musulman pratiquant, estimait que son rejeton aurait ainsi droit à la meilleure éducation possible. Sans compter que ses années de jeunesse se sont épanouies dans un quartier juif. Son père, commerçant dans le vieux Mellah de Fès, avait élu domicile dans le quartier où il travaillait. Et Slim y a grandi et appris à connaître les coutumes et les pratiques religieuses juives. À les apprécier aussi. De son père, il a hérité ce profond respect qu'il leur voue et qui est dû à sa conviction qu'il faut être juif pour être bon commerçant.

Quand Slim a rencontré Judith, de dix ans son aînée, intelligente, riche, cultivée — actionnaire principale d'une maison d'édition de renom —, parfaite femme d'affaires, elle n'a démenti en rien ses certitudes. D'autre part elle avait " des plus " en comparaison des filles qu'il avait connues jusque-là ; plus mûre, plus femme, plus avisée, plus introduite. Même " ses moins " étaient " des plus ", moins midinette, moins prude, moins envahissante, moins revendicative.

Belle rencontre, en vérité.

Une vraie femme, déjà bien mariée, mère de famille, et résidant à Paris. " Tout ce que vous avez toujours rêvé d'avoir en amour et que vous n'avez jamais eu ", dit Slim à ses amis qui le jalousent.

De ses trois femmes, c'est Judith que préfère Slim. C'est également elle qu'il voit le moins. Leurs rencontres, fréquentes au début de leur relation, se sont espacées.

Judith flatte l'égo de Slim.

La présence d'une femme de sa trempe dans sa vie le valorise aux yeux de son entourage. Elle est pour lui un atout non négligeable.

D'un autre côté, elle ne cesse de le complimenter, comme savent si bien le faire les femmes " plus ", sur la qualité de son travail — et elle s'y connaît-, et même sur son physique pourtant sans attrait particulier. Elle lui assure qu'il a un physique intéressant. Ce qui est mieux que si elle lui avait dit qu'il était beau.

Ce qu'il ne sait pas, c'est que Judith, en femme cultivée, a un jour lu un texte de Jean Giraudoux dont elle a fait sa devise en matière d'hommes. Giraudoux dit : " Quand vous voyez une femme escortée en tout lieu d'un état-major de servants, ce n'est pas tant qu'ils la trouvent belle, c'est qu'elle leur a dit qu'ils sont beaux. "

Et Judith n'est pas belle.

Bouthaïna partie, Slim peut enfin prendre sa douche tranquillement. Le jet d'eau est brûlant. Il se dit que, bientôt, il n'aura plus de sensations. Même si l'odeur de Bouthaïna est présente pour lui prouver le contraire. L'appartement sans bruit, sans voix, mais l'odeur de Bouthaïna. Sa chambre, imprégnée d'elle. Il est en retard. Son métier est tout ce qui arrive encore à le motiver. Devenir journaliste a été la seule ambition de sa vie. On dit de sa plume que c'est l'une des meilleures de la profession. Caustique, objective, libre, parfois sans scrupules, comme lui.

Rien à perdre ! Telle est la devise de Slim dans la vie.

Aujourd'hui, il a de quoi faire. Deux marches sont prévues dimanche, annonce un quotidien connu. L'une à Rabat, l'autre à Casablanca.

Slim lit : " Deux clans antagonistes de la société marocaine vont manifester, les uns, qu'on appelle les modernistes, leur adhésion au nouveau plan d'intégration de la femme au développement, les autres, qu'on appelle les islamistes, leur rejet de ce même plan . "

Il hausse les épaules.

Slim sait qu'il veut tenter l'impossible : mieux comprendre les positions des uns et des autres, sans préjugés, ni parti pris. Tâche véritablement ingrate parce qu'en guise d'objectivité, il ressent une hargne profonde pour les islamistes, ennemis fervents et déclarés de la bouteille.

Par ailleurs Judith arrivera le lendemain, lundi treize mars deux mille. Il ne s'agit pas de lui faire faux bon. Elle lui manque. Ses compliments aussi. Avec elle au moins, il n'a pas l'impression d'être un sous-homme.

Un dernier coup d'œil à l'appartement qui exhale l'odeur de Bouthaïna, puis Slim sort en marmonnant : elle aurait pu mettre de l'ordre avant de partir tout de même !

II

Bouthaïna avance d'un pas décidé. Elle respire à pleins poumons l'air pollué de Casablanca. Les rues sont bondées de gens encore plus pressés qu'elle. Le boulevard Mohammed V apparaît dans toute sa splendeur. Elle a l'habitude, chaque fois qu'elle passe par là, de marcher le nez en l'air. Mais aujourd'hui, l'angoisse lui coupe le souffle. " Pourquoi est-ce que je continue à entretenir cette liaison foireuse ? " se demande-t-elle. " Qu'est-ce que je lui trouve, à cet abruti ? Tout est devenu tellement… faux. Sans intérêt. Slim est fuyant, brutal, excédé. Oui, excédé. J'ai l'impression qu'il me supporte de moins en moins. " Bouthaïna fouille dans sa mémoire. " Quand a-t-il fini de m'aimer et a-t-il commencé à me supporter ? " La réponse s'impose à elle, brutale. " Quand il s'est rendu compte que je me suis attachée à lui au point de devenir dépendante, midinette pathétique. "

" Il m'avait mise en garde. Ne deviens jamais attendrissante à mes yeux si tu veux que je continue à t'aimer, lui a-t-il dit, un jour de grande éloquence verbale. "

Pourtant tout a commencé comme dans une tragédie shakespearienne. Tout et tous étaient contre leur liaison. On s'est accroché pour la sauvegarder. "

Aujourd'hui, de ce lien interdit qui les a unis, il ne reste plus grand-chose.

Bouthaïna s'arrête. Elle n'arrive plus à avancer. Les souvenirs déferlent, émouvants.

Elle hèle un taxi.

Les versets coraniques sont partout maintenant, même dans les taxis, constate-t-elle en découvrant Aïate El Coursi, petit carré de papier chiffonné collé sur la vitre arrière.

Le chauffeur lui demande où elle va. Elle lui répond machinalement d'une voix qu'elle ne reconnaît pas. Il continue à lui parler de la pluie qui n'est pas tombée cette année, des paysans qui souffrent. Elle ne l'entend plus.

C'était il y a à peine trois ans. Bouthaïna n'était pas heureuse, mais pas malheureuse non plus. Une vie rangée. Un mari, une petite fille au sourire encadré de fossettes. Un mariage comme tant d'autres avec son cortège de lassitudes. En contrepartie, la sécurité d'un foyer confortable.
Mais Bouthaïna est une adepte des passions. Et les passions ne sont ni sécurité ni paisibles certitudes.

Candidate idéale au rôle de Madame Bovary version orientale, il a suffi de peu -le sourire qui n'en est plus un d'un poète déchu qui ne l'a jamais vraiment été parce qu'il n'a jamais été poète-, et la voilà qui se pose la mauvaise question qu'elle croit la bonne : dois-je larguer ce mariage qui n'en est pas un et qui jusqu'ici a puisé sa force dans la léthargie ? Sa mère, qui a les deux pieds sur terre, et qui, vite fait, en femme avertie, flaire les entourloupes, lui recommande de garder le mari indésirable mais vrai dans un premier temps et, ma foi, puisque telle est sa lubie du moment, de garder aussi l'amant désirable mais faux. La futée tablait sur le temps et le bon sens de sa fille.

Deux erreurs impardonnables quand on connaît Bouthaïna. Pas assez garce pour jouer longtemps les Madame Bovary, et trop entichée. Elle décide donc de se libérer de ses chaînes pour son amant éploré. Oui, éploré ! et blessé d'avoir été deviné et rejeté par son ex-future belle-mère.

Dès lors, la guerre est déclarée, la passion aussi.

Divorce à la marocaine.

Amour toujours. Enfin… Tant que tout le monde est contre.

Plus tard. On se calme. Les amours jadis interdites se métamorphosent en amours concédées voire licites. Et c'est le début du flop.

Bouthaïna s'accroche. Slim décroche.

Elle s'est trompée d'histoire d'amour. Une passion née des transgressions. Une adolescence finalement peu vécue qui rejaillit du passé pour enfin s'épanouir dans les rébellions. Une mère à qui elle s'oppose pour se poser. Et une méprise qui s'appelle Slim.

Chéri, chéri, je t'en supplie, ne me quitte pas.
Je crois bien que j'adore être au plus bas.
The last blues song.

La belle et la bête, nouvelle version.

Il y a bien des hommes, dit la belle, qui sont plus monstres que vous, c'est vous que je préfère malgré votre apparence…

Bouthaïna s'imagine, comme tant d'autres avant elle, qu'en aimant Slim au-delà de tout, au-delà de sa laideur, d'un amour désintéressé, parfait et tolérant, le miracle se produira, la bête se transformera en prince charmant.

Elle s'évertue à ne pas voir sa cruauté, son indifférence, ses abus.

Elle ne voit pas que Slim est affectivement inaccessible, incapable d'aimer.

Elle ne se voit qu'elle, avec son dévouement, sa servilité aveugle et sa peur de ne pas en faire assez pour le sauver de la déchéance.

On ne s'improvise pas sauveuse d'âme. Les concepts d'éthique islamo-judéo-chrétiens selon lesquels il faut aider ceux qui sont plus malheureux que soi, ne pas les juger, mais les aider, faire de cette aide une obligation morale, sont hors de propos dans ton histoire Bouthaïna !

Et voilà que la princesse est tirée vers le bas. Humiliée, mille fois trahie, mille fois abandonnée, délirante, elle coule… Et boit.

Le calice jusqu'à la lie.

Tassa.

Autrement dit, la gentille bouteille de Slim

— la plus forte de ses deux muses — se plaît à lui faire découvrir à quoi elle a voulu s'attaquer.

Flou artistique. Nuits blanches et grises. Rouge de la violence. Noir de l'encre d'un scénario revu et corrigé. La palette colorée de son poète chassé du paradis de la clairvoyance devient sienne.

Dieu merci, il lui reste ses jours. Et Bouthaïna se prépare, dans le cadre de l'association de lutte pour les droits de la femme, à se rendre à la marche de Rabat manifester son adhésion au plan d'intégration de la femme dans le développement.

Ne riez pas !

Elle a envie d'y croire.

Bouthaïna, vous l'avez deviné, est une romantique et une idéaliste. Un cœur dans les étoiles, comme elle dit.

Obsolète.

Debout en retrait dans la salle du local de l'association, la réunion l'exaspère.

— Nos slogans, beugle une militante forcenée doivent être mobilisateurs et interpellants. Les Islamistes gagnent du terrain. Ils envahissent nos champs d'action. Notre engagement à notre cause doit être clair et déterminé. Et cela doit se voir.

Pourquoi préparer des slogans ? se demande Bouthaïna. Il faut laisser parler les cœurs. La souffrance ne s'exprime bien que dans la spontanéité.

De quoi souffrons-nous ?

Le nous militant la fait sourire. Quelle est la cause pour laquelle elle combat ?

Bouthaïna a vu à la télé, il y a longtemps, aux infos, à l'occasion d'un changement de gouvernement dans un pays africain, un ministre, sous les feux des projecteurs, hésiter à répondre à un journaliste qui lui demandait de lui parler de ses nouvelles fonctions et demander d'une voix complètement paniquée à un de ses confrères : je suis ministre de quoi déjà ?

La présidente de l'association, en fine politicienne, future ministre de quelque chose, devine le désarroi de Bouthaïna. Elle file du mauvais coton, celle-la en ce moment, songe-t-elle, et nous avons besoin de tout le monde.

— Bouthaïna, dit-elle, si tu veux bien, c'est toi qui porteras la banderole avec Farah. Vous marcherez en tête du cortège. Alors, nous sommes bien d'accord ? poursuit-elle en s'adressant à tous, Non à la pauvreté ! Non à la violence conjugale ! Nous voulons le changement de la Moudawana. L'Islam est une civilisation, non un abattoir pour les bouchers. Bouthaïna ! Tu m'écoutes ?

Bouthaïna acquiesce. Elle a la tête ailleurs. Dans l'appartement de Slim. Elle vient de se rappeler avec effroi qu'elle est partie sans faire le ménage.

III

Ihsane se lève du lit avec difficulté. En rentrant hier tard dans la nuit du *Abou Nouas*, le bar où elle bosse, elle n'est pas arrivée à s'endormir. Elle a préféré attendre l'aube pour faire sa première prière de la journée. Du foyer pour jeunes filles où elle crêche, elle entend distinctement le muezzin appeler à la prière d'al fajr. Elle est restée un long moment sous la douche, car comme après toutes les nuits où elle rentre du boulot, elle ne s'est pas contentée des ablutions classiques, l'oudou sghir, qu'elle devrait exécuter pour la prière. Elle s'est appliquée à se laver méticuleusement en accomplissant le rituel de l'oudou lékbir, que normalement, les musulmanes n'accomplissent qu'après un acte sexuel ou à la fin de leurs règles. Ihsane se sent souillée par les regards concupiscents des ivrognes du *Abou Nouas*. Elle n'a pas eu le choix. Il fallait qu'elle travaille pour aider sa mère à nourrir ses frères et sœurs et pour pouvoir poursuivre ses études supérieures. L'avantage d'un travail de nuit, c'est qu'il rapporte plus : les pourboires des pochards ne sont pas négligeables. Il lui arrive de se faire jusqu'à cinq cents dirhams la soirée. Par ailleurs, ce job lui laisse les journées libres pour aller à la fac.

Dieu merci, il y a la fac, réservoir de toutes les éruditions, de la connaissance, de la lumière. Elle a dû souffrir et se battre pour passer son bac et intégrer l'université. Son père n'était pas d'accord.

Son père est un de ces débauchés comme elle en rencontre tous les soirs au *Abou Nouas*. Il a la violence et la tendresse des ivrognes. Slim la fait penser à son père, avec ses gros yeux tour à tour pleurnichards et menaçants selon ce que lui a inspiré sa muse, " la boureille ". Encore un mot de son invention. Entre bourré et bouteille.

Chaque fois qu'Ihsane pense à son père, sa gorge se noue. Mais elle a appris à ne plus pleurer.

Quand elle était enfant, elle passait son temps à pleurer. Sa grand-mère maternelle la surnommait sekkaïa, fontaine.

Sa grand-mère partageait avec sa mère une haine viscérale pour son père. Il faut dire que, quand son père rentrait à la maison ivre, il lui arrivait de cogner sa mère. Cette dernière ne se défendait pas. Elle se contentait de protéger son visage de ses mains. Pour le reste, elle se laissait faire.

Ihsane, quand elle était réveillée par les gémissements de sa mère, se levait pour lui porter secours, la peur au ventre. " Ce n'est rien, ma fille, lui disait-elle pour la rassurer, va te recoucher. Ce n'est pas de sa faute, c'est ce maudit chrab. "

C'est aussi ce maudit chrab qui, plus tard, a poussé son père à la regarder d'une drôle de façon. Ihsane avait treize ans mais en paraissait plus. Il lui semblait que sa poitrine était énorme et provocante tant son père la fixait de ses yeux troubles.

Un jour, il a décidé de ne plus aller boire dehors. Il ramenait sa bouteille à la maison et exigeait que ce soit elle qui le serve. Bizarrement, sa mère était contente. Les regards lubriques de son mari sur sa fille ne la dérangeaient pas.

Ihsane avait peur de lui.

Il ne l'a jamais touchée. Il se contentait de la regarder. Elle se sentait déshabillée par ce regard. Ihsane avait honte d'elle-même et de son corps. C'est à cette période que sa mère est de nouveau tombée enceinte.

Son père a fini par se lasser.

Puis, il l'a haïe. Il a voulu qu'elle arrête de fréquenter le collège. L'insulter, l'humilier, était devenu son passe-temps favori. Ihsane se faisait toute petite et discrète pour qu'il l'oublie. Mais il la cherchait. Alors, elle a décidé d'aller vivre chez sa grand-mère. Complice, sa mère a prétexté que Ihsane avait contracté une maladie grave qui exige des soins et qu'elle n'avait pas le temps de la soigner.

Désormais considérée comme une pestiférée, son père l'a laissée tranquille et elle a pu continuer ses études.

Il est mort le jour des résultats du bac. C'était un lundi. Elle n'oubliera jamais ce jour, ni son état d'âme, entre la joie et la peine.

" Tu es l'aînée, il va falloir que tu travailles pour m'aider ", lui a dit sa mère.

Oui.

" Mais pas question de ne pas m'inscrire à l'université ! ", lui a-t-elle répondu d'un ton ferme.

Ihsane a dû quitter la chaleur réconfortante du foyer de sa grand-mère. Elle ne pouvait pas se permettre de rentrer toutes les nuits à des heures tardives ni lui avouer qu'elle travaille dans un bar.

Un bar ! Lieu de débauche et de perdition. La figure de la modernité par excellence. Liberté ? Non. Libertinage. Panthéisme. La face cachée et hideuse de ce qu'ils appellent " la tolérance de l'Islam ". Quelle honte ! agréer de pareils agissements dans un pays musulman. La hantise de Ihsane est que ses frères et sœurs musulmans, ses compagnons de lutte pour une société saine, découvrent un jour qu'elle passe ses soirées dans cet endroit.

Ihsane les a rencontrés à la fac. Elle était un peu perdue. La mort de son père. Le bar. La fac. Le foyer de jeunes filles. Jeunes filles, façon de parler. Un ramassis de putes à deux sous.

Les culpabilités.

Coupable d'avoir affriolé le regard de son père. Coupable de travailler dans un bar. Coupable d'exister en dehors de sa logique profonde, sans repères sécurisants.

Et les repères, elle les a trouvés grâce à son identité de musulmane. Dans un projet de société musulmane. Pas telle qu'elle existe actuellement. Biaisée par des valeurs qui ne sont pas les siennes. Travestie par la mondialisation. Un mot chic pour dire impérialisme. Il n'y a que le nom qui change, l'objectif reste le même, comme l'a affirmé une des militantes du groupe : éradiquer l'identité des peuples pour les domestiquer à travers une laïcité mondiale. Ihsane soupire. Toutes ces connes qui vont aller manifester pour ce plan d'intégration de la femme dans le développement. Sont-elles aveugles ? Ne voient-elles pas le danger ? Ont-elles oublié qui elles sont et d'où elles viennent ? Ne voient-elles pas les détracteurs ? La machination ?

Les solutions sont dans l'Islam, pense Ihsane, C'est notre seule possibilité de protéger notre dignité et d'assurer nos droits. Ne pas empiéter sur notre passé. Ne pas colorer nos valeurs des couleurs de l'occident. Les restituer dans leur véritable contexte, une société arabo-musulmane, jalouse de son identité.

Vite ! Quitter le foyer. Rejoindre les rangs des défenseurs de la vraie liberté, celle de l'Islam.

IV

Affalé sur son divan, le regard rivé sur le poste de télévision, Slim décide qu'il fera un effort pour se réveiller tôt demain.

Il hésite. Rabat ou Casablanca ?
Deux scénarios se mettent en place dans sa tête.

La manif de Casa , les hommes d'un côté, les femmes de l'autre. islamistes.
Rangs serrés.
Obéissance et discipline.
Les femmes à voiles et à vapeurs.

Le manif de Rabat, tous les brassages.
Les féministes. Panachages de couleurs bigarrées.
Mélanges d'hommes, de femmes et d'enfants.
Alliances de toutes sortes.
Complexité et joie de vivre.

Il en est sûr, c'est comme ça que ça va se passer.

Le choix n'est pas difficile. C'est pourquoi il hésite. Parce qu'il ne doit pas penser à son bien-être mais comprendre. Or il n'arrive pas à adopter cet état d'esprit dans lequel il met de côté sa subjectivité. Va-t-il renoncer ? Arrivera-t-il à pulvériser sa hargne ? À défaire son mépris pour ces femmes qui réfutent leurs droits ? Et s'il n'avait rien compris ? Après tout, il n'est pas une femme. Mais, oui, il est contre la polygamie, contre la violence, contre les abus. Oui, il pense que le développement ne peut se faire sans les femmes. Oui, de tout temps, la femme est le centre et au centre de tout.

Oui, il ira à Rabat.

Non, il ne renoncera pas à comprendre. Il n'ira pas à Casablanca, mais il trouvera un moyen pour rencontrer ces femmes qu'il se refuse pour l'instant à traiter d'obscurantistes.

Aouita la navette ferroviaire Casa Rabat affiche complet. Slim ne regrette pas son voyage à Rabat. Il entend " les modernistes " parler. Des bribes de conversations éparpillées, à leur image. Leur langage est teinté de libertés, d'espoir mais aussi de doutes. Serons-nous nombreux ? Où en sommes-nous ? Danger ! Il faut agir.

Et cet espoir lumineux qui les anime, qui les unit, est assombri par des ombres de voiles, fantômes jaillis de leur passé, pour eux, spectres de l'obscurantisme.

Slim somnole. D'une oreille distraite, il écoute deux femmes parler.

— Les intégristes ne sont plus une menace. À l'échelle internationale, ils ont échoué. Les détracteurs du monde musulman doivent se réorienter. Tu verras, c'est par le biais des organisations non gouvernementales qu'ils vont attaquer, maintenant. Les agents de la mondialisation s'infiltrent dans les associations. Le Nord nous envoie ses chômeurs pour soi-disant nous accompagner dans le processus de développement. En réalité, ils ne veulent plus être accompagnateurs, mais acteurs. Petit à petit, ils prennent la place des Marocains et s'y installent.

— C'est terrible ce que tu dis. La militante islamiste qui est passée à la télé hier n'a pas tort.

— Qu'a-t-elle dit ?

— Que l'Occident veut domestiquer les peuples à travers une laïcité mondiale ou encore une mondialisation laïque pour des intérêts économiques purement et simplement. Pour comprendre ce qui se passe, il ne faut plus raisonner qu'en termes de marché.

— Oui, j'ai lu dans un hebdo le point de vue d'un enseignant qui dit la même chose. Il donne pour exemple Israël. Les Israéliens qui sont fiers de leur culture n'adoptent pas celle des Etats-Unis qui les protégent. Ils utilisent l'hébreu jusque dans le domaine nucléaire. Ils ont compris que la voie du progrès d'une nation est étroitement liée à la fierté de sa propre identité culturelle.

—Identité culturelle ? Es-tu capable de définir la tienne aujourd'hui ? Te sens-tu arabo-musulmane ? Citoyenne du monde ? Les deux ?

— Moi, je suis arabo-musulmane. Mais ce que j'aime dans l'Islam plus que dans tout autre religion c'est le libre-arbitre. C'est mon interprétation de l'Islam qui fait sa valeur. Le choix d'une religion est individuel. Le rapport avec Dieu est individuel. C'est ce qui détermine sa force et sa qualité. L'histoire a prouvé qu'un projet de société musulmane est voué à l'échec. L'Iran en est un exemple. L'interprétation des textes sacrés à des fins politiques, leur application les dépouillent de leur perfection. Les paroles de Dieu s'humanisent. La Moudawana n'est pas un texte sacré à ce que je sache. Dans le Coran, j'ai compris personnellement, par exemple, que la polygamie n'a pas lieu d'exister. Ou alors c'est surestimer le sens de l'équité des hommes. Un vrai musulman devrait avoir l'honnêteté de lutter contre la polygamie. Il sait mieux que personne, et en tant qu'être humain, quels abus il peut en tirer. En s'interdisant d'être polygame, il choisit de ne pas avoir la possibilité de céder aux tentations.

— Un peu simplet tout ça et confus. Moi, je reste convaincue que la laïcité peut être une solution à nos problèmes même si, je pense, nous ne sommes pas prêts pour ça. Beaucoup ne comprennent pas bien ce que ce mot signifie. Il faut le redéfinir, lui donner un contenu spécifique, arriver à la laïcité, petit à petit, sans heurts. En douceur. Prendre le temps d'y réfléchir.

Slim ricane. Nous ne sommes pas sortis de l'auberge ! Il détourne son attention vers le paysage verdoyant qui défile par la fenêtre du train. Discours et paysage immuables. Tout semble avoir été déjà pensé, dit et vu. Ces enfants qui courent là-bas, en se découpant sur le ciel, sont les mêmes que tout à l'heure.

Il se sent comme en liberté provisoire. La nuit le libère de sa loi pour un jour. Mais il la sent toute proche. Elle regrette déjà cette permission et lui souffle à l'oreille : que fais-tu ici ? Ce n'est pas ta place ni ton milieu. Tu vas suffoquer. Je t'attends. Fais vite !

Dix heures trente. Rabat. Place Bab El Had. Comme Slim l'a imaginée ; des hommes, des femmes, des chérubins. Une ambiance bon enfant. Fleurant bon les libertés, la diversité des aspirations, l'espérance, la vie. Une seule voix tout de même. Enthousiaste. Fervente.

Des artistes. Des intellectuels. Des associations. Des monsieur et madame tout le monde.

Slim, agoraphobe, suffoque. Slim, démocrate, respire.

Il essaie de trouver un rythme, se laisse guider par le rythme de son souffle. Je ne pouvais pas être ailleurs, songe-t-il. Ma place est ici. Dans la complexité. Dans la richesse. Dans le Maroc d'aujourd'hui et de demain.

V

Allongé sur le lit de la chambre d'hôtel, nu, la télécommande à la main, Slim zappe tout en regardant discrètement Judith défaire sa valise.

Il regarde.
Le corps de Judith, mince et musclé par les salles de sport luxueuses qu'elle fréquente à Paris.
Il hume.
Le parfum coûteux de Judith embaumant le jasmin.

Avec ça, il y a, la pâleur du mensonge. Le bleu gris des cernes. La fatigue de l'adultère consommé. Et du noir partout. Judith ne s'habille qu'en noir. Veuve d'un jour. Veuve de tous les jours. Belle de nuit.

Il hurle. En silence. Mais il hurle. Détresse. La vie n'est que chaos. Injustice. Désordre. La seule femme qui le fait vibrer si lointaine ! Le goût de la vie qui s'échappe. Pourquoi est-elle si… Si fonctionnelle ?

Elle lui rappelle lui quand il est avec Bouthaïna. Détaché. Il le connaît bien cet état d'âme sans âme. Une lucidité oppressante. L'envie de fuir ce qui, quelques minutes auparavant, était l'objectif ultime.

Il se pose des questions. Que cherche-t-elle en moi ma juive marocaine ? L'exotisme d'un pays abandonné, retrouvé ? Le goût des interdits ? Le carburant de la jeunesse ?

Suis-je le frère ennemi ? L'amant fougueux ? Sa réconciliation avec l'autre partie d'elle-même ? Celle qu'elle camoufle honteusement et douloureusement dans le refuge de sa vie de bonne femme bien mariée, bien installée, bien mère de famille. Et ce mari fantoche de ses nuits sans amour pour qui elle a " beaucoup de tendresse ", fantoche de ses nuits sans amour, qui est-il ?

- Toute ma vie ! dit Judith en brandissant un carnet de rendez-vous. Sans lui, je ne suis rien. C'est ma mémoire.

- Je croyais que tu ne venais que pour me voir ! s'exclame Slim, vexé.

- Mais oui ! Je voudrais aussi simplement profiter aussi de ma visite pour rencontrer quelques personnes. Tu ne vas pas en faire un drame. Toi aussi tu as ton travail. Et d'après ce que je vois, tu as du pain sur la planche ! Mon Dieu ! regarde toutes ces femmes voilées. Ça ne te fait pas peur ? demande-t-elle en fixant l'écran de télévision.

- C'est la marche de Casablanca. Je n'y étais pas. J'ai préféré couvrir celle de Rabat. Moins impressionnante. Mais je me sentais plus concerné.

Sur l'écran, le long et vaste Boulevard Mohammed V est envahi par une foule dense qui avance posément, opiniâtrement. " Démonstration de force ", commente le journaliste. Les Islamistes sont au rendez-vous, en masse. Des quatre coins du pays. Une organisation à toute épreuve.

Slim écarquille les yeux. Il vient d'apercevoir le visage de Ihsane jaillir du flux humain, tâche lumineuse, irréelle, parce que connue et reconnue.

Un instant, tout s'évanouit.

Un instant, même Judith n'existe plus. Ses gestes sont en suspens.

Slim se sent trahi.

Un instant, puis tout se remet en mouvement.

Et il découvre que Ihsane n'a rien à faire dans cette chambre d'hôtel. Sa présence y est indécente. Sa trahison, ordinaire, lui importe peu finalement. Elle s'éloigne aussi promptement qu'elle s'est imposée.

— Vous vivez des moments exaltants, dit Judith.

Et Slim la déteste pour ces mots. Le vous globali sateur est péremptoire.

Mais Judith est belle dans ses légèretés.

Une fois, au milieu de la nuit, Slim avait réveillé Bouthaïna délirante dans un cauchemar. Elle criait le nom de sa fille. En ouvrant les yeux, elle vit le visage de Slim et ne le reconnut pas. Elle le repoussa violemment. La haine déformait ses traits. Il ne l'aima jamais autant que cette fois là.

Mais Judith est-elle éphémère ? Dans ses propos ?

Pour l'heure, elle se maquille devant le miroir. Elle se sait décolorée. Ses lèvres brunes s'enluminent de rouge vif, ses yeux de noir charbon.

Disgracieux, le visage de Judith.

Il n'y a que Slim pour lui trouver du charme.

Un front bombé, des yeux creux, une bouche large avec des lèvres minces et - ce qui fait le désespoir de Judith - des cheveux crépus, héritage de ses origines africaines. Pas des boucles soyeuses, non, des ressorts. Son coiffeur se donne un mal de chien pour les détendre. Heureusement, Il y a son corps. Elle en prend grand soin, le structure par le sport, l'adoucit de crèmes parfumées et soyeuses, l'habille de dessous sophistiqués et affriolants. Résultat : il s'en dégage une sensualité raffinée, travaillée, prometteuse.

Slim aime contempler Judith qui se déplace dans la chambre, nue. La grâce de ses mouvements. Son assurance. Son aisance. Elle sait qu'il la regarde. C'est sa façon à elle de lui appartenir.

— C'est pour toi que je me fais belle, lui dit-elle. Où allons-nous ce soir ? Je n'en peux plus de cette chambre d'hôtel, si luxueuse soit-elle. L'air conditionné m'indispose. Pourquoi ne veux-tu pas me recevoir chez toi ? C'est si… impersonnel ici !

— C'est toi qui ne veux pas. Aurais-tu oublié ?

— Peu importe. Toi, moi… Je ne veux pas rencontrer malencontreusement tes petites amies.

— Je n'ai pas de " petites amies ".

— Elles sont grandes alors ? dit Judith en plaisantant gentiment.

— Arrête de me traiter comme ça !

— Comment, comme ça ?

— Comme un enfant ou un dégénéré.

— Mais tu es un enfant ! Délicieux. Capricieux. Fantaisiste. Authentique. Beau. Incompris. Ma bohème à moi.

— J'aimerais être plus.

— Revendicatif !

— Tu me castres.

— Ce n'est pas vrai. Tout à l'heure…

— Arrête ! Tu comprends ce que je veux dire.

— fait déjà partie du passé. Je serai la plus heureuse quand je pourrai tenir dans mes bras ton enfant. Un petit Slim ! quel bonheur ! Moi, c'est trop tard. Je ne peux plus te faire un enfant.

— Qui te parle d'enfant ? Je n'en veux pas. Et arrête de te prendre pour ma mère.

— Je ne suis pas ta mère. Ni ta femme. Ne cherche pas l'impossible. Vis notre histoire comme je la vis. En dehors de tout. Libre. Fabuleuse. En marge de tout conformisme, de toute attache, de toute contrainte. Sans le quotidien, la lassitude, l'usure. Une histoire parallèle à la vie, comme n'en faisant pas partie. Pas condensée, ni étouffante. Déployée dans le temps. Précieuse. En vagues déferlantes. En rareté. En moments privilégiés. Insaisissable. Immortelle.

— C'est comme ça que tu la vois ?

— Comme ça… Et autrement.

— M'aimes-tu ?

— Evidemment !

— As-tu d'autres amants ?

— Est-ce que je te pose ce genre de questions moi ?

— C'est un oui ?

— Slim, ne gâche pas tout. Habille-toi et sortons.

Le vaste hall de l'hôtel Hayat Regency connu précédemment sous le nom d'hôtel Casablanca, grouille de personnes de tous horizons, Saoudiens en habit traditionnel, Américains en jeans et baskets, poules de luxe à talons et en décolleté. Slim et Judith demandent un taxi. Slim a la bouche sèche. Il se rend compte qu'il ne s'est même pas servi un verre dans le mini-bar de la chambre.

— Commençons par aller boire un verre quelque part, dit-il à Judith en la prenant par le bras.

VI

Ce jour sur le déclin, ni tout à fait d'hiver ni tout à fait de printemps est de plus en plus Mortel, pense Bouthaïna. Et Slim qui n'appelle pas. Son portable est éteint.

Que faire ?

Commencer par rentrer à la maison. S'occuper de Hind. Les devoirs. Le bain. Le dîner. Puis prendre le temps de se rassembler.

Dans la rue, elle frissonne, trébuche. Elle est éblouie par la luminosité. L'anarchie de la circulation. Elle émerge. De ses pensées. De sa léthargie. De son mal-être.

Son cabinet d'architecte a connu des jours meilleurs.

Et si ce n'était qu'un cauchemar. Si tout ça n'était pas vraiment arrivé ? Si elle se trompait ?
Elle rentrerait chez elle. Elle trouverait son mari, sa fille, ensemble à l'attendre. Une soirée tranquille.

Rassurante.

Sans Slim.

Invraisemblable.

Il suffirait pour retrouver la paix, de croire, pour s'apaiser, que la vie ne peut plus rien prendre. Accepter ses manques. Dessiner de nouveaux rêves qui propulsent en avant. Et marcher, marcher jusqu'à épuisement. Jusqu'à ce que le rêve, même dans l'illusion, prenne forme et chasse le désespoir. Oui mais voilà, Bouthaïna ne cesse de trébucher. Encore et encore. Elle se dit que sa vie n'est qu'une série pathétique de trébuchements.

Dès le départ, elle s'est sentie cernée par elle ne sait quels manques. Enfant déjà, elle était insatisfaite. Et pourtant, son itinéraire d'enfant gâtée ne prédisposait en rien à ces mélancolies et à ces abattements. Peut-être, faut-il chercher du côté du père, lui a dit un jour une amie psy.

" Mon père, songe Boutaïna.

Un homme complexe. Silencieux. Travailleur. Se complaisant dans le labeur. Y puisant sa force et sa rigueur blessante. Un regard intransigeant.

Méprisant quoi que je fasse. Etait-il réellement méprisant ? Moi, sa fille, ai-je le droit aujourd'hui de le juger alors que j'ai raté ma vie ?

De la sienne, il a fait un hymne à l'épanouissement de ses enfants. Nous avons eu tout ce qu'il était possible d'avoir. L'éducation. Les voyages. La culture. Les livres. Le cinéma. Les expositions. Le théâtre. Les sports.

Peut-être manquait-il la tendresse ?

La tendresse qui nourrit l'âme des petites filles les grandit, fait plus d'elles tard des femmes à part entière. Mon père, cet être extraordinaire à mes yeux, qui m'a comblée de savoirs, m'a servi de modèle, a été le premier homme de ma vie, n'a jamais su me dire : je t'aime ".

La vie serait-elle tout bêtement un éternel recommencement ? La reproduction d'un schéma qu'on se serait gravé sur la peau comme une blessure, marque affichée de nos parcours passés présents et futurs. Loufoque ! Si c'est vrai et si on le sait, chaque acte est lourd à porter, chaque être démystifié.

" Une sensation nouvelle. Celle de la proximité de la mort. C'est chez Slim et avec Slim que je l'ai connue, pense Boutaïna. À la fois fascinante et abjecte. Toujours présente. Implacablement. Née du désir. De ce qui m'a semblé être la vie ".

Délire ?

Course contre le temps ?

Fuite en avant ?

Envie de vivre ou de mourir ?

Bouthaïna caresse le visage rond et rose de sa fille. Lina lui sourit de son sourire brèche-dents. Sa mère est si peu présente. Même quand elle est là, elle n'est pas là. Ses gestes ne sont pas doux. On dirait qu'elle se fiche d'elle. Ce qui est important, c'est de la laver, de la faire manger et surtout qu'elle dorme. Lina a de plus en plus de mal à s'endormir. Plus sa mère veut qu'elle dorme, plus le sommeil lui échappe. Elle a beau compter les moutons comme elle lui dit ou essayer de penser à des choses agréables, elle n'y arrive pas. Sa maman est tout le temps énervée. Elle la voit qui pleure. Lina veut être gentille pour la voir sourire. Elle fait son possible, s'applique en tirant la langue pour faire ses devoirs. Peine perdue. Sa mère est triste.

— Lina, ma chérie, dépêche-toi. Il est déjà neuf heures. Quand vas-tu dormir ?

— Tu vas me raconter une histoire ?

— Oui, oui ! si tu fais vite.

— Celle de Leila et le loup ?

— D'accord.

— Dis maman, tu vas sortir ?

— Pourquoi tu demandes ?

— Pour savoir.

— Je ne sais pas encore, ma chérie. Ça dépend.

— Ça dépend de quoi ?

— Je ne sais pas. Dors.

Pas de nouvelles de Slim.

Appeler une copine.

Sortir ! Prendre l'air. Faire comme lui.

Boire.

Le retrouver dans l'odeur de l'alcool, le brouhaha des bars, les vapeurs de la nuit.

Malika.

Toujours prête à faire la fête.

Malika et Bouthaïna décident d'aller à la Bodéga. Tout le gratin de Casablanca est là. Les youpies. Les minets. Les minettes. Les super-womens. Quelques artistes. Des journalistes. Ils sont partout ceux-là.

Une ambiance ibérique ou latino, va savoir. Tapas. Musique étouffée par les ouï-dire des uns et des autres sur les uns et les autres. Un air de liberté. Des bouffées de fumée.

Bouthaïna et Malika s'installent au bar.

Malika est en chasse.

Son dernier petit copain a largué les amarres pour convoler en justes noces avec une vague cousine.

Elle zyeute.

Bouthaïna avale son premier verre comme si c'était la panacée à tous ses maux. Elle en redemande.

— Doucement ma belle ! lui hurle Malika.

— OUblie-moi, lui répond Bouthaïna en vidant son deuxième verre.

Détendue, elle sirote son troisième. Deux hommes proposent de leur offrir une tournée. Malika se pâme. Bouthaïna bougonne. Elle n'en a rien à foutre de ces deux cons. Du large ! Elle leur offre son dos.

Blottie dans sa souffrance, Bouthaïna tente de faire diversion à ses états d'âme en s'acharnant sur les détails de ce qui s'offre à sa vue. Un couple énamouré. La fille : La trentaine, les yeux embués la mine déjà défaite, le cœur au bord de ses lèvres entr' ouvertes. Le garçon : La trentaine, quémandeur, idiot parce que quémandeur de ce qui est déjà acquis, la queue au bout des yeux.

Bouthaïna aussi a la trentaine. Dit comme ça, on dirait une maladie. Mais à trente ans, sa vie vient à peine de commencer.

Des perspectives.

Elle aime bien ce mot porteur d'espoir et d'ouvertures. L'éducation des sentiments passe par l'apprentissage du désespoir. Après le désespoir, l'espoir. L'alcool commence à lui faire du bien. La vie change de look. Elle a envie de rire.

Au fond de la salle, un autre couple. Le garçon, une allure vaguement familière. La femme, sa mère ? Bouthaïna se fige. C'est Slim. Avec une femme. Il est différent. Elle ne l'a jamais vu comme ça. Presque normal.

Elle prend la fuite. C'en est trop pour elle. Malika a vu. Elle la laisse partir.

— Je te téléphone, lui dit-elle, tout à coup grave.

Complicité entre femmes.

" Merde ", je ne suis même pas allée à cette marche à Rabat, gémit Bouthaïna en sortant de la Bodéga.

VII

Ihsane est recroquevillée dans son lit, devant la fenêtre. Sa main caresse lentement la vitre et, derrière son geste, elle voit la pluie tomber, déchaînée. Elle se tasse encore plus. Pourquoi penser à lui ? Il ne fait pas partie de sa vie. Avec ses gros yeux tendres. Chaque fois qu'il la prend, elle se sent pénétrée de sa souffrance.

Ihsane se lève. Elle se dirige vers le grand miroir sur le mur. Ses mains gobent ses seins menus, s'imprègnent des contours de son corps. Il la trouve belle. Elle l'est.

Il prononce son prénom avec une douceur qui l'irrite.

Slim ne sait pas comment dormir avec elle. Souvent, il se lève au milieu de la nuit, s'assied au bord du lit, et la regarde. Elle fait semblant de dormir, de ne pas le voir. Il arrive aussi à Ihsane de se réveiller. Elle tente alors, en lui caressant le dos, la nuque, de l'inciter à se rallonger.

Il est constamment épuisé. Sa respiration saccadée.

Elle ne comprend pas pourquoi elle l'a suivi le premier soir chez lui. Pourquoi elle s'est laissée dénuder.

Il aime la regarder se balader nue dans la maison. Ihsane jusqu'alors refusait d'avoir conscience de son corps. À cause du regard de son père. La première fois qu'elle a fait l'amour, elle s'en souvient, c'était l'année de son bac, l'année de la mort de son père. Avec un garçon insignifiant. Une après-midi terne. Sur un coup de tête. Pour survivre. Étreinte brutale qui lui avait ravi sa virginité et qui l'avait laissée sur sa faim.

Avec Slim, tout est différent.

Il lui fait l'amour maladroitement, cherchant coûte que coûte à la satisfaire, y parvenant, mais incapable de jouir lui-même. Il s'accuse, se lamente, pathétique. Impuissant à faire jaillir de lui la vie.

Il lui arrive aussi de la faire s'asseoir, de s'agenouiller devant elle, de poser les lèvres entre ses cuisses, sur son sexe, de la supplier d'accepter ce baiser indécent comme gage de son adoration, de se retrancher de la course au plaisir, de l'y mener.

Étrange et déroutant.

Elle se demande quelles cicatrices marquent son cœur.

Ihsane ne lui parle que rarement, ne trouvant rien à lui dire, consciente qu'un monde les sépare. Il cherche désespérément à extraire d'elle quelques paroles, en les quémandant.

Elle lui offre son demi-sourire, pâle et froid.

Comment lui expliquer qu'elle a l'impression de ne plus avoir une larme en elle. Un éclat de rire. Elle n'a que ce poids dans la poitrine qu'elle traîne et qui fait que ses gestes sont lents, son regard absent.

Ihsane s'observe dans le miroir.

De longs cheveux bruns et soyeux, qui lui caressent les fesses et qu'elle cache comme une tare tous les jours sous ses voiles. Des yeux en amande, ouverts et sans lumière. Un visage à l'ovale parfait, qui émeut. Une bouche large, pleine. Jamais l'ombre d'un fard.

Oui, elle est belle.

Elle le sait, Slim ne peut pas se contenter longtemps d'une image sans vie. Il est en manque de vie.

Après tout qu'attend-elle de lui si ce n'est ces parties de plaisir intense mais sans joie ?

Il n'y a que cette détresse qui les rapproche, faisant d'eux les amants de la désespérance, le triste couple d'*Abou Nouas*.

Retour en arrière.

Le boulevard Mohammed V était couvert de monde.

Ihsane a honte.

Honte de penser à son corps, de le sentir quand c'est son âme qui devrait l'occuper. Honte de s'avouer qu'aucun des hommes qui étaient présents à la marche n'aurait la faculté de l'exciter, ne la fouillerait de sa langue jusqu'à ce qu'elle jouisse.

Peut-être devrait-elle faire des choix ?

S'abstenir de rentrer avec Slim chez lui la prochaine fois qu'il le lui demandera ?

Quitter le *Abou Nouas* ?

De quoi vivrais-je ? s'interroge Ihsane au fond, satisfaite de trouver cette excuse.

Avec des gestes vifs et précis, presque rageusement, elle tord ses cheveux, les ramasse en chignon bas derrière la nuque, les épingles. Elle enserre sa tête dans un foulard noir en s'appliquant à ne pas laisser dépasser une mèche.

Dehors, la pluie continue à tomber, droite et drue. Sa chambre large et claire lui paraît étroite. Aucune image n'orne les murs. Un lit d'une place, son chevet, un petit bureau, sa chaise sur le dossier de laquelle le tapis de prière sont les seuls meubles de la pièce. Ihsane ouvre la fenêtre pour aérer. Elle prend le Coran sur son chevet et l'effleure de ses lèvres. Puis elle enfile rapidement une jellaba et sort.

Dans le couloir, deux filles rient en se racontant leurs dernières prises, celles de la veille.

— Il fallait voir le mien ! Il salivait à la perspective de me mettre dans son lit, dit la petite brunette à son amie.

En voyant Ihsane, elles chuchotent quelque chose que Ihsane n'entend pas entièrement.

— La voilà… Foulard… Triste…

Ihsane passe devant elles, majestueuse. Elle ne leur adresse jamais la parole, à ces filles de mauvaise vie. Elles sont si… vulgaires !

Dans la rue, Ihsane frisonne. Le vent froid lui pince le visage. La tête baissée, d'un pas pressé, elle se dirige vers la station de bus. Personne ne la voit, ombre à forme indéfinie. Le bus s'arrête. Elle se fraye un passage dans la foule, poinçonne son ticket, soupire. Elle a promis à sa mère de lui rendre visite aujourd'hui.

VIII

Ryad Zitoun. Le meilleur restaurant marocain de Casablanca, d'après l'intelligentsia locale. Pas de décor des mille et une nuits comme ailleurs. De la simplicité. Une jolie terrasse. Des murs peints en rose de Marrakech. Quelques lampes, joyaux de l'artisanat marocain. Des garçons en habit traditionnel. Un patron élégant et prévenant.

Slim boit.

Judith retrouve les mets délicats des jours de fête de son enfance. À bien plus de mille et une nuits de son amant. Concentrée sur les saveurs. Celles, exquises des plats qu'on lui sert et celles, nostalgiques de ses jeunes années enfuies.

Slim n'a pas vu Bouthaïna à la Bodéga, ni son départ précipité. Il ne l'a pas vue non plus les suivre jusqu'au Riad Zitoun, les guetter, défigurée par la jalousie, le visage bouffi par les larmes.

Et pourtant, à ce moment précis où elle attend dehors, figée par le dépit, il pense à elle.

Ce serait si bon de pouvoir l'aimer comme elle le désire ! De lui faire cet enfant que Judith aurait tant de bonheur à tenir dans ses bras.

Mais il est trop tard. Pas seulement pour Judith. Pour lui aussi.

Judith ferme les yeux. Elle ne veut pas voir la réalité. Celle de la perte de Slim. Il dépérit de jour en jour, songe-t-elle.

" Moi père ? s'indigne Slim en silence. Quelle blague ! A mon âge, juste bon à être grand-père. Et encore. Il me manquerait les gestes tendres de l'âge mûr, la patience qui les accompagne gagnée à coups de déboires ".

Dans ses rêves - il lui arrive encore d'en avoir - c'est d'une petite fille que Slim aimerait être le papa. Pas un garçon. Une mignonnette. Ronde et rose. Gorgée d'éclats de rire. Joviale. Malicieuse. Il l'appellerait Amal et elle serait la raison d'un nouveau combat de tous les jours. L'ennemie déclarée de sa mort. Sa vie.

Mais il est trop tard.

Personne ne le sait mieux que lui. Encore moins les femmes qui l'aiment.

— Arrête de boire, dit Judith d'une voix plaintive. Mange quelque chose. Tout est si bon ici !

— Je n'ai pas faim, mon cœur, répond Slim, la larme à l'œil.

— Force-toi. Je te veux solide, pas défaillant.

— Tu me tues. J'en ai marre de cette histoire qui m'use.

— Alors on arrête tout. À vrai dire je suis venue avec l'intention de t'en parler. Cela fait dix ans que nous sommes ensemble. Je suis persuadée que notre liaison t'empêche de faire ta vie, de te marier, d'avoir des enfants. Et ça, je ne le veux pas. Je ne veux pas que tu aies à le regretter un jour, que j'aie à me le reprocher.

Suit un de ces silences où chacun peut gamberger de son côté.

Slim n'est pas en état de répondre. Il se tient debout devant Judith, blême, flageolant, cassé, les yeux plus brouillés que jamais.

— Slim ça va ?

Il ne peut pas répondre, les mains posées à plat sur la table, les jambes vacillantes avec l'air de ne pas savoir qui est Judith. En face de lui, à quelques mètres de là, fixant le dos de Judith, Bouthaïna est pétrifiée. Dans son regard, sa haine pour l'humanité.

Nouveau silence.

Bouthaïna tourne les talons et s'en va.

Judith s'inquiète.

— Slim ça va ?

Curieusement, à ce moment-là Slim songe qu'il faut plus d'une femme pour réussir un homme.

— Partons, dit-il.

— Tu as un malaise ? demande-t-elle compatissante.

— Partons, répète Slim agacé.

Maintenant que Bouthaïna a découvert les infidélités de Slim, tout ira de mal en pis. C'est sans issue. D'ailleurs qui trompe-t-il ?

Il serait volontiers allé rejoindre Bouthaïna, mais il ne trouve pas de prétexte à sortir à Judith pour justifier son départ.

Réflexion faite, pas de compromis.

Que chacun et chacune s'assument. Après tout il n'a jamais rien promis à personne. Quant à Bouthaïna…

La souffrance est la conséquence du libre jeu des parties du système, pense Slim en se référant à Houellebecq. Je le sais et je le dis.

Toutes les choses souffrent jusqu'à ce qu'elles soient. Toute souffrance est bonne. Toute souffrance est utile. Toute souffrance est productive. Si on décide de rester vivant. Et Bouthaïna a le profil de l'éternelle rescapée.

Dans un excès d'euphorie soudaine, Slim propose à Judith de prolonger la soirée dans un cabaret.

— Tu vas aimer, tu verras, lui garantit-il pour la convaincre.

— Non Slim, tu es sinistre. Arrête de boire et rentre avec moi te coucher.

— Non.

— Alors bonne nuit ! dit-elle agressivement en montant dans un taxi.

Le taxi s'éloigne, rouge et noir.

Slim décide d'aller au *Abou Nouas*. Avec de la chance, Ihsane le consolera.

IX

De retour dans sa chambre de jeune fille, Bouthaïna déguste un breuvage - qu'elle a trouvé dans le réfrigérateur - aux fruits de la passion. D'une traite. Les yeux fermés. Voluptueusement.

Elle se sent trop petite.

Pour l'Amour.

Pour la souffrance.

Et même pour Dieu.

Elle tète goulûment la bouteille. Le goût sucré et velouté du sirop la rassure. Lina dort dans le lit. C'est comme si elle avait deviné qu'aujourd'hui Bouthaïna n'est pas sa mère mais sa petite sœur. Ou alors peut-être bien est-elle venue chercher sa mère, se blottir dans la chaleur rassurante de sa chambre.

Bouthaïna ne la touche même pas. Elle l'ignore.

Bouthaïna a toujours su que Slim n'est pas homme à se contenter d'une seule femme. Trop dispersé. C'est d'avoir vu , de dos l'autre qui la désarçonne.

Elle découvre avec étonnement qu'elle aurait voulu servir d'alter ego à Slim dans sa vie polygame. Lui ouvrir les jambes des inconnues, les lécher consciencieusement pour les lui préparer. Elle s'occuperait des prémices et lui du reste. Ils ne formeraient plus qu'un dans l'acte d'amour. Et l'autre resterait l'autre. Leur partenaire. L'objet de leur désir. Étrangère à leur fusion.

C'est peut-être mon corps qui ne lui plaît pas, songe-t-elle. Elle se souvient des paroles de son père : c'est sur ta tête que tu dois compter, ma fille. Oublie le reste, lui a-t-il dit un jour. Il l'avait surprise entrain de se vernir les ongles dans sa chambre à coucher. Et il n'aimait pas ça. Bouthaïna s'était sentie dépouillée de sa féminité. Et depuis, elle relègue au second plan tout ce qu'elle considère comme faisant partie des choses superflues de la vie, les séances en institut de beauté, les visites répétées chez le coiffeur, le maquillage et autres bricolages spécifiques à la gente féminine. Pourtant, elle le sait, elle attire les regards, ne laisse pas indifférent. Lina lui ressemble. Les mêmes grands yeux clairs, kaki, dit sa mère. Les mêmes cheveux auburn que Bouthaïna coupent court par souci de commodité et que Lina porte longs et bouclés, refusant systématiquement par coquetterie de les raccourcir. Le même menton volontaire. Le même profil parfait. Une peau de rousse, blanche, lisse.

Bouthaïna est plutôt grande. Elle a des petits seins et des fesses rebondies que les hommes lorgnent avec une lueur grivoise dans les yeux.

Sa mère ouvre la porte de sa chambre, interrompant sa rêverie.

— Où étais-tu ? lui demande-t-elle avec un air accusateur.

— Dehors, répond Bouthaïna d'un ton sec.

— Encore avec ce minable ?

— Ca ne te regarde pas.

— Décidément, ma pauvre fille, tu es folle à lier. Tu n'as pas encore compris que ce type n'est pas pour toi. Ni pour personne d'ailleurs. Essaye au moins de ne pas t'afficher avec lui partout et surtout dans ces bars sordides qu'il affectionne. Fais-le pour ta fille. Et par respect pour ton père.

— Se serait-il plaint à toi ?

— Tu le connais. Il ne dit jamais rien. Mais là, tu y vas un peu fort. Il n'ose même plus aller à la mosquée le vendredi depuis qu'un de ces illuminés qu'il y rencontre lui a dit qu'il n'a pas su t'éduquer correctement. Il t'a même traitée de débauchée. Ménage ton père. Après tout, tu lui es au moins redevable de ce que tu es aujourd'hui.

— La belle affaire !

— Non Bouthaïna, quoi que tu en dise, c'est ton père et il t'aime. Il ne veut pas qu'on te montre du doigt.

— Il ne veut pas qu'on le montre du doigt, rectifie Bouthaïna.

— Et alors ? Même si c'est vrai, il a le droit de se protéger. Ce n'est pas parce qu'il a eu la sottise de te laisser faire ce que tu veux dans la vie qu'il faut qu'il en pâtisse. Il ne te reproche jamais rien. Ton père t'a toujours appuyée. Invariablement. Même dans ce divorce ridicule. Et maintenant il est obligé de supporter les conséquences de cette liaison ignominieuse.

— Slim m'aime.

— Slim ne s'aime même pas. Il est incapable d'aimer. Sors-toi de cette histoire tant qu'il en est encore temps. Tu as tout pour être heureuse. Tu es libre, jeune, belle, intelligente. Et il te fait douter de toi-même et de tes capacités. Tu as une petite fille adorable que tu négliges. Quitte ce cauchemar qui chaque jour t'affaiblit un peu plus. Quand tu seras à bout, usée, tu seras seule à porter le fardeau de ta détresse. Personne, même avec toute la volonté du monde, ne pourra t'apporter une aide. Secoue-toi. Ouvre les yeux. Tiens, tu peux me dire quel type de relation il entretient avec sa famille ?

— Il ne les voit jamais. Il lui arrive de trouver un mot de ses frères ou sœurs, glissé sous sa porte, mais il n'en fait pas cas.

— Même sa mère, il ne demande pas de ses nouvelles ?

— Pas à ma connaissance. Des fois, j'ai l'impression qu'il lui en veut pour quelque chose. Il n'a plus l'âge de dépendre de ses parents.

— Ne confonds pas tout. Ce n'est pas une histoire de dépendance et tu le sais bien. Nous ne sommes pas en Occident ici. Nous sommes au Maroc. L'attachement aux parents, leur prise en charge, ne serait-ce qu'affective, est sacrée. On va au moins leur rendre visite de temps en temps, s'inquiéter de leur santé. On ne les abandonne pas à leur vieillesse, hchouma. Il n'y a que les voyous pour faire ça.

— Ce que tu peux être vieux jeu.

— Tu es de mauvaise foi, Bouthaïna. Tu sais que j'ai raison. Quelqu'un qui ignore ses parents, c'est quelqu'un qui n'a pas de cœur ni de reconnaissance. Il ne faut jamais rien attendre de bon de lui.

— Tu en fais un portrait au vitriol. Tu pourrais lui chercher des circonstances atténuantes. Une enfance malheureuse. Des problèmes existentiels. Peut-être ne voit-il pas ses parents pour les ménager.

— Oui je te l'accorde, je veux bien penser que c'est un malade mental, un alcoolique suicidaire trop lâche pour se tuer. Pervers aussi. Et toi, tu n'as rien à faire dans cette galère. Tu n'es pas son psy. Ni sa mère. Tu es la mère de Lina. Ne l'oublie pas. Ne fais rien que tu pourrais te reprocher amèrement plus tard. Je sais que ça ne me regarde pas, que c'est ta vie. Mais j'ai peur pour toi, ma fille. Ce dément va te détruire. J'ai du mal à l'imaginer te faisant l'amour. Il doit en être incapable.

— Maman ! Tu deviens indécente.

— Réfléchis. Analyse. Et tu verras. Tu finiras par me donner raison.

— Je crois que c'est plus compliqué que ça. Slim est un être qui a au fond de lui une immense tendresse. C'est un enfant. Ecorché. Trop sensible. Pas fait pour ce monde. Il a peur de tout, ne supporte pas le moindre problème, fuit dès qu'il en flaire un. Ça fait longtemps qu'il a déposé les armes. Il ne fait que passer. Même dans ma vie. J'en suis consciente et je ne lui en veux pas. C'est un solitaire. Il ne peut plus faire autrement. Et moi, je l'aime comme ça.

De son côté, je le sais, il essaye de marcher vers moi, lentement, de contourner les obstacles mais il se laisse prendre par l'air du temps, l'éphémère, parce qu'il a peur.

Bouthaïna se tait et baisse les yeux pour les relever avec défi. Dans la lumière de la lampe de chevet, ses cheveux sont presque roux, flamboyants. Elle est belle, dure, insolente.

— C'est triste n'est-ce pas ?

Sa mère mordille le coin de sa lèvre.

— Je vais dormir, lui dit-elle. Tu ferais bien d'en faire autant.

Sa mère ne sait plus la consoler comme quand elle était petite et qu'elle se blottissait contre sa poitrine. Elle lui caressait les cheveux, lui racontait une histoire et l'angoisse s'envolait, une douce chaleur l'envahissait.

Aujourd'hui elle se sent congelée. Elle n'a plus confiance. L'idée qu'elle se fait du bonheur ressemble à un moule confortable trop étroit pour Slim.

Bouthaïna quitte sa chambre, sort dans le jardin fumer une cigarette. Au début de leur relation, Slim lui téléphonait tous les jours à des heures surprenantes. Il la réveillait au milieu de la nuit, lui demandait de le rejoindre dans des endroits de Casablanca pas toujours tranquillisants. Elle s'habillait à la hâte et courait vers lui comme si sa vie en dépendait. Quand elle arrivait, Slim lui disait en riant qu'il avait enfin trouvé plus fou que lui.

Bouthaïna grimace.

Demain est un autre jour, se dit-elle.

X

Ihsane le voit rentrer titubant, s'asseoir sur un tabouret et s'accouder au bar. Il commande un verre de scotch. Double. Elle le sert en silence. Slim, la tête légèrement penchée sur le côté, la fixe intensément. On dirait presque qu'il somnole. Autour de lui rien ne bruit ni ne vit.

Sa solitude transperce Ihsane.

La résolution de Ihsane de ne plus rentrer avec Slim chez lui quand il le lui demande s'évapore.

Elle a envie de prendre la tête de Slim entre ses mains et d'enfoncer ses doigts dans la soie de ses cheveux longs comme ceux d'une fille. D'où peut-il venir pour chuter ici dans cet état ? se demande Ihsane. Il est pire que d'habitude.

— Viens Slim, rentrons chez toi. Je t'emmène, lui murmure-t-elle à l'oreille.

— Non, laisse-moi, dit Slim en la repoussant maladroitement. Tu travailles, toi.

— C'est fini, Slim. Le *Abou Nouas* va fermer. Il est une heure.

Slim la regarde sceptique, sa tête ballote, ses yeux chavirent.

— Prends ma bouteille avec toi. Tu es belle, Ihsane. Je t'aime. Tu ne me crois pas ? Je te dis que je t'aime, hurle Slim.

— Mais oui, mais oui. Partons.

Tant bien que mal, Ihsane hèle un taxi, y installe Slim, s'y engouffre avec la bouteille dissimulée dans un sachet en plastique noir.

Slim taquine le chauffeur de taxi, lui déclare sa tendresse dans une envolée lyrique, compatit au sort de tous les chauffeurs de taxi du monde, les erreurs… non ! Les errants de la nuit.

Dans l'appartement de Slim, Ihsane l'aide à s'allonger sur le canapé, lui enlève ses chaussures.

— Sers-moi un verre, ma beauté. Tu crois que je suis saoul ? Jamais ! Allez, sers-moi un verre, mon cœur. Et mets de la musique. Le CD de Chab Mami.

Mali, mali, mali haaakda ? chante Slim en faisant des grimaces. Plus fort, Ihsane ! Plus fort ! Je n'entends rien.

— Les voisins…

— Je m'en fous, des voisins. Je m'en fous de tout. Je ne fais jamais de mal à personne, moi. Je ne suis pas un fils de pute. Ma mère m'a éduqué dans les règles de l'art. Je n'ai rien à me reprocher. Tu m'as déjà vu faire du mal à quelqu'un ? Dire du mal de quelqu'un ?

— Non.

— Alors fais ce que je te dis. Je ne demande jamais rien à personne. Quand on a vu des enfants mourir, plus rien n'a d'importance.

— Tu as vu des enfants mourir, toi ?

— Au Liban. En reportage. Je ne veux pas en parler, marmonne-t-il, en chassant de la main un fantôme.

Écoute Chab Mami. Il chante la vie de tous les jours, la réalité, notre réalité.

— Tu parles de la tienne.

— Non Ihsane, tu te trompes. Écoute-le bien. C'est toi aussi qu'il chante, ta génération.

— Je ne me sens pas concernée.

— Tu n'y comprends rien alors. Danse, Ihsane ! Laisse-toi prendre par le rythme. Lâche tes cheveux. Ils sont si beaux. Pourquoi tu les ramasses toujours ? Tu t'emprisonnes. Tu es si belle, Ihsane. Libère-toi. Laisse la vie te pénétrer.

Je t'ai vue à la télé dimanche, à la marche. C'était toi, n'est-ce pas ? À Casablanca. N'est-ce pas ? insiste Slim.

— Oui, répond Ihsane, étonnée que Slim l'ait reconnue avec le foulard.

— Tu es folle ou quoi ? rugit Slim. Qu'est-ce que tu foutais avec ces malades, ces fanatiques ? Ce n'est pas toi, ça, Ihsane. Toi si douce. Quand tu fais l'amour avec moi, tu n'es pas ça, tu es différente.

— Non ! C'est quand je suis avec toi que je ne suis pas moi.

Slim l'observe, hésite.

— Tu es en colère, feint-il de découvrir. C'est normal. Ça te passera, dit-il en chassant de la main un deuxième fantôme.

De quoi as-tu peur ? poursuit-il. Regarde-toi. Rien ne peut t'atteindre. Baise-les tous. Pas de pitié. Et moi aussi, baise-moi.

— Slim, tu divagues. Tu ferais bien d'aller dormir. Je vais faire ton lit.

— Ne me laisse pas seul, pleurniche Slim, la mine défaite. Tu dors avec moi, n'est-ce pas ? demande-t-il, prêt à la supplier.

— Ne t'en fais pas, je reste avec toi. Arrête de pleurer.

— Tu n'aimes pas quand je pleure ? Je pleure tout le temps, tu sais. Mon chagrin est immense.

Ihsane le regarde d'une drôle de façon.

Slim a découvert Houellebecq récemment.

Houellebecq écrit : " Lorsque vous susciterez chez les autres un mélange de pitié effrayée et de mépris, vous saurez que vous êtes sur la bonne voie. Vous pourrez commencer à écrire. Vous êtes bien parti dans votre carrière de poète. Si vous ne parvenez pas à articuler votre souffrance dans une structure bien définie, vous êtes foutu. La souffrance vous bouffe tout cru, de l'intérieur, avant que vous ayez eu le temps d'écrire quoi que ce soit. La structure est le moyen d'échapper au suicide ".

Slim pense à une chanson de Brel :

J'aurais aimé ma belle
T'écrire un long poème
T'écrire un long je t'aime
Mais le temps de prendre une plume
Le temps de la tailler…

— Je vais en finir, dit Slim à Ihsane. Je ne suis pas poète. Je dois mourir.

Bouthaïna aurait pensé : tu es trop lâche pour te suicider, Slim.

Un jour, il lui a demandé ce qu'elle ferait s'il mourait. Elle lui a répondu sur un ton mi-tragique, mi-moqueur : j'irai cracher sur ta tombe.

Ihsane le prend par le bras et le conduit à sa chambre. Elle le déshabille, le borde, puis s'allonge à côté de lui, raide. Elle ne le comprend pas. Il oublie Dieu. Dieu est là. De tous les instants. Elle pose sa main sur le cœur de Slim endormi et balbutie un verset du Coran. Puis elle prie pour Slim. Mon Dieu, montre-lui le chemin qui mène à toi, supplie-t-elle de toute son âme.

XI

Quand Slim se réveille, il est seul. Il se lève, la tête prise dans un étau, la démarche vacillante. Sous la douche, il tente de reprendre ses esprits. Il s'est passé beaucoup de choses hier. Judith. Puis Bouthaïna... Puis Ihsane. " Voilatilisée ", celle-là, ricane Slim.

Slim se dépêche.

Il n'aime pas flâner dans son appartement quand il est seul. En réalité, il n'aime pas son appartement. La première fois que Bouthaïna est venue chez lui, elle lui a dit :

— Ton appartement est triste. On s'y sent mal à l'aise. Il est gris et sans vie.

Slim l'a meublé à la va-vite, chez Kitéa. Il l'a voulu pratique, fonctionnel. Pas le temps de choisir autre chose. Il n'est pas homme à vivre dans une maison.

Résultat : un décor aux couleurs neutres, des meubles sans véritable attrait, aucune touche personnalisée. Un peu comme les hôtels Ibis ou

Campanile en France. Un lieu de passage pour homme pressé.

Sa mère est venue un jour, en son absence, et a nettoyé de fond en comble. Il lui avait laissé la clef chez le concierge.

Puis elle est partie. La conscience tranquille. Sans essayer de le voir, lui, Slim.

Quand il était enfant, c'était pareil, elle prenait le temps de le laver, de l'habiller, de le nourrir. Elle accomplissait son devoir mécaniquement, était quitte vis-à-vis de Dieu et des hommes, satisfaite.

Et la tendresse, bordel ! comme dit l'autre.

Un jour, Slim a quémandé sa tendresse. Sa sœur aînée lui avait parlé du vieil adage qui dit que le paradis se trouve sous les pieds des mères. Et Slim a voulu avoir un avant-goût du paradis en embrassant les pieds de sa mère. En se remémorant la scène, Slim s'apitoie sur le petit enfant au cœur gonflé d'affection qu'il était, à la recherche d'un câlin de cette mère lointaine et sans cesse affairée. Elle l'a repoussé brutalement. Excédée. Dix enfants, c'est beaucoup pour une seule femme.

Quand Bouthaïna, dans son cauchemar, l'a repoussé en criant le nom de sa fille, Slim l'a aimée.

Cherchez la femme dans tout ça !

Slim décide de passer au Hayat Regency avant de se rendre au journal. Judith doit lui en vouloir. Il ne veut pas perdre Judith.

À la réception de l'hôtel, un individu à la mine patibulaire et au regard soupçonneux lui annonce solennellement qu'elle est partie et lui tend avec dédain un morceau de papier chiffonné.

— Madame Cohen vous a laissé un message, l'informe-t-il d'une voix neutre.

Slim déplie le morceau de papier chiffonné. Quelques mots écrits précipitamment par une Judith certainement exaspérée parce que tout ne se passe pas comme elle l'avait prévu.

Slim,

Je suis partie. Je ne supporte plus de te voir comme ça. Mon amitié, tu le sais, t'est acquise. Pour le reste, il est temps de mettre un terme à une liaison qui te laisse insatisfait (Judith a commencé par écrire malheureux puis l'a barré et remplacé par insatisfait). Trouve-toi une fille, pas une fille de bar, une fille bien, qui s'occupera de toi et te fera des enfants. Je l'envie déjà, cette inconnue qui saura te satisfaire.

Bien à toi. Judith.

— À quelle heure est-elle partie ? demande Slim au réceptionniste.

— Ce matin à dix heures.

Slim soupire. Elle ne l'a donc pas attendu. Il n'y a qu'une femme pour conseiller à un homme de chercher une autre fille pour, l'instant d'après, lui avouer qu'elle envie déjà cette inconnue qu'elle lui suggère de rencontrer. Slim se demande pourquoi elle l'envie déjà. Parce qu'elle aura l'incroyable faculté de savoir le satisfaire et donc des qualités pour ça que Judith estime ne pas avoir, ou bien, parce qu'elle l'aura lui, Slim ? Que cherche Judith ?

À lui faire du bien. Elle est même prête à se sacrifier pour mon bonheur, conclut Slim qui décidément croit connaître les femmes ; c'est une femme merveilleuse. Irremplaçable.

Appeler Bouthaïna ?

Non, pas encore. La laisser mariner. Elle reviendra. Sans que je fournisse le moindre effort, songe Slim. Elle revient toujours.

Peut-être que, si elle ne revenait pas, ce serait différent. Il irait la chercher. Slim n'aime pas l'idée de la faire souffrir. Mais avec Bouthaïna, on ne peut pas faire autrement.

Slim l'interpelle comme si elle était là avec lui.

Pourquoi me renvoies-tu cette image de tortionnaire que je ne suis pas ? Pourquoi réveilles-tu en moi des instincts que je ne me connaissais pas ? Tu ne me laisses même pas le temps de savoir si je te veux vraiment ou pas. Constamment présente. Aimante. Pas amoureuse, aimante. Et si forte ! A toi seule, Bouthaïna, tu es capable de bouffer dix hommes comme moi.

Slim a rendez-vous à la brasserie La Presse. Sur le boulevard Roudani. La plus ancienne brasserie de

Casablanca. Mi-bar, mi-restaurant, n'y débarquent que les habitués, les fidèles et même, de temps en temps, les infidèles, les journalistes (encore !), et autres amateurs de la plume et du monde de la culture en général. Bien sûr comme partout ailleurs, on peut y rencontrer aussi les autres, les étrangers de passage, les buveurs d'un verre puis de deux, les mangeurs d'entre midi et deux, les égarés. Mais en général, de La Presse on dit que c'est, comme son nom l'indique, le rendez-vous de la presse de Casablanca. Lieu enchanteur en vérité. À sauvegarder dans la mémoire de Casablanca comme faisant partie du patrimoine. Son côté bas quartier de luxe. Ses garçons berbères, et donc droits, pas colonisables. Toute l'histoire du Maroc y a été débattue, analysée, réécrite. On peut y rêver d'incorruptibilité, de liberté d'expression et de discussions politiquement correctes. Un côté canaille aussi. Pas pour déplaire.

Manque peut-être pour Slim qui affectionne les phénomènes de mode du monde de la modernité un côté chébran.

Perché sur le tabouret du bar, le flic attend Slim. Ces journalistes toujours en retard ! On leur rend service et ils trouvent moyen de ne pas vous respecter, songe-t-il exaspéré. Cette affaire de pots-de-vin va déclencher un gros scandale. Une commune est impliquée. Et même des flics. L'inspecteur Nacer se régale à la perspective d'aider Slim à dénoncer toute cette pourriture. Ça ne fait pas longtemps que l'on peut se permettre de divulguer ce genre d'affaires où des hommes de pouvoir sont impliqués. Il y a bien eu l'affaire Tabit. Mais c'était autre chose. Une vilaine histoire de réseau porno. Là, c'est différent. Tout le monde a été arrosé. J'espère qu'il tiendra sa promesse et qu'il ne révélera pas mon identité, s'inquiète Nacer prêt à partir si Slim ne se manifeste pas dans la minute qui suit.

Nacer a rencontré Slim dans un bar, lieu de prédilection des flics et des journalistes, source intarissable de renseignements. Et zone d'échanges de bons procédés.

Nacer était avec une pute qui connaît Slim. Slim les a salués. Puis il leur a offert des verres. Nacer lui a rendu la politesse en l'invitant à se joindre à eux.

Slim amuse Nacer. Avec son humour singulier, ses idées avant-gardistes, son air d'être toujours au courant de tout ce qui se passe, et son sourire qui n'en est plus un.

Nacer renseigne Slim comme il peut. Et, ce que Slim fait semblant de ne pas comprendre, Slim renseigne Nacer. Tout le monde est content. Le Maroc est en marche.

Au moment où Nacer se lève pour partir, Slim arrive essoufflé.

— Tu partais sans m'attendre, canaille ! s'exclame Slim en tapant grassement sur le dos de Nacer.

— J'allais aux chiottes, répond Nacer finalement content de boire un coup et de refaire le monde avec Slim.

— C'est une femme qui m'a retardé, avoue Slim de son air désabusé.

Slim et le journalisme.

I

Quand Slim intègre le monde du journalisme en mille neuf cent quatre-vingt-deux, il a vingt et un ans. Une année auparavant, il a passé son bac avec mention bien. Puis une année à la faculté de médecine l'a à jamais dégoûté des études supérieures. Une de ses premières petites amies à qui il écrivait des lettres enflammées — elle fut bien la seule d'ailleurs — riches en mots savants, sans doute pour l'impressionner, l'a convaincu qu'il a en sa possession un don de Dieu, l'un des plus enviés de tous, le don de l'écriture. Fort de cette certitude, Slim présente sa candidature pour un poste de rédacteur au journal qui le déçoit le moins à l'époque : *Le point de vue*. Un ennui tout de même ; journal partisan, *Le point de vue* est censé défendre une cause qui n'est pas celle de Slim. Mais qu'à cela ne tienne ! Faisant preuve d'une intelligence et d'un sens de la modération qu'il perdra après, il considère et clame avec beaucoup de sagesse et d'humilité qu'il a moult choses à apprendre de ses aînés. Et il a appris. Slim a travaillé avec les plus grands et a su en tirer profit. Certains d'entre eux l'ont même pris sous leurs ailes. Avec l'âge et l'expérience, son écriture s'est affinée et l'on a commencé à vanter les vertus de sa plume.

Plus tard, son caractère belliqueux, ses réactions impulsives et son orgueil mal placé ont fait de lui, et de loin, le journaliste le plus mobile de la profession. De ce fait, il est passé par tous les canards de la place.

Dix-huit ans plus tard, plus professionnel que jamais, désillusionné, calmé, mais aimant toujours son métier, Slim a également appris à monnayer ses compétences. Le voilà donc responsable du service société dans l'un des hebdomadaires indépendants les plus lus du pays. Poste longtemps convoité et gagné voire largement mérité grâce à une détermination et à un travail acharné que personne ne conteste.

Peu populaire dans le milieu du journalisme, Slim y est réputé pour être une forte tête, sans scrupules quand il s'agit de collecter l'information ou de décrocher une exclusivité. Ses confrères ne l'aiment pas.

Ailleurs, on le redoute. On l'évite. Il faut dire qu'il n'épargne personne. Sa langue est acérée. Ses billets sans complaisance. Réputé pour être incorruptible, il dérange par son intégrité.

Certaines langues malintentionnées déclarent même haut et fort qu'il a de la chance d'avoir débarqué dans la profession après les années de plomb.

Slim sort de la brasserie La Presse satisfait de son entrevue avec Nacer. Ce dernier lui a livré toutes les informations qui lui manquaient pour écrire son article.

On a beau dire que rien ne lui fait peur, il sait qu'il a toujours eu du mal à ne pas s'autocensurer. L'autocensure fait partie des règles implicites du métier. Elle a pris place, lui a dit un de ses maîtres à penser, à un moment de l'histoire de notre pays où il a fallu choisir entre elle et la torture. Puis elle s'est installée en nous jusqu'à devenir un mécanisme inconscient, une démarche intellectuelle inévitable. Aujourd'hui c'est d'une thérapie que nous avons besoin pour nous en débarrasser.

Slim achète une poignée d'hebdomadaires dans le kiosque du coin, jette un coup d'œil sur les titres. Il n'en revient pas de ce foisonnement de nouveaux titres, " fruit du processus démocratique ", comme ils disent.

Ils lui donnent la nausée. La mise en scène du Maroc qu'ils présentent est la plus hypocrite manière d'en parler. Et il a l'impression de participer, quoi qu'il fasse, à cette duperie. Réapprendre à s'exprimer est une priorité incontournable et nécessaire maintenant qu'il est devenu possible de le faire.

Apprendre à parler vrai en paragraphes clairs. Mettre en pages des vérités.

Apprendre et enseigner l'amour des vérités.

À moins de stagner et donc de reculer.

Il a un jour longuement parlé à un journaliste palestinien qui vivait aux Etats-unis. De l'exil. De la souffrance, qui en résulte. Mais le jeune Palestinien lui a avoué qu'il était heureux. " Parce que je sers, comprends-tu, je sers à ma façon, en dénonçant, en cultivant l'amour de la vérité ", lui avait-il dit les yeux illuminés.

Slim a l'impression d'être seul et de ne servir à rien, ce jeudi d'avril. Il a honte de ses peurs. Qu'est-ce que sa vie sinon une accumulation de fuites ?

Tourner la page, tourner la page, tout le monde ne parle plus que de ça.

Oui. Mais lisons-la d'abord. Faisons le point. Sauvegardons notre mémoire. Notre mémoire est le phare qui illuminera notre avenir. Elle ravivera notre envie d'avancer. Dissimuler, toujours dissimuler. Nous ne savons faire que ça. Les murs de la honte. Les crimes. Les disparitions. Les tortionnaires en liberté. Les voiles.

Slim soupire. Ihsane l'aidera peut-être à mieux comprendre ces femmes de la marche de Casablanca. Pour cela, il faut qu'il écoute ce qu'elle dit, qu'il entende. Qu'elle veuille parler aussi.

Slim arrive au journal. Jaouad le reçoit quelques minutes dans son bureau de rédac chef de l'hebdo, faisant mine de l'écouter tout en répondant au téléphone, souriant, affable. Puis il le raccompagne jusqu'à la porte.

— Je suis sûr que c'est très intéressant. Je lirai ton billet avec attention quand tu l'auras écrit. As-tu parcouru ma chronique de cette semaine ? J'aimerais beaucoup avoir ton point de vue. Elle devrait te plaire.

Slim hoche la tête. Il n'arrivera jamais à s'habituer à ce jeu stupide. Ces mondanités hors propos.

Il traîne dans les couloirs, passe la tête par les ouvertures des portes des bureaux, salue ses confrères.

— On se voit à la réunion de rédaction, lui dit Salah en se sauvant.

Puis il revient.

— Tu ne connais pas la nouvelle ? Jaouad est dans la merde. Il ne dirige plus rien. Ils ont fait venir quelqu'un d'autre pour soi-disant contrôler. Ils veulent lui enlever la direction de publication. Noureddine de son côté lèche les bottes du nouveau. Il voit déjà loin. Moi, je ne veux pas qu'on touche à mes pages. Ou alors je me barre.

L'excitation de Salah ne semble pas gagner Slim. Slim regarde Salah comme s'il ne se sentait pas concerné.

— Eh ! réveille-toi, Slim. Tu m'écoutes ?

— Tu ne sais pas où sont mes scribouillards ? demande Slim.

— Ils sont à la salle de rédaction. Tu t'en fous de tout ça, toi, n'est-ce pas ?

— À vrai dire je ne sais pas encore, répond Slim, dubitatif.

Il rejoint la salle de rédaction. Ses trois collaborateurs y sont. Ils chuchotent, debout, en cercle. En voyant arriver Slim, dans un même élan, ils parent leurs faciès de rictus censés reproduire des sourires de bienvenue.

— Où en êtes-vous ? demande Slim sans même les saluer.

— Nos papiers sont faits, répond Nadia, sa préférée.

— Faits, c'est une façon de parler, raille Slim. Voyons ça.

Slim s'empare des feuillets que lui donnent ses collaborateurs et se retire dans son bureau. Nadia revient à la charge.

— Une certaine Bouthaïna t'a téléphoné, lui dit-elle l'air complice.

— Merci Nadia. Je vous verrai plus tard.

" Elle est mignonne cette petite, songe Slim, mais si incompétente ! Ambitieuse avec ça. Il va lui falloir travailler dur pour apprendre à écrire correctement.

En attendant, elle me fait les yeux doux. Ne jamais mêler le travail et le cul. Les autres le font suffisamment comme ça. On a l'impression que tout le monde baise avec tout le monde ici ".

Slim corrige en rouge les textes, appelle le photographe qui prétend être occupé et s'apprête à partir quand il se souvient du coup de fil de Bouthaïna. Plus que deux jours pour le bouclage. Elle attendra.

II

Royal Mansour, dix-neuf heures. Happy hour. L'heure de l'apéro en musique dans le majestueux hôtel de l'avenue des Forces Armées Royales plus communément appelée l'avenue des FAR. Slim s'installe au bar, commande un scotch on the rocks, et cherche des yeux les habitués du lieu. Dans le tas, il apprécie de bavarder avec un vieux loup de la presse qu'il est sûr de trouver là tous les soirs. Une musique d'ambiance, mélange infâme de jazz et de raï ? - jouée par un petit orchestre fortement excité et incompétent- donne au magnifique bar du Royal Mansour un cachet de " bar d'hôtel de luxe d'un pays maghrébin en voie de développement ". Des hommes d'affaires, le cigare à la bouche, le verre et la chevalière à la main, parlementent actions et, tels des chirurgiens plastiques snobinards, débattent de la meilleure façon de remodeler le visage jeune et pourtant ingrat de la Bourse de Casablanca. Quelques Moyen-Orientaux lorgnent, ouvertement libidineux, les poules de luxe, derniers prototypes sur le marché de la drague — arrivage frais de la campagne Marocain — au look refait à la va-vite à partir de photos de top-modèles européennes exposées dans les kiosques. Les Claudia Schiffer aux formes épanouies et au maquillage approximatif se félicitent de leurs investissements dans le monde de la mode et se pâment déjà à l'idée de l'enveloppe qu'elles espèrent empocher la nuit même. Avec ça, perdu et éperdu, un jeune couple visiblement de milieu modeste — vraisemblablement, le promis a choisi de conter fleurette à sa promise dans un lieu on ne peut plus enchanteur —, deux Françaises, classe moyenne, sans doute des infirmières ou des sages-femmes qui ont découvert la meilleure formule vacances de leur vie à un prix im-bat-table !

Slim déguste son deuxième verre quand il aperçoit Saïd.

Grand, chauve, déglingué, le visage pâle et les yeux profondément enfoncés dans la tête, Saïd avance, son corps légèrement penché vers la gauche comme si un poids invisible pesait sur son épaule. Slim lui fait signe, son sourire qui n'en est plus un figé sur sa bouche.

— Comment vas-tu, mécréant ? lui demande Saïd de sa voix chevrotante.

— Bof !

— Comme d'habitude quoi.

— J'ai lu ton billet : les limites du gouvernement El Youssoufi. C'est pas mal. Tu es bien le seul à lui trouver des circonstances atténuantes.

— Ouais. Nous n'avons pas attendu près de quarante années qu'un gouvernement de gauche soit aux commandes pour lui tomber dessus comme des dégénérés. Laissons- lui le temps de trouver des voies.

— Tu sais que le Magazine a été censuré cette semaine ?

— Ils sont allés trop loin. Donner la parole à un membre du Polisario, ce n'est pas très futé. Tu sais bien que cela fait partie de la sacro-sainte trinité inviolable. Dans l'euphorie de la découverte de la liberté d'expression, ils se sont oubliés.

— C'est le gouvernement El Youssoufi qui a pris la décision de la censure. Seul.

— La presse est divisée. Les uns disent qu'il faut établir des règles à la profession. Ils parlent de maturité et de pondération. Les autres, la jeunesse, se sentent investis d'une nouvelle mission parce qu'ils doivent se démarquer de leurs aînés et qu'ils se déclarent " produits d'un processus historique de démocratisation ". Le débat n'est pas simple mais nécessaire.

Par ailleurs, L'USFP a toujours été très nationaliste. Je me souviens quand j'étais étudiant, dans une assemblée générale de l'UNEM, un membre de la jeunesse Ittihadia a failli tuer un étudiant qui avait osé parler d'autodétermination du peuple sahraoui. Un scandale épouvantable. Tous les membres présents de la jeunesse Ittihadia se sont levés et ont chanté l'hymne national. Le pauvre gosse n'a plus remis les pieds dans une réunion. À l'époque l'USFP et le PPS faisaient bloc contre ceux qu'ils appelaient les gauchistes ou les traîtres. Belle époque en vérité ! s'exclame Saïd nostalgique. Celle de la jeunesse et des grandes illusions. Nous, au moins, nous savions rêver. Regarde-les aujourd'hui. Va faire un tour dans les universités. Tu y verras un ramassis de barbus et de voilées, juste bons à invoquer la puissance divine. Quelle tristesse ! Il faut dire que la scène politique est désespérément vide. Les jeunes n'en peuvent plus de la langue de bois et des promesses non tenues. C'est le chômage et la pauvreté qui les attend au bout. Et avec ça cette mondialisation qui les nargue et qui ne profite qu'aux détenteurs de richesses. En vérité, nous avons besoin de penseurs. C'est la réflexion qui nous fera avancer. Il est temps de se mettre au travail. Je me demande ce que foutent les enseignants dans les universités.

— Ils enseignent.

— Oui.

saïd part d'un éclat de rire retentissant puis change de sujet.

— Il paraît que ton patron se fait marcher sur les pieds ? interroge-t-il.

— Il paraît.

— C'est quoi cette histoire ? Une crise de confiance ?

— Je ne sais pas, répond Slim en haussant les épaules.

— Avec toi on est tranquille. Tu ne sais jamais rien.

Slim ricane. Il n'en dirait jamais plus même s'il savait. Il est toujours resté en dehors des médisances et des jalousies qui sévissent dans le milieu. Les journalistes passent leur temps à se taper dessus. Parfois par billets interposés. Il est même arrivé que ça aille très loin. Slim refuse de participer d'une manière ou d'une autre aux polémiques. Quand il écoute ses confrères s'entredéchirer, des lueurs sadiques dans les yeux, ils lui donnent envie de gerber. Il a pris l'habitude chaque fois que ça arrive de déserter et la conversation et le lieu où elle se passe.

— Slim ça va ? Tu me donnes toujours l'impression que tu ne fais que survivre, dit Saïd.

— Mais qui ne survit pas ? répond Slim en se levant pour partir.

Slim debout à côté de Saïd distingue la calotte claire de la calvitie de son ami.

Il en éprouve un plaisir amer.

Il doit comprendre qu'il n'est lui aussi qu'un survivant, songe-t-il en s'éloignant.

III

Il ne reste à Slim que deux jours pour le bouclage. Deux jours pour écrire son papier. Il le sait, il le fera comme d'habitude à la dernière minute. D'une traite et sans effort majeur. Il suffit de maîtriser une technique. Avec le temps et l'expérience, il est rodé. L'information, une pointe d'humour, quelques jeux de mots qu'ils ne comprennent pas toujours, un côté chébran, ça c'est sa spécificité, et le tour est joué. Les lecteurs ne sont pas trop exigeants. Avec ce qu'on leur sert à côté, c'est normal. Slim reçoit de temps en temps des lettres de félicitations pour ses écrits. Ça le fait marrer. Ailleurs, ce serait différent. Il le dit souvent à Judith. Cette dernière le rassure, l'encense. Elle adorrrre ce qu'il écrit. Et pour prouver sa bonne foi, elle lui a même proposé de l'appuyer pour travailler dans un grand hebdomadaire en France. Bouthaïna, en revanche, n'aime pas toujours ses billets. Il le voit bien, même si elle ne le lui dit pas. Tiens, elle lui manque celle-là ! Slim décide de la rappeler après le bouclage. Si elle ne l'a pas fait entre-temps. Ce qui est plus que probable.

" Jaouad a des problèmes. Peut-être devrais-je lui téléphoner ", Se dit slim. Il n'y a pas si longtemps que ça c'était un ami.

Retour en arrière.

Slim a connu Jaouad des années auparavant quand il était à la tête d'un nouveau canard, le Citoyen. Belle aventure que celle de lancer un nouveau journal. On a l'impression que tout est permis, qu'on va changer la figure de la presse, qu'on sera les seuls à être de vrais pros, qu'on va définir de nouvelles règles pour le métier et que tous les confrères vont les adopter. Jaouad avait confiance en Slim. Slim était enthousiaste. Ils formaient une équipe gagnante.

Slim abattait le travail de dix personnes. Il était responsable des cahiers société et culture, supervisait avec Jaouad les autres rubriques et accomplissait la tâche ingrate de secrétaire de rédaction. Évidemment, il provoquait la jalousie des autres. Mais à l'époque, il s'en foutait et Jaouad aussi. Ce qui comptait, c'était le nombre de lecteurs, à chaque numéro plus important, les innovations, les originalités, le professionnalisme. Et cette ambiance euphorique dans laquelle ils travaillaient chaque jour, cette complicité n'avaient pas de prix. Slim n'a jamais autant aimé son métier qu'à cette période où Jaouad et lui se comprenaient à demi-mot.

Par ailleurs ils n'avaient plus de vie privée. Plus le temps.

C'est aussi au cours de cette période que Slim a doublé sa consommation d'alcool.

Jaouad ne boit plus.

Jaouad a goûté à l'argent facile, s'est embourgeoisé. Ses enfants ont grandi. Il a fallu leur payer les meilleures études. Sa femme a voulu habiter dans une villa comme celles de ses sœurs. Il a pris maîtresse.

C'est Jaouad qui a fait appel à Slim et lui a demandé d'intégrer le Progrès. Ne serait-ce qu'au nom de leur passé commun inoubliable, Slim ne pouvait pas refuser son offre. Slim a même accepté, lui, le pro confirmé, de passer des tests pour accéder au poste qu'envisageait pour lui Jaouad. Une exigence des financiers que Jaouad n'a pas pu lui éviter. Bouthaïna n'aime pas Jaouad à cause de ça. C'est une trahison ! s'indigne-t-elle chaque fois qu'elle en a l'occasion. Et les occasions ne lui manquent pas. Parce qu'il a été jadis son ami et que tout le monde le sait, parce que c'est lui qui a offert ce poste à Slim, Jaouad se croit obligé à chaque réunion de rédaction d'être particulièrement infect avec lui. Et Slim, malheureux, abattu, en parle souvent à Bouthaïna.

— Je ne mérite pas ça, lui dit-il de sa voix plaintive des grandes occasions. J'ai toujours été là pour lui. Il m'humilie devant cette bande d'abrutis juste pour leur prouver qu'il ne fait pas de favoritisme.

— C'est de ta faute. Quand tu es avec lui, tu n'es plus le même. On dirait qu'il t'hypnotise. Il le sait et il en abuse. Sa carrière passe avant tout. Et son fric aussi, dit Bouthaïna avec mépris. On dit même qu'il fricotait avec le ministre de l'intérieur précédent. Ce tortionnaire ! Jaouad acceptait de se laisser museler à l'époque. Il était même prêt à se museler lui-même. D'où crois-tu que lui vient tout ce fric ? De ses petits salaires de journaliste ?

— Non Bouthaïna, tu te trompes. Sa villa, il la paie à crédit, comme tout le monde.

— Et le reste ? Les vêtements signés de sa femme ? Les études de ses gosses à l'étranger ? Les cadeaux pour sa maîtresse ? Et pas n'importe quoi, une Alfa Roméo dernier cri. La ferme à Bouskoura ? Et… Tout ce qu'il cache ? Tu trouves encore le moyen de le défendre ? Je ne te comprends pas.

— Il n'y a rien à comprendre. Ça ne te regarde pas.

— Dans ce cas ne m'en parle plus, finit invariablement par dire Bouthaïna.

Jaouad a des problèmes. Slim hésite à l'appeler. Jaouad est capable de nier, de l'envoyer sur les roses, de faire comme s'il n'avait besoin de personne. Slim sait, malgré tout ce que peut dire Bouthaïna, que Jaouad aime son métier par-dessus tout. Le Progrès est son bébé. Il veille sur lui avec passion, vérifie personnellement toutes les étapes de son impression, lit et corrige dix fois les mêmes papiers, soucieux de leur qualité, passe la nuit dans les locaux s'il le faut, ne répond plus au téléphone à sa femme et à sa maîtresse le jour du bouclage pour vérifier que tout se passe bien et finalement emmener avec lui le journal. Jaouad ne prend même plus en considération sa santé quand il est question du Progrès. Ne serait-ce que pour ça, Slim le respecte infiniment. Jaouad est le seul ami qu'il ait jamais eu dans le milieu du journalisme et en dehors, celui qu'il estime le plus. Et ni Bouthaïna ni aucune femme n'est capable de comprendre cette étrange tendresse qu'il a pour l'homme qui, l'espace de quelques numéros du Citoyen, lui a permis de prendre goût à l'illusion et de vivre au lieu de survivre.

Judith le comprendrait, peut-être. Elle comprend tout, celle-là. Non il ne l'appellera pas. Jaouad sait qu'il sera toujours là pour lui, quoi qu'il arrive.

IV

Conférence de presse suivie d'un cocktail dînatoire. D'habitude, Slim charge Nadia de ce genre de corvée. Mais aujourd'hui, Jaouad a tenu à ce que ce soit Slim lui-même qui représente Le Progrès à cet événement.

Ils sont tous là. Les loups de la presse.

Ils rôdent, l'inévitable verre à la main, salivant déjà pour le second.

Il y a aussi les petits derniers. Ceux qui se considèrent comme la nouvelle race de journalistes, " produit d'un processus historique ", comme ils disent, et qui méprisent poliment leurs aînés. Ces louveteaux qui ont troqué la langue de bois héritée des anciens pour une langue bien pendue.

Oui, incontestablement, ils sont tous là.

Certains rasent les murs. D'autres se pavanent. Surtout ceux de la télé. Les nouvelles stars du petit écran. Kamal du vingt heures, Selma de " l'homme du jour " et d'autres.

Il y a même les renégats, ceux qui ont décidé qu'ils sont trop bons pour se mêler au tas, les plumes reconnues qui ont choisi les îles désertes de l'anonymat. Parmi eux, Rachid. Look à la BHL. L'écharpe blanche, flottante. Philosophe. Talentueux. Improductif. En fuite. Méprisant la médiocrité. Préférant les délices de la paresse et… La réflexion solitaire, dans l'ombre, à jamais inaccessible aux esprits dans le manque de lumière. Avec ça, beau garçon, retenu, vivant le moins possible de peur de péter les plombs. Un véritable gâchis.

En compagnie de Slim, Rachid a toujours l'exquise sensation de s'encanailler. C'est pourquoi dès qu'il l'aperçoit, il s'empresse de le rejoindre.

— Rachid ? Que fais-tu ici ? demande Slim surpris.

— J'ai monté une boîte de com, répond Rachid désappointé.

— Toi ? Une boîte de com ?

— Il faut bien bouffer.

— Et elle marche, ta boîte de com ?

— Mon rêve c'est qu'elle marche encore mieux. Je pourrais la céder et enfin me consacrer à l'écriture.

— Joli rêve !

— Mais un rêve.

— Moi, je te verrais bien à la télé animant une émission littéraire.

— Je ne suis le copain de personne.

— Toute l'équipe de la troisième chaîne vient de changer.

— Je ne suis le copain de personne. Le nouveau responsable ne peut pas me sentir. Et puis il a des désirs de production qu'il ne peut plus mettre en œuvre maintenant qu'il est aux commandes. Je le gênerais dans ses fantasmes. Si je lui propose un projet d'émission qui l'emballe, il en sera malade. Il pensera que je lui ferai de l'ombre même si ça ne se passe que dans sa tête.

— Peut-être faut-il essayer quand même ? Nous avons besoin d'émissions de qualité. Tu n'as rien à perdre.

— Si. Bien plus que tu ne le crois.

Slim et Rachid se dirigent vers le bar, saluent au passage quelques têtes connues.

— Sais-tu comment Lahsane les appelle ? demande Rachid à Slim.

— Non mais tu vas me le dire.

Lahsane, universitaire, romancier à ses heures. Lahsane étonne Slim. Cet homme au visage mou, austère, à la voix un peu mielleuse, a une énergie inépuisable. Il enseigne, écrit, publie, préside des associations, intervient aussi de temps en temps dans la presse. Il a ses pions, place ses hommes, est très respecté dans le milieu universitaire.

— Les chiens bâtards, ajoute Rachid, en riant cette fois, découvrant ses dents trop blanches, parfaites, et leur perfection est comme un gros canular auquel on n'a pas envie de croire. S'il était présent, poursuit-il, il nous dirait : la meute est là. Cette sous-race de chiens qui imagine pouvoir comprendre, expliquer et juger les vrais loups. Tout juste bons à japper. S'ils avaient des crocs, ils changeraient la face de la scène politique.

— Et lui, il la change ?

— À sa façon. Sa seule voix est mieux entendue que toutes celles qui sont ici réunies aujourd'hui.

— Il fut un temps où il était ministrable.

— On dit ça. Personnellement, je ne le crois pas. C'est un éternel opposant. C'est ce qui fait sa valeur. Au pouvoir, il perdrait de sa superbe. Tu n'imaginerais jamais ce que je l'ai surpris en train de faire un jour. Il rayait avec les clefs de sa Fiat Uno les carrosseries des voitures de luxe de ses amis chez qui il était invité à dîner.

— C'est un ami de Jaouad. Ils ont été à la fac ensemble.

— Je sais. Jaouad est le seul qu'il épargne de ses sarcasmes. Au nom de je ne sais quel passé commun.

— Ils voulaient refaire le monde.

— Toute une génération !

Slim s'immobilise. À deux mètres de lui, Bouthaïna est en grande conversation avec un groupe de journalistes. “ Que fait-elle ici ? se demande-t-il. Je la croyais morte. ”

Slim ne bouge pas. Il est gêné. Il pense que la quitter constituerait une lâcheté de plus.

N'est-ce pas une lâcheté de quitter la vie comme il le fait, à petit feu ?

“ Finalement, pense Slim, je n'ai survécu que parce que je l'ai décidé. Si je perds ma volonté, je m'effondre. ”

Mais il le sait, il a la vie chevillée au corps et se méprise suffisamment pour ça. Les jours passent. Il survit. Il vivra donc.

Bouthaïna, songe-t-il, vit comme elle respire. Elle se projette avec tant d'élan dans son existence qu'elle va jusqu'au bout de sa vie en un seul souffle.

— Ce n'est pas Bouthaïna ? demande Rachid à Slim. Et Judith que devient-elle ? poursuit-il sans attendre la réponse de Slim.

— Elle médite.

— Elle t'édite ? Tu nous sors quelque chose ? Un roman ?

_ Ma vie est un mauvais roman. Et je n'ai plus de mémoire.

Slim pense que s'il ne buvait pas jusqu'à épuisement, c'est la nuit qui serait pour lui le temps de la mémoire. Sa tête contiendrait des bribes de chapitres qui, même s'ils relataient des scènes gaies, deviendraient des pages de calvaire, parce que la fin de l'histoire serait connue d'avance.

Bouthaïna le voit, détourne la tête, soudain très pâle. Ses mains tremblent. Elle entend son cœur battre la chamade. " Tu t'attendais un peu pourtant à le rencontrer en débarquant ici, se dit-t-elle. Reprends-toi, ma vieille, tu es pathétique. "

Slim la prend par le bras et lui chuchote :

— Barrons-nous d'ici.

Rachid les regarde s'éloigner, perplexe. Quelque chose d'inharmonieux dans le couple l'embarrasse. Il pensait que Bouthaïna était une fille de bonne famille, pas le genre à fréquenter un type comme Slim ni à partir sans dire au revoir. Une gentille fille qu'il imaginerait derrière des fourneaux, mère au foyer travaillant à mi-temps, juste pour pouvoir dire à ses copines qu'elle travaille. Qu'est ce que slim peut bien lui trouver d'intéressant ?

V

Slim ouvre la porte de son appartement et entre suivi de Bouthaïna. Ils n'ont pas échangé une parole. Même pas dans la voiture. Bouthaïna a pris le chemin de chez Slim en silence, sans lui demander son avis. Elle a conduit nerveusement, sans retirer sa main du levier de vitesse, rétrogradant souvent, indifférente aux sons aigus du moteur.

Et maintenant, Bouthaïna s'affaire, mécaniquement. Elle va à la cuisine, ouvre le réfrigérateur, sort les glaçons de leur bac, place deux verres sur un plateau, cherche la bouteille, la trouve, emmène le tout au salon, allume la chaîne stéréo, met la cassette de Chab Mami, sert un verre à Slim, se sert, s'assied enfin.

Slim la regarde, abattu.

Il aurait aimé l'atteindre vraiment. Mais elle ne cesse de se dérober. Elle est dans un délire et rien ne peut l'en sortir. C'est comme ça que Slim sent les choses. Bouthaïna épuiserait n'importe quel adversaire. Il n'y a qu'elle qui soit capable de s'emmurer comme ça dans un silence agité de gestes brusques, précis, hors de propos.

— Tu m'as manqué, finit-elle par avouer.

— J'étais occupé.

— Je sais.

— Ce n'est pas ce que tu penses.

— Je ne t'ai rien demandé.

— C'est une amie.

— Je ne veux pas savoir.

— Tu préfères inventer une histoire, te complaire dans je ne sais quel rôle merdique de victime affligée ?

— Tu ne comprends rien. Ce qui m'importe c'est notre couple, toi et moi. Le reste…

— Couple ?

— Tu n'aimes pas ce mot, je sais, mais…

— Arrête tout de suite ! Tu t'es trompée de bonhomme, Bouthaïna. Je regrette.

— Tu veux me quitter ?

— Je ne te quitterai jamais, Bouthaïna, j'en suis incapable. C'est toi qui le feras. Un jour tu en auras assez de moi et tu t'en iras.

— J'ai tout quitté pour toi.

— Est-ce une raison suffisante ?

— Je t'aime.

— Il y a des moments où je me demande…

— Tu en doutes ?

— Je n'ai pas dit ça, Bouthaïna. Tu ne me laisses même pas finir mes phrases. Tu serais capable de dire les questions et les réponses. Tu ne m'entends pas. Dans quel monde es-tu ?

— Le nôtre, mon amour.

— Quelle misère !

— Pourquoi dis-tu ça ?

— Tu es aveugle ou quoi ? Tu t'es trompée d'histoire. Je suis incapable d'être celui que tu veux que je sois, quand même je le voudrais.

— Et Amal ? Nous la ferons notre petite fille, n'est- ce pas ?

— Amaaal ! Si je pouvais faire un enfant, c'est avec toi que je le ferais, Bouthaïna.

— Qui t'en empêche ?

— Tu ne poses pas la bonne question, mon cœur.

— C'est cette femme ?

— Nous y voilà ! Cette femme s'appelle Judith. Cela fait dix ans qu'elle fait partie de ma vie. Elle a beaucoup compté pour moi. Aujourd'hui c'est fini. Son rêve c'est que je me marie et que j'aie des enfants. Tu t'entendrais très bien avec elle.

— Tu l'aimes toujours ?

— Bouthaïna, ne sois pas stupide. Viens à côté de moi. J'ai besoin de toi. Comment va ta fille ?

C'est elle, l'amour de ta vie, tu sais

— Tu es cruel. Il n'y a que toi. Plus personne ne compte en dehors de toi.

— Je t'interdis de dire ça. Ta fille est ce que tu as de plus précieux. Il n'y a que ton enfant que tu as le droit d'aimer plus que moi. Je ne te mérite pas, mon amour. Écoute ce que chante Mami : je ne suis qu'un voyou, vas te chercher un garçon bien pour faire ta vie.

— Tu es un garçon bien.

— Non mon cœur. Tu ne sais pas grand-chose de moi. Je suis un mauvais garçon, dit Slim en étouffant un sanglot. Pourquoi m'aimes-tu, Bouthaïna ? Pourquoi ? répète-t-il. Dis-le moi. Je ne te mérite pas. Tu es trop belle pour moi.

Bouthaïna baisse la tête, une mèche de cheveux devant les yeux. Elle le sait, elle n'est rien pour lui.

Maintenant Slim la traque du regard. Elle baisse les paupières.

Slim, en pleure-misère avide de tendresse, déraisonne. Peut-être ne l'aime-t-elle pas ?

Elle entrouvre les yeux avec toute la force de sa conviction d'être la femme de sa vie. L'œil sirupeux la guète, la happe. Vaincue, elle prend Slim dans ses bras et le berce comme un enfant. Dans sa tête, elle entend sa mère lui dire : tu as déjà un enfant, Bouthaïna, c'est de ta fille que tu devrais t'occuper. Son étreinte se fait moins forte.

Slim se redresse.

Bouthaïna détourne la tête, se dérobe.

— Tu m'aimes ? demande Slim.

— Je ne sais pas, répond-elle.

Slim cesse de la fixer. Pour une fois, il sait qu'elle est sincère.

À ce moment-là, son portable se met à sonner. Slim s'éloigne pour répondre.

Et lui, que sait-il de moi ? se demande Bouthaïna.

Il ignore qu'il m'arrive de m'allonger à même le sol, et de caresser de mes lèvres le carrelage froid juste pour sentir que j'existe.

Il ignore que les enfants me dérangent par leur présence bruyante et leurs jeux incessants.

Il ignore que je ne sais même pas si j'aime mes parents.

Slim revient.

— C'est Jaouad. Il nous invite à prendre un verre dehors.

— Il est seul ?

— Non, il est avec sa copine.

— Slim, promets-moi que si nous sommes mariés un jour, tu ne mèneras pas une double vie.

— Je te le promets, mon amour. Partons, ils nous attendent.

VI

Jaouad et Mouna attendent, assis à une table en retrait, dans la somptueuse salle de l'assiette gourmande. Chaque vendredi soir, Jaouad passe chercher Mouna et l'emmène dîner à son restaurant favori. Rien ni personne ne peut contrarier ce rituel que le couple illicite a décidé de vivre comme " une parenthèse enchantée ".

La propriétaire du restaurant le sait et réserve invariablement, chaque veille de week-end, à " son couple d'amoureux " la table la plus discrète de l'assiette gourmande. De temps en temps, une personne vient les rejoindre, rarement la même.

Mouna était la secrétaire de Jaouad. De vingt ans plus jeune que lui, elle s'est facilement laissée séduire par " ce quadragénaire (à l'époque) aux tempes grisonnantes, au caractère impossible, au charme irrésistible et au portefeuille bien garni ", et ce sont les propres mots de Mouna, soufflés un jour à l'oreille de Bouthaïna.

De son côté, Jaouad ne supportait plus les vociférations de sa femme quand il rentrait chez lui tard, épuisé par son travail. Il a trouvé en Mouna une jeune compagne discrète, non revendicative, présente sans être envahissante, indulgente, attentive. Elle l'écoute. Elle est devenue, grâce aux confidences qu'il lui a faites sur l'oreiller, une spécialiste du monde de la presse. Comme il ne voulait pas mêler travail et sentiments, il a préféré l'entretenir. Un appartement sur le boulevard Moulay Youssef qui lui a coûté la bagatelle d'un million de dirhams et qu'il continue de payer jusqu'à aujourd'hui, des voitures de plus en plus coûteuses, quelques meubles chez les antiquaires, des émoluments variables selon ses revenus, et le tour est joué. Il faut savoir que Mouna ne demande jamais rien. Elle se contente de l'aimer. leur liaison s'est étirée jusqu'à somnoler et, dix ans plus tard, ils sont devenus ce vieux couple adultère mais ronronnant, ces deux êtres lassés l'un de l'autre mais satisfaits d'être ensemble, chacun pour une raison différente. Mouna est riche d'un appartement que Jaouad a tenu, au temps de vaches grasses, à mettre à son nom. Et Jaouad est content de trouver une oreille et une couche complaisantes qui somme toute avec le temps ne sont pas si onéreuses que ça.

L'arrivée de Slim et de Bouthaïna perturbe la propriétaire de l'assiette gourmande pour qui la présence d'un autre couple à la table de ses amoureux légitime une relation qui n'a d'attrait que si elle est clandestine. Mais Slim et Bouthaïna ne comprendront jamais pourquoi la maîtresse des lieux les a reçus avec cet air pincé et cette froideur inopinée.

Slim affiche son sourire des grandes circonstances qui n'en est plus un. Bouthaïna boude. Jaouad parle. Mouna prête l'oreille.

_ On veut me mettre des bâtons dans les roues, confie Jaouad à Slim. Ils n'ont pas trouvé mieux que cet imbécile de Salhi qui ne connaît rien au métier. Il fourre son nez partout sans avoir peur du ridicule. Et le plus grave, c'est que je ne peux pas réagir. Quand c'est un canard partisan, c'est à l'idéologie du parti qu'on est soumis ; quand c'est un canard indépendant, c'est aux détenteurs du fric.

— Fais ton journal.

— Tu rigoles ? Tu m'as regardé ? Ils m'ont bouffé toute mon énergie. Je n'ai plus de souffle. Place aux jeunes.

— Tu plaisantes ? Ton métier, c'est toute ta vie. Je suis bien placé pour le savoir. Tu ne vas pas abandonner ?

— Je crois que si. Personne n'a le droit de m'humilier à mon âge et avec mon expérience.

— Si tu quittes le Progrès, je quitte aussi.

— La question n'est pas là, Slim. Et puis tu irais

où ? Le problème est le même partout. Je quitte la presse. Une retraite anticipée. Je préfère vendre des cacahuètes que d'être traité de cette manière.

— De quelle manière exactement ?

— Ils veulent me retirer la direction de la publication. Je ne garderais que la direction de la rédaction. Et c'est cet empoté de Salhi qui deviendrait directeur de publication. Une marionnette qu'ils manipuleront comme ils veulent.

— Tu peux refuser.

— Cela voudrait dire que je déclare la guerre. Je n'en ai pas la force.

— Alors essaye de gagner quelque chose de tout ça, ne pars pas perdant. Vends-leur la direction de la publication. Au prix fort.

— Il y a des moments où tu m'étonnes, Slim. C'est épatant après toutes ces années. J'y ai pensé bien sûr. À mon avis, c'est la seule solution qui me reste.

— Et si on oubliait tout ça un instant et qu'on s'amuse, ce ne serait pas bien aussi, roucoule Mouna qui a senti que c'est le bon moment pour intervenir.

— Oui, chérie, tu as raison. Cela fait longtemps que nous n'avons pas passé une bonne soirée avec Slim et… sa fiancée, dit Jaouad qui hésite sur le mot adéquat mais surtout ne se souvient pas très bien du prénom de Bouthaïna.

— Je m'appelle Bouthaïna et je ne suis pas sa fiancée, rétorque la jeune femme avec insolence.

— Bouthaïna ! Comment ai-je pu être assez idiot pour oublier un prénom pareil. Alors Bouthy, où aimerais-tu que nous allions ?

— Au Balcon, s'empresse de répondre Mouna à sa place. Je crois que Slim et Bouthaïna n'ont pas encore dîné et c'est le seul endroit où l'on peut manger correctement à cette heure. La cuisine est excellente, il y a de la bonne musique.

— C'est bourré de putes, chérie ! Mais si ça peut te faire plaisir…

À la porte du Balcon, les flics saluent Jaouad et Slim. Le portier les fait entrer avant tout le monde. On leur donne une table. Une des meilleures. Jaouad commande une bouteille de Black Label. Slim et Bouthaïna jettent un coup d'œil sur le menu.

Vingt-trois heures. Aznavour en sourdine, chante La Bohème. La discothèque n'a pas encore fait le plein. Quelques filles sont pourtant déjà là, sans doute pour repérer le client. Les plus belles de Casablanca et les plus chères, jusqu'à deux mille dirhams la passe. Tout à l'heure, elles vont se déhancher sur la piste principale de la boîte et il faut qu'elles sachent qui elles vont avoir dans le champ de mire. Elles ont l'air de toutes connaître Slim. Discrètement, parce qu'il est accompagné, elles lui font un petit signe de la tête ou un clin d'œil pour le saluer. À plus de minuit, on ne trouve pas sa place au

Balcon. Certaines mauvaises langues racontent que le plafond de la discothèque est truffé de gris-gris. Sorcellerie ou pas, la magie qui se dégage de la boîte est bel et bien là. La musique, disco, orientale, raï, rock ou techno est toujours à propos, les lumières, que ce soient celles des petites lampes posées sur les tables ou celles des pistes de danses, offrent l'éclairage approprié, les garçons sont pros et vous servent comme si vous étiez leur unique client. L'ensemble est merveilleusement kitch.

Jaouad continue à appeler Bouthaïna Bouthy. Elle a l'impression qu'il se moque d'elle. Sans doute finit-il par comprendre qu'il se trompe d'attitude, à la manière dont elle le regarde puis baisse la tête avec irritation et aux coups de genoux que lui donne Mouna sous la table. Slim ne parle plus. Il boit.

_ Regardez qui vient d'entrer, dit Mouna. C'est ce porc de Rfihi, le rédac chef de L'Echo, avec une de ses filles du journal. Il paraît qu'elles passent toutes à la casserole. Il joue au caïd. Tout le monde lui fait des courbettes. Et avec ça il se croit irrésistible. L'imbécile !

— Le plus gros tirage des quotidiens du pays, commente Jaouad.

— Normal, c'est le journal officiel, rétorque Mouna.

— Ses journalistes lui mangent tous dans la main, dit Jaouad.

— Des lèches-culs. Ils ont la vie facile. Ce n'est pas à L'Echo qu'ils vont faire école. Ils ont le taux d'absentéisme le plus élevé de la presse. J'en sais quelque chose, j'ai une amie qui travaille avec ce rigolo, explique Mouna. Regardez, il se trimbale toujours avec sa cour.

— Dis-moi, Slim, tu avances sur cette affaire de pots de vin ? demande Jaouad pour changer de conversation.

— Je dois voir le flic demain. Il a des témoins à me présenter. Je crois que c'est du solide.

— Fais gaffe quand même.

— Depuis le temps que tu me connais, m'est-il déjà arrivé de faire une boulette ?

— Non. Je te fais confiance.

— Je te tiendrai au courant.

La voix de Natacha Atlas interrompt la conversation. Deux ou trois filles remplissent la piste de danse de leur présence agitée. Slim se lève et dit à Bouthaïna : partons. Bouthaïna obtempère. Ils sortent dans la cohue tant bien que mal après avoir salué Jaouad et Mouna.

— Drôle de couple, dit Mouna à Jaouad.

VII

Slim a donné rendez-vous à Nacer au *Abou Nouas*, avec l'espoir de revoir Ihsane et de l'emmener chez lui pour y passer la nuit. Elle l'a à peine salué quand il est entré. Dans les lumières tamisées, il la regarde servir les clients comme une automate. Elle fait tache dans le décor ; l'ambiance glauque du bar, la présence de ses propriétaires — trois frères aux allures de maffiosi -, les tenues légères des autres filles, leur attitude racoleuse. De temps en temps, entre deux commandes, elle lui jette un regard furtif, mais elle ne s'approche pas.

Nacer arrive en retard et en compagnie de deux hommes. Le premier est plus grand que lui, arborant le visage un peu pataud des campagnards, des vêtements de laine fruste, trop étriqués pour lui, une calvitie naissante et des chaussures à faire hurler un dandy. Le second, plus petit, massif, carrément chauve, vraisemblablement myope et sans lunettes à cause de la marque qu'il a sur le nez entre les yeux, habillé décemment, avec cet air " d'en savoir long " des fonctionnaires de l'administration.

— Slim, je te présente Zaki et Ahmed, dit cérémonieusement Nacer. Ils sont prêts à t'apporter tous les éléments qui te manquent et à te dire tout ce que tu as envie de savoir sur cette affaire… Celle qui t'intéresse et de laquelle nous avons parlé l'autre jour.

— Oui, tout, affirme en hochant la tête de haut en bas et en clignant des yeux, Ahmed, le myope sans lunettes.

Puis, en se penchant, appuyant familièrement de sa main sur l'épaule de Slim, l'immobilisant, il reprend cette fois-ci en lui chuchotant à l'oreille : " Nacer m'a dit que vous voulez mettre votre nez dans l'affaire B. ça m'intéresse et j'en ai beaucoup à raconter. "

— Ce sont des preuves, des faits qu'il me faut, pas des ragots, dit Slim.

— Bien sûr ! je sais qui vous êtes. Vous connaissez votre métier, vocifère Ahmed en lui tapant sur l'épaule, puis il rajoute plus bas : J'ai en ma possession des chèques, de grosses sommes, des documents compromettants et même un témoignage en la personne de Zaki que voilà.

— Et vous, vous seriez prêt à témoigner ? demande Slim à Zaki qui ballotte son corps de gauche à droite en les observant.

— Puisque je vous le dis ! s'exclame Ahmed. Parlez-lui en arabe, il ne parle pas bien le français.

— Et de quoi va-t-il témoigner ? demande Slim.

— C'est le chauffeur de B. B l'envoyait remettre les enveloppes, de l'argent liquide, beaucoup d'argent, parfois des mallettes, n'est-ce pas, Zaki ? Sacré Zaki va ! Il livrait tout ça aux types des communes et des administrations concernées. Tout le monde devait être arrosé dans cette histoire, vous le savez. B ne prenait pas beaucoup de risques. Il mouillait tout le monde avec lui.

— Je suppose qu'il lui donnait de l'argent à lui aussi, dit Slim en désignant Zaki de la tête.

— Kan kaï tfalla alaïa (Il se payait ma tête), dit Zaki intervenant enfin dans la conversation. Il me disait que je faisais partie de sa famille, qu'il serait toujours là pour moi. Quand ma mère est tombée malade et qu'il a fallu la soigner, il n'a pas fait un geste. Alors, je suis retourné dans le bled quelque temps. C'est à ce moment-là qu'il a eu des problèmes. Dieu est grand.

— Tu es resté combien de temps à son service ? demande Slim.

— Quinze ans ! Monsieur. Quinze ans de loyauté. Je faisais tout ce qu'il me demandait. Je n'étais pas que son chauffeur. J'étais l'homme à tout faire. J'ai mon certificat d'études primaires, moi, Monsieur. Je lis et j'écris correctement l'arabe.

— Et tu l'as revu après ?

— Non. On ne revoit pas un homme qui ne vous aide pas quand votre mère est mourante. Alors que vous avez été son larbin toutes ces années. Une mère, c'est sacré. Je dirai tout ce que vous voudrez savoir. Pas de pitié pour les mécréants.

— Quant à moi je vous ai apporté les preuves que vous vouliez, les chèques et les documents, dit Ahmed.

— Il va falloir que nous restions en contact, dit Slim.

— Je m'en occupe, lui répond Nacer. Je leur ai déjà donné ton numéro de téléphone. Et toi si tu veux les voir, je t'y emmènerai. Tu sais où me trouver. Bien, puisque tout est clair, buvons un verre à notre collaboration.

Zaki s'en va. Il ne boit pas. Slim, Nacer et Hamid s'installent à une table. Un instant après, Kaoutar les rejoint. Grande, pleine et blanche, plutôt vulgaire, maquillée de couleurs écarlates, vêtue d'une jupe noire qui découvre ses jambes longues et bien en chair et d'un boléro rouge décolleté. Kaoutar est le prototype de la prostituée qu'affectionnent les flics comme Nacer, songe Ihsane en la voyant arriver.

— Regarde, Slim. Ça c'est de la femme, dit Nacer en caressant les cuisses de Kaoutar et en riant grassement. Quand tu tiens ses belles fesses rondes et douces, poursuit-il en glissant ses mains sur le postérieur de la fille, tu t'enfonces comme dans du beurre. Et c'est la sensation la plus excitante que puisse éprouver un homme. Elle a une copine encore plus appétissante qu'elle. Tu veux essayer ?

— Non merci, répond Slim.

— Et toi Hamid, tu veux ?

— Je suis marié, dit Hamid timidement.

— Moi aussi, mon vieux. Mais ni vu ni connu. Si on ne peut plus s'amuser… Allez Kaoutar téléphone à Camilia et dis-lui de venir tout de suite. Tu verras Hamid, tu ne le regretteras pas. C'est un morceau de choix. J'ai passé une nuit avec les deux filles que je n'oublierai pas de sitôt. Slim, tu peux nous emmener chez toi comme l'autre fois ? L'avantage d'avoir un ami célibataire ! On se rend service, n'est ce pas ?

— Ce soir, je ne peux pas, j'attends quelqu'un.

— Cachottier va ! C'est sérieux ? Tu vas finir par te marier un jour ?

— Quand tes poules auront des dents.

— Ha ha ha ! Tu ne changeras jamais, reste comme tu es, c'est comme ça qu'on t'aime.

Slim se lève pour aller aux toilettes, s'arrête à côté de Ihsane au passage.

— Tu viens avec moi tout à l'heure ? lui demande-t-il, en la prenant par le bras.

— Je ne peux pas, répond-elle en se dégageant.

— Tu me manques.

— Excuse-moi, j'ai à faire.

Désappointé par la froideur de Ihsane, et ne désirant pas rentrer seul, Slim finit par inviter Nacer et sa bande chez lui. Après tout, se dit-il, il m'a rendu service, je ne peux pas lui refuser ça.

VIII

Slim entre dans le bureau de jaouad, un dossier à la main. Jaouad relève la tête, ses lunettes de vue sur le bout de son nez, l'air préoccupé.

— Tu as un moment ? Je t'apporte le dossier de B pour que tu y jettes un coup d'œil.

— Tu as eu tout ce que tu voulais ?

— Apparemment tout y est. C'est du béton. J'ai même un témoin. C'est le chauffeur de B. Il lui en veut de l'avoir exploité et quand il a eu besoin de lui pour faire hospitaliser sa mère, B L'a ignoré.

— Fais gaffe quand même. Les vieilles rancœurs ne sont pas de mise dans ce genre d'affaire.

— J'ai des garanties, dit Slim en pensant à Nacer.

— Alors fonce. Je te fais confiance.

Jaouad se remet à lire les papiers posés sur son bureau.

— Je suis désolé, Slim, J'ai beaucoup à faire. Ce n'est pas le moment de flancher pour moi, et tu le sais.

— Bien, bien, je m'en vais, dit Slim en fermant la porte derrière lui.

" Voilà un billet qui va asseoir définitivement ma réputation de fouteur de merde, songe Slim. C'est la première fois que je m'attaque à un si gros morceau et en plus j'ai carte blanche, que demander de plus ? Remarque, depuis le temps que je travaille avec Jaouad, il sait que je ne prends jamais rien à la légère. "

Slim se sent presque bien en marchant dans les couloirs du Progrès. Dans un élan de générosité, il téléphone à Bouthaïna.

— C'est moi, lui dit-il de sa voix la plus tendre. On dîne ?

— À la maison alors. Je m'occupe de tout, répond-elle trop heureuse de l'invitation inattendue.

— Vingt heures ?

— Ne me laisse pas attendre dans la rue, se plaint-elle déjà.

— Oui, oui. À tout à l'heure.

Bouthaïna a l'art de tout gâcher, se dit Slim en souriant de son sourire qui n'en est plus un.

Slim entre dans la salle de rédaction où il trouve ses collaborateurs en pleine conversation à propos des rumeurs sur le départ de Jaouad.

— Il est discrédité, entend-il Ali dire.

— Ne sois pas stupide, rétorque Nadia. Un

homme de la trempe de Jaouad n'est pas facile à déquiller. Ils ne l'auront pas comme ça.

Nadia voit Slim arriver et le reçoit comme d'habitude avec son air mi-aguicheur, mi-professionnel.

— Cet ensemble te va bien, lui dit-il gentiment. Puis il ajoute rapidement comme s'il regrettait de lui avoir fait ce compliment ; J'espère que je ne vais pas avoir à faire trop de corrections sur vos papiers, je n'ai pas le temps. Et puis pour une fois, démerdez-vous avec le secrétaire de rédaction. Je suis dans mon bureau. Ne me dérangez qu'en cas d'extrême urgence.

Installé dans son bureau, Slim réexamine une à une toutes les pièces du dossier, s'assure qu'il a tous les éléments en main, puis commence à rédiger son billet. Contrairement à son habitude, il passe du temps à choisir ses mots, détaille avec le plus de précisions possibles chaque cas de corruption, cite des noms. Nacer, sur la base de la requête du chauffeur de B lui a demandé de ne pas mentionner le nom du témoin. Il respecte donc le vœu d'anonymat de Zaki. Au moment où il met le point final à son article, vers dix-neuf heures trente, son portable sonne.

C'est Judith.

Elle appelle pour demander de ses nouvelles, lui parle longuement de tout et de rien, l'écoute lui raconter l'affaire B, puis le voyant amical, voire détaché, lui annonce qu'elle a un nouvel homme dans sa vie, un jeune écrivain espagnol très intéressant.

— Torturé, profond, bourré de talent, une vraie plume dont on entendra parler, lui dit-elle enthousiaste. Puis elle rajoute : " Et, avec ça, le charme et la sensualité des andalous, la jalousie des méditerranéens, leur sens de la passion aussi. Je suis comblée.

— J'en suis heureux pour toi Judith, lui dit Slim. Je suis désolé de devoir t'interrompre, mais j'ai un rendez-vous tout de suite. Rappelle-moi une autre fois.

— Un rendez-vous galant ?

— En quelque sorte. Je t'embrasse.

Slim traverse rapidement les couloirs maintenant déserts du Progrès en pensant à B : J'aurai sa peau à ce minable.

En bas de l'immeuble adjacent à celui où il habite, à vingt heures dix, Bouthaïna chargée de paquets l'attend, la mine renfrognée.

— Tu ne sais plus où j'habite ou quoi ? Lui demande Slim.

— C'est ce petit merdeux de concierge. Je n'aime pas qu'il me reluque pendant que je t'attends. En plus, il me pose une quantité de questions et je n'ai pas envie de lui répondre.

— Quel genre de questions ?

— Si nous sommes fiancés, si mes parents sont au courant de notre liaison, et je ne sais quoi encore.

— Il fait son boulot.

— C'est un flic ?

— Tous les concierges sont des flics, mon cœur.

— Ca avance, ton histoire de pots de vin ?

— Pas mal.

— Jaouad est content ? J'espère qu'il se rend compte qu'il n'a que toi dans ce canard. Tu devrais demander une augmentation de salaire.

— Ce n'est peut-être pas le moment.

— C'est ça ! Ça ne sera jamais le moment. Tu vas encore te faire avoir.

— Et si nous passions une soirée tranquille pour une fois, tu veux bien ?

— Oui mon amour, je suis désolée. Tu dois être crevé. Je vais m'occuper de toi.

— Bouthaïna, arrête de te prendre pour ma mère. Sois plus femme. Et pas femme au foyer. Ça me castre, dit Slim en claquant la porte de son appartement.

IX

Slim relit son billet pour la troisième fois. Il est installé sur la terrasse du petit café qui se trouve à côté de chez lui et que Bouthaïna appelle " le café des lapins ". Il est vrai qu'il lui en a posé, des lapins, dans ce lieu ! Et ailleurs aussi. Elle reste à l'attendre pendant des heures. Slim lui a pourtant dit de ne jamais l'attendre. " Si au bout de trente minutes je ne suis pas là, pars ", lui a-t-il suggéré. Mais elle ne veut rien entendre. Elle choisit de se faire du mal.

Son papier est à la une. Jaouad l'a laissé s'occuper de tout. Et Slim est satisfait du résultat. La photo de B en première page. Avec son air suffisant de satrape. Les mots du titre et du chapeau ont été pesés, sélectionnés, placés avec soin. Il n'y en a pas un de trop. Le texte est précis, serré, acéré, sévère. Pas un seul jeu de mots ni le moindre calembour. Sobriété de rigueur.

Oui. Jaouad devrait être content.

Peut-être Bouthaïna n'a-t-elle pas entièrement tort après tout. Peut-être devrais-je demander une augmentation ? Songe Slim. Jaouad ne se rend pas compte à quel point je lui suis indispensable. Une paye de misère avec l'expérience que j'ai. Et ce test qu'il m'a imposé ! Je ne peux pas l'oublier.

— Dans ta course contre la vie, tu n'as plus aucune exigence, lui a dit Judith un jour. Tout t'échappe.

— Tu donnes l'impression que tout ce qui te concerne ne revêt pas d'importance à tes yeux. C'est comme si tu étais indigne de tout avantage, de toute douceur, lui a dit Bouthaïna de son côté de tout droit ; tu te plais à partir perdant,

" Oui. Et alors ?

J'ai suffisamment fait de conneries comme ça. Maintenant, il est trop tard. Je paye.

Je suis le seul à savoir.

Mes errances. Mes égarements. Mes méprises.

Mes défaillances.

Je suis pernicieux avec ceux qui m'aiment. Destructeur. "

Mourad.

Une plage, un jour d'été. Mourad avait tout juste vingt ans. Il était Amoureux. Slim jouait. Il l'a planté là sur cette plage, pensant qu'il était jeune, insouciant, qu'il avait toute la vie devant lui, qu'il s'en remettrait.

Slim n'a pas vu sa détresse. Le drame qui se préparait. Mourad est mort.

" Par ma faute ", se dit slim.

Il baisse la tête, se ronge les ongles, ce qu'il en reste. La sonnerie de son portable le fait sursauter.

— Débarque tout de suite dans mon bureau ! beugle Jaouad.

— Que se passe-t-il ? demande Slim qui a du mal à émerger de sa vision du corps de Mourad échoué sur le sable, brisé.

— Débarque ! répète Jaouad, puis il interrompt la communication.

Quinze minutes plus tard, Slim traverse les couloirs du Progrès. Sur son passage, les yeux de ses collègues sont tous braqués sur lui. On chuchote. On l'évite.

La porte du bureau de Jaouad est largement ouverte.

— Nous sommes dans la merde, lui hurle-t-il en le voyant arriver. B nous fait un procès pour propos diffamatoires. Tes preuves n'en sont pas. Le dossier a été monté de toutes pièces par ton flic véreux et je ne sais qui. Nous sommes dans de sales draps. Mon poste de directeur de publication ne vaut plus un clou.

— Calme-toi. Qu'est ce que tu racontes ? Nous avons un témoin, des documents…

— Du pipeau ! Le dossier est fabriqué. J'ai appelé toutes les personnes que je connais et qui sont susceptibles de nous renseigner. C'est un coup monté. Tu t'es fait avoir comme un bleu.

— Je vais appeler Nacer. Il doit y avoir une erreur. Je vais lui demander de venir avec les deux autres.

— Surtout pas. Ne fais plus rien. Barre-toi. Prends un congé. Disparais un mois quelque part. Je vais voir comment je vais faire pour étouffer cette affaire. Ma direction de publication va y passer mais c'est un moindre mal par rapport à ce qui pourrait nous arriver.

— Je ne comprends pas.

— Moi si. Il ne s'agit plus de comprendre mais d'agir. Je ne veux plus te voir dans les parages. Demande à ta Bouthy de t'emmener à Marrakech ou ailleurs. Je t'appellerai pour te tenir au courant de la suite de cette histoire. Allez, va t'en, dit Jaouad d'une voix moins dure, sa colère tempérée par la pâleur du visage de Slim.

Slim s'enfuit plus qu'il ne sort du *Progrès*.Il est ahuri. Il lui faut quelque chose de fort.

À boire. Un verre. Vite.

X

Deux heures du matin. Slim est ivre. De cette ivresse qui alourdit son corps, anesthésie son cerveau et l'immobilise. Il est incapable de rentrer chez lui dans cet état. Ihsane n'est pas au *Abou Nouas*. Elle a appelé les frères mafiosi pour les prévenir qu'elle serait absente ce jour-là parce que malade.

Slim a du mal à l'imaginer malade. Qu'est ce qui lui prend, à celle-là ? Elle déserte ?

Avec des gestes lents et maladroits, il compose le numéro de téléphone de Bouthaïna. Elle répond d'une voix endormie.

— Je te dérange, dit Slim, la langue pâteuse. Tu dors.

— Non. Où es-tu ?

— Viens tout de suite. J'ai besoin de toi.

— Mais où ? demande-t-elle affolée.

— Je t'attends place de Verdun à côté du King Burger. J'ai faim, dit-il, la tête dans le brouillard.

— J'arrive tout de suite, s'empresse de répondre

Bouthaïna. Le temps de m'habiller et de sortir la voiture.

— Dépéche-toi, je vais m'écrouler.

Bouthaina essaie d'être la moins bruyante possible pour na ne pas réveiller Lina ou sa mère. Elle sait qu'elle va passer la nuit dehors et qu'à son réveil, sa mère va s'apercevoir de son absence, devoir s'occuper de Lina, la changer, l'emmener à l'école. Et sa mère n'a plus envie d'être mère.

Quand elle arrive place de Verdun, Slim est là. Elle soupire. Bouthaïna ne compte plus les fois où il lui a demandé de le rejoindre et où elle ne l'a pas trouvé. Il tient à peine sur ses jambes.

— Tu es là ? lui dit-il.

— On rentre, lui répond-elle.

Dans l'appartement de Slim, Bouthaïna s'empresse de procéder au rituel qu'elle connaît si bien. Lui enlever ses chaussures, l'aider à s'allonger, lui servir un verre, même si c'est pas très indiqué, mettre de la musique, de préférence Chab Mami.

— Je suis un mauvais garçon, se lamente Slim.

— Que se passe-t-il ? demande Bouthaïna.

— J'ai trahi la confiance de Jaouad, répond Slim abattu. C'était foireux. Je me suis fait baiser.

— C'est cette histoire de pots de vin ?

— Oui. Je veux foutre le camp. Allons-nous-en quelque part loin d'ici. Rien que toi et moi. Tu es la seule, Bouthaïna… Tu sais ? Tu es la seule.

— La seule ?

— Partons !

— Où veux-tu que nous allions ?

— À Marrakech. Je te présenterai à des gens très bien, tu verras. Nous allons passer un bon moment.

— Il faut que je m'organise.

— Non ! Partons cette nuit. Maintenant.

— Je ne peux pas. Il faut que je prévienne ma mère. Qui va s'occuper de Lina ?

— Tu ne m'as pas dit qu'il n'y avait que moi ? Que je suis ta vie ?

— Oui.

— Alors partons, dit Slim en fermant les yeux et en se mettant à ronfler.

Slim endormi, Bouthaïna erre dans l'appartement silencieux. Elle se sent chez elle ici. Peut-être plus que Slim.

Chaque recoin a déjà été exploré, fouillé, senti. Mécaniquement, elle sort une valise du placard de la chambre à coucher, l'emplit de vêtements, y adjoint la trousse de toilette, sans oublier le parfum de Slim. Il ne peut pas se passer de son parfum aux senteurs sucrées.

Nous prendrons la route demain matin quand il se réveillera, songe-t-elle. Je téléphonerai à ma mère, elle s'occupera de Lina. Ou alors, elle demandera à son père de s'occuper d'elle. Il peut le faire de temps en temps quand même, s'indigne-t-elle.

SLIM ET LA MORT.

I

Marrakech apparaît au loin, comme dans un rêve. Bouthaïna accélère. Elle tend le bras hors de la voiture. L'air est doux et sec. Slim à demi allongé sur la banquette arrière, en est à sa dixième bière. Il bat la mesure, de sa main sur la vitre. Les Rolling Stones chantent " Miss you ". Bouthaïna lui jette un regard dans le rétroviseur. Il fait mine de l'embrasser. Elle rit.

— Nous sommes arrivés, mon prince, lui dit-elle.

— Où allons-nous crécher ? demande Slim.

— Il y a un hôtel que tu préfères ?

— Allons au Jardin de Marrakech. Tu te souviens de la première fois où nous y avons logé ? Tu étais mariée et tu ne voulais pas donner ta carte d'identité nationale à la réception.

Bouthaïna fait une grimace.

— Mon prince était là, dit-elle attendrie, il a suffi qu'il intervienne et tout était réglé.

— Je me suis arrangé pour qu'il n'y ait pas de trace de ton séjour au Jardin de Marrakech. Je garde un souvenir inoubliable de ce voyage. Tu étais belle. Et si gaie ! Tu n'arrêtais pas de m'embrasser. Je t'ai appris à jouer au Yam. Tu m'as fait découvrir tes talents de masseuse. Personne ne m'a jamais massé les pieds comme tu l'as fait. C'était bon. J'ai dormi comme un bébé.

— Je me sentais coupable.

— Tu n'en avais pas l'air.

— J'étais heureuse.

— Tu ne l'es plus.

— Si, comme on peut l'être dans un vieux couple ! hurle Bouthaïna en lâchant le volant, joviale.

— Je voudrais que nous retournions au Jardin de Marrakech. Cette fois-ci, je leur dirai que tu es ma femme et que nous sommes en voyage de noces. Je vous présente ma femme ! dit-il, théâtral. Une femme respectable, ajoute-t-il, moqueur.

Le directeur de l'hébergement, une vague relation de Slim — Bouthaïna comprend qu'ils se sont rencontrés dans un bar à Casablanca où ils ont partagé de grosses cuites - les reçoit avec des transports d'enthousiasme. Il s'extasie d'apprendre que Slim a enfin trouvé l'âme sœur, leur propose la suite nuptiale au prix d'une chambre normale et avec cinquante pour cent de réduction, leur offre une bouteille de champagne et une corbeille de fruits.

Le balconnet de la suite ouvre sur un magnifique jardin d'orangers, quelques palmiers, et d'un parterre de roses panachées. Leur parfum embaume agréablement la large pièce dans laquelle le lit trône, immense, démesuré. Slim s'y vautre, invite Bouthaïna à le rejoindre.

— Il y a trop de lumière ici, lui dit-il. tire les rideaux et viens à côté de moi.

— Tu veux du champagne ?

— Du champagne ! Moi ? s'exclame-t-il, outré. Cherche plutôt dans le mini-bar s'il y a de la vodka. Le champagne est pour toi, ma belle.

Bouthaïna sert un verre de vodka — les deux mignonnettes du mini-bar - avec un glaçon à Slim et fait sauter le bouchon de la bouteille de Champagne. Slim prend le bouchon, puis le met dans la main de Bouthaïna.

— Promets-moi que tu le garderas toujours en souvenir de notre voyage de noces, lui dit-il affectueusement.

— Tu nous la joues quoi ? demande Bouthaïna troublée.

— Chut ! Ne gâche pas tout. Fais-nous couler un bain avec plein de mousse.

Bouthaïna s'étend dans la spacieuse baignoire ronde bordée de marbre rose, contre Slim. Un grand miroir lui renvoie l'image de leur couple. Tendrement, Slim lui caresse les seins. Puis il la prend avec douceur.

Coucher du soleil sur Marrakech vu de la terrasse panoramique de La Renaissance. Le garçon à la veste défraîchie. Le ticket à quinze dirhams. Le vieil ascenseur. Et cette atmosphère à la fois glauque et lumineuse. L'histoire du suicide. Le ciel de Marrakech. Ses couleurs. La Koutoubia, majestueuse.

Bouthaïna, son walk man à la main, chante avec Dalida " Bambino ".

— L'amour et la jalousie, bambino, bambino, ne sont pas des jeux d'enfant, chante Bouthaïna en pointant son doigt sur Slim.

— Comment peux-tu écouter ça ? lui demande-t-il, l'air dédaigneux.

— Tu ne comprends rien à Dalida. C'est un personnage, elle...

— Je ne veux pas savoir, dit Slim en l'interrompant.

— Écoute ça, lui dit-elle ravie, puis elle chante : " Il venait d'avoir dix-huit ans...

— Je te verrais bien vieillissante, baisant à fesse que veux-tu en cachette avec un garçon de dix-huit ans, derrière des bottes de foin à la campagne pendant que ton mari ronflerait dans une chambre d'auberge.

— En l'occurrence, le mari serait toi.

— Moi ? Je serais mort et enterré.

— Alors, il n'y aura pas de mari.

— Tes réponses sont tellement prévisibles que je commence à m'ennuyer.

— Je t'aime.

— Qu'est-ce que je disais !

Slim compose un numéro sur son portable.

— Je vais appeler des amis que je voudrais te présenter. Lui, c'est un artiste peintre talentueux. Elle, une originale. Cultivée, intelligente, un peu excentrique, attachante.

— Elle te plaît ?

Slim hausse les épaules.

— Tu ne peux pas oublier d'être conne des fois ?

La voix grave de Leila lui répond.

— Quelle entrée en matière mon cher ! Tu m'épates.

— Leila ! Je suis à Marrakech…

— Laisse-moi deviner. Avec celle qui doit oublier d'être conne ?

— Avec ma femme.

— Tu t'es marié ?

— En quelque sorte.

— Alors je meurs d'envie de la rencontrer. Vous êtes ici après-demain soir ? Nous recevons quelques amis.

— Une soirée mondaine ?

— On peut dire ça comme ça.

— Je suis toujours content de vous revoir, ma chérie. Nous y serons.

Slim se tourne vers Bouthaïna.

— Où veux-tu que nous dînions ce soir, mon amour ?

— Dans la chambre. Sur la petite table du balcon.

— Vendu ! Moi non plus je n'ai pas envie de sortir ce soir.

Slim caresse la joue de Bouthaïna. Il veut qu'elle soit heureuse.

Je vais faire un effort, songe-t-il, je voudrais qu'elle garde un bon souvenir de ce séjour à Marrakech.

II

Les Ammor habitent un riad splendide dans la vieille médina de Marrakech. L'enchantement vous saisit dès que vous franchissez leur porte et que vous découvrez ce que dissimulent les hautes murailles, un fouillis de plantes grimpantes. Des roses, des orangers, des citronniers, des grenadiers, des hibiscus rouges, une fontaine en marbre rose de laquelle gicle une eau pure, illuminée par un jeu de lumières. Des lampes aux lueurs vacillantes, en fer forgé, éclairent faiblement un chemin en zelliges corail qui mène à l'entrée de la qobba principale, grande ouverte par deux portes en sapin rouge ciselé d'ornements.

À l'intérieur, un plafond haut, soutenu par des poutres en bois sculpté d'arabesques, des murs en qerati et mzihri aux multiples couleurs, des objets d'art, des toiles signées de noms connus, un décor luxueux, travaillé.

Le maître de maison les reçoit en grand seigneur. Il est vêtu d'une gandoura tunisienne en soie blanc cassé, ses yeux sont soulignés au khôl. Sa femme, Leila, porte un caftan en organsin mauve et des mules assorties, brodées ton sur ton. À sa cheville droite, l'unique bijou qu'elle arbore, un khalkhal en argent incrusté subtilement de pierres bleutées.

— C'est donc vous qu'il nous cache, dit Leila à Bouthaïna de sa voix à l'accent mondain, en la prenant familièrement par le bras et en l'entraînant vers les autres convives. Et ça fait longtemps que vous connaissez cet énergumène ? C'est sérieux entre vous ? Comme si Slim pouvait être sérieux ! N'est-ce pas ? ajoute-t-elle complice, en se dirigeant vers un autre invité et sans attendre la réponse.

Slim est accueilli par une ovation générale. Même le joueur de luth dépose son instrument un instant pour le saluer. Bouthaïna reconnaît quelques célébrités, un chanteur, des compositeurs, une jeune actrice en vogue, la fameuse Selma de l'homme du jour. Le théâtre aussi est représenté, par Taleb Sefrioui, un auteur à succès.

Une cinquantaine de personnes sont rassemblées dans le salon. Elles semblent toutes, avoir déjà rencontré Slim.

Mieux. Slim est la star de la soirée. Et il se pâme, rit aux éclats, gonflé d'importance, frisant le ridicule, comme un enfant gâté dont on fête fastueusement l'anniversaire. Et Bouthaïna, au titre de " femme de la star ", récolte ici et là quelques attentions, des regards curieux, d'autres intéressés, des hommages discrets.

Trois heures du matin. Leila a éteint les grandes lumières pour ne laisser que quelques lampes. Le dîner n'a toujours pas été servi. Personne ne le réclame d'ailleurs. Slim a trop bu. Tout ce beau monde a trop bu et continue de boire.

On roucoule.

On jacasse.

On danse.

On se pelote.

Mais surtout on se disperse en petits groupes de deux ou de trois. Les uns sortent dans le jardin sous prétexte qu'il fait meilleur dehors. Et effectivement dehors l'air est doux, parfumé. Ce ne sont pas encore les grosses chaleurs à Marrakech. Les autres se faufilent par les portes ouvertes des autres qobbates, autour du jardin.

Leila a vite abandonné Bouthaïna.

— Je vous la confie, a-t-elle dit à un homme élégant qui semble prendre soin de tous les invités.

La maîtresse de maison a une allure féline - plutôt tigresse que chatte. Toute la soirée, elle a tourné autour de Slim. De sa démarche souple. Ses yeux étirés vers les tempes par un maquillage habile.

Elle a ignoré Bouthaïna.

Le maître de maison de son côté flirte dans un coin avec un magnifique garçon d'une vingtaine d'années.

Slim aussi semble avoir oublié Boutaïna. Assis par terre aux pieds de Leila, il lui caresse les mollets en bavardant avec elle. La maîtresse de maison lui sourit, aux anges.

Quel âge peut-elle avoir ? se demande Bouthaïna. Quarante ans ? Peut-être plus. Elle est très sensuelle, finit-elle par s'avouer avec amertume.

Bouthaïna les yeux exorbités regarde Leila se lever de la banquette, puis s'asseoir sur les genoux de Slim. Ils échangent un long baiser.

Bouthaïna cherche le mari de la maîtresse de maison, ne le trouve pas. L'éphèbe aussi s'est volatilisé.

— Laissez-les s'amuser. Ils ne font rien de mal, lui dit son élégant voisin qui a remarqué son air interloqué. Prenez un verre, détendez-vous, vous le retrouverez, votre Roméo. Elle ne vous le prendra pas. Prêtez-le lui une soirée. Ça ne pourrait vous faire que du bien.

Leila continue d'embrasser Slim. Puis, d'un bond, elle se lève et l'invite à la suivre dans une autre pièce. Ils disparaissent tous les deux derrière une porte.

— Vous n'êtes jamais venue, constate le gandin. Vous savez, tout le monde passe la nuit ici. Il suffit de se trouver un endroit confortable.

— Je m'en vais, dit-elle en se levant.

— Votre ami sera fâché.

— Qu'il se fâche !

Bouthaïna quitte le riad en trébuchant, s'égare. Elle passe à côté d'une pièce. Par la porte entr'ouverte elle aperçoit le maître de maison à genoux, léchant le ventre de son jeune amant pendant que de ses mains il lui pétrit les fesses. Ils sont nus tous les deux et semblent prendre beaucoup de plaisir.

Allongée sur le grand lit de la suite nuptiale, Bouthaïna n'arrive plus à se rappeler comment elle est arrivée à l'hôtel. Les images de Slim et Leila enlacés et du maître de maison léchant le ventre de son jeune amant la poursuivent. Elle a honte, parce que, malgré elle, elle se sent émoustillée par ces visions.

Elle finit par s'endormir, le corps en feu.

À dix heures du matin, Slim la réveille. Il est en colère. Toujours ivre.

— Pourquoi es-tu partie ? hurle-t-il.

— J'en avais marre, répond-elle en se redressant.

— Marre de quoi ?

— Fous-moi la paix !

— Je vais te la foutre. Lève-toi. Nous partons. Tout de suite.

— Allons déjeuner d'abord.

— Si tu veux manger, commande quelque chose ici. Et pour moi ça sera une bouteille de vodka.

Slim s'assoit sur le fauteuil en face du lit.

— Viens ici ! ordonne-t-il.

Elle obtempère.

Slim glisse ses mains sous le tee-shirt de Bouthaïna, puis, comme elle ne bouge pas, qu'elle se raidit, du bout de ses doigts, il pince la pointe de ses seins. Elle a envie de crier, mais elle se mord la lèvre, désirant qu'il lui fasse encore plus mal. Elle le fixe, arrogante. Il la prend par les cheveux et l'oblige brutalement à se mettre à genoux devant lui.

— Suce-moi, dit-il. Tu es ma femme et je fais de toi ce que je veux, ajoute-t-il hargneux.

III

Bouthaïna conduit nerveusement. La route est dangereuse la nuit ; la lumière aveuglante des phares, les camions nombreux. Elle a bu. Pas beaucoup, mais suffisamment pour ne pas avoir les idées claires. Slim a tenu à ce qu'ils rentrent à Casa le jour même.

À eux deux, ils ont vidé la première bouteille de vodka, puis la moitié de la deuxième. À travers la vitre du balconnet de la chambre nuptiale, le crépuscule s'annonçait. C'est à ce moment-là que Slim a décrété qu'il fallait partir. Bouthaïna se sentait un peu ivre. Elle a protesté. Faiblement. Slim est devenu odieux. Il a menacé de l'abandonner là, dans cette chambre d'hôtel qui était censée abriter leur lune de miel zama. Elle a fini par céder.

" C'est décidé, je vais le quitter ", songe-t-elle, en le regardant dans le rétroviseur boire au goulot la dernière moitié de la bouteille de vodka. D'un geste précis, elle sort son portable de son sac à main et compose le numéro de ses parents. Lina lui répond, apparemment joyeuse d'entendre sa voix.

— Je rentre ce soir, ma chérie. Ne m'attends pas. C'est moi qui te réveillerai demain matin et qui t'emmènerai à l'école. Je t'aime.

Slim rit de son rire extravagant.

— Tu ne l'aimes pas assez, dit-il.

Bouthaïna ne lui répond pas. Elle est impatiente d'arriver chez elle et de le larguer chez lui. Elle accélère, double une voiture sans tenir compte de la ligne continue.

Slim ne comprend pas ce qui s'est passé. Un bruit phénoménal. Il s'est senti projeté vers l'avant, puis, il ne sait pas comment, il s'est accroché au dossier de Bouthaïna. La voiture a dérapé sur la gauche et a fait deux tonneaux.

Maintenant, il distingue un fouillis avec déjà des gens qui s'attroupent. Il perd connaissance, se réveille sur une civière. Un homme en blouse blanche est penché sur lui.

— Il s'en sortira, l'entend-il dire. C'est la fille qui est mal en point.

Bouthaïna. Mal en point ? Slim ferme les yeux. Il n'arrive pas à parler. Une lumière aveuglante, le corps de Mourad désarticulé sur le sable. Et maintenant, Bouthaïna.

Bouthaïna ne voit plus rien, n'entend plus rien. Mais elle vit. Son corps flotte, sans consistance. Sa tête est lourde. Elle lui fait mal.

Le sourire brèche-dent de Lina.

" Lina ! Je lui ai promis de l'emmener à l'école demain matin. Ça fait si longtemps ! Je suis en train de mourir ? C'est ça la mort ? Je ne dois pas mourir. Aidez-moi ! La trentaine. Des perspectives. Ma fille. Je l'aime. Il n'y a qu'elle. Ma mère ne peut pas s'en occuper. "

" Une voix. J'entends une voix. "

— Vous m'entendez ? demande la voix. Nous vous emmenons à l'hôpital le plus proche. Ne vous endormez pas. Restez avec nous, poursuit-elle, votre mari va bien.

" Mon mari ? Nadir ? Il n'est plus mon mari.

Slim ! "

" La mort ne veut pas de lui. "

" Mon Dieu, laissez-moi vivre ! Je m'occuperai de ma fille. Je serai une bonne mère. "

" La sirène. Ils ont mis la sirène. Ça veut dire que c'est grave. "

L'homme en blouse blanche serre la main de Bouthaïna dans la sienne. " Quel âge peut-elle avoir ? se demande-t-il. Vingt-sept, vingt-huit ans ? Ils ont bu de l'alcool tous les deux. " Ce qui a sauvé le garçon c'est qu'il était installé sur la banquette arrière. Il a dû s'accrocher à elle. " Quel gâchis ! "

L'hôpital.

L'officier de police demande à Slim si Bouthaïna est sa femme. " C'est ma fiancée ", répond Slim. Puis il lui donne le numéro de téléphone de ses parents.

— Vous voulez bien les appeler. J'en suis incapable.

Bouthaïna est dans la salle de réanimation. Elle a perdu connaissance.

Slim l'a vue.

Bouthaïna a des tuyaux pleins de sang, des tuyaux pleins d'oxygène qui pénètrent son corps de partout par des aiguilles, des canules, des drains. Elle est pâle comme une morte. Avec des tuméfactions sur son visage.

Slim ne la reconnaît pas.

Bouthaïna est vivante. Elle ne peut pas mourir.

Il y a un écran de contrôle sur lequel est affiché les battements de son cœur, sa respiration entrecoupée de silences.

Bouthaïna est dans le coma.

— Tu as tué mon enfant ! hurle la mère de Bouthaïna à slim. Je le savais. Je savais que tu la tuerais. Tu as fait de sa fille une orpheline. Tu es un monstre !

slim la regarde ahuri.

La peur jaillit en lui, la peur d'avoir touché à la vie. Peur du sacrilège.

Bouthaïna morte ? Jamais !

L'homme à la blouse blanche est désolé. Il a tout essayé. Une hémorragie cérébrale.

La mère de Bouthaïna s'écroule.

Slim quitte l'hôpital. Il ne veut pas assister à la suite des événements.

Settat est déserte la nuit. Il fait noir. Tout est fermé. Slim marche longtemps. Il faut qu'il trouve un taxi pour rentrer à Casablanca.

" Je suis coupable ! se dit-il. Mon destin est à ce point déterminé ? Pourquoi ? Ça n'a pas de sens. Il doit y avoir une issue. "

" Ihsane ! Je dois voir Ihsane. Il faut qu'elle sache. "

Dieu est définitivement mort.

IV

Slim s'est enfermé chez lui pour ne pas entendre parler de la mort de Bouthaïna.

Slim ne va jamais aux enterrements.

Il a devinée que c'est aujourd'hui que va avoir lieu cette cérémonie absurde.

Aujourd'hui, Bouthaïna, enveloppée dans son linceul, va enfin sortir de chez ses parents, dans un cercueil, escortée des youyous des femmes et des versets du Coran psalmodiés par les tolbas.

Aujourd'hui, la mère de Bouthaïna, habillée de blanc, les yeux couleur sang, à moitié morte de chagrin, va venir renforcer les rangs de ses ennemis.

Aujourd'hui, Lina, la fille de Bouthaïna, va comprendre le sens de la vie.

Et lui, Slim, est las.

Il boit et boit encore.

Mais, le flou, son fameux flou artistique a fait long feu.

À sa place, une réalité lisse et sans tache.

Son appartement que, décidément l'odeur de Bouthaïna ne veut pas quitter. Quelques affaires lui appartenant - elle laissait toujours traîner quelque chose derrière elle -, une boucle d'oreille sur la table de chevet. Un tee-shirt XXL dont il avait horreur — seulement pour dormir, disait-elle -, froissé et jeté négligemment sur le lit de la chambre à coucher. Et même une paire de sandales rouges au talon cassé. Kitsch.

Slim finit son verre de vodka d'une grande gorgée.

" C'est bizarre, se dit-il, Je ne ressens rien. "

D'un bond, il se lève, prend son blouson et sort.

V

Au *Abou Nouas,* les frères mafiosi apprennent à Slim que Ihsane ne viendra plus.

— Elle se marie, paraît-il, lui dit le frère aîné en ricanant. Ihsane a daigné confier cet événement de sa vie à une fille d'ici. Peut-être pour lui prouver qu'elle est différente. Camélia ! poursuit-il en appelant la fille en question. Viens raconter à Slim ce que t'a dit Ihsane.

Camélia avance vers eux en se déhanchant encore plus que d'habitude, gonflée de l'importance que lui donne le propriétaire des lieux.

— Elle épouse un garçon qui est avec elle à la fac. Ils vont s'installer à Kénitra.

— Elle habite toujours au foyer de jeunes filles ? demande Slim.

— Non, elle est repartie vivre chez sa grand-mère. Son fiancé ne voulait plus qu'elle reste là-bas. C'est un garçon de bonne famille, paraît-il. De milieu aisé. Elle a dit qu'il est fou d'elle. Personnellement, je ne vois pas ce qu'il lui trouve. Elle fait tout le temps la gueule. Rien que de la regarder, ça vous sape le moral. Il n'y a pas mieux que les filles bonnes vivantes comme moi, conclu-t-elle en riant.

— On ne t'a pas demandé ton avis, répond le frère aîné, retourne travailler. Elle n'a pas tort la garce ! poursuit-il à l'attention de Slim, cette petite était d'une tristesse qui parfois me donnait la chair de poule. Elle semblait t'apprécier. Je l'ai rencontrée un jour en ville. Vous ne me croirez pas si je vous le dis… Elle était voilée ! Je ne l'ai même pas reconnue au début. Il a fallu qu'elle s'approche. Elle a fait semblant de ne pas me voir. Je ne lui en ai pas voulu, elle n'était pas seule. Je me suis dit qu'elle était peut-être avec quelqu'un de sa famille. La plupart des filles n'avouent pas aux membres de leur famille qu'elles travaillent dans un bar. Du moment qu'elles sont majeures, moi…

— Ihsane est une belle femme, dit le frère cadet d'un air entendu. N'est-ce pas Slim ?

— Elle est plus que ça, répond Slim.

— Serais-tu mordu ? demande le frère aîné. Il faut faire gaffe mon vieux. Elles ont toutes des grigris ici. Ne te laisse pas avoir.

— Elle va me manquer.

— Tu en trouveras une autre ! Regarde la petite nouvelle, celle qui remplace Ihsane. Dans le genre " virginal, sainte-nitouche, qui n'exerce ce métier que parce qu'elle y est obligée ", elle fait l'affaire elle aussi. Je me suis dit qu'il fallait rester dans le même registre. C'est qu'elle ne plaisait pas qu'à toi la belle Ihsane ! Elle avait ses fidèles. Les inconditionnels de Ihsane ! Certains ne venaient ici que pour la voir. Et elle le savait.

— Ihsane n'est pas intéressée, dit Slim.

— Avec toi peut-être. Crois-moi, avec les autres, elle ne faisait pas sa grande dame, elle s'est fait du fric au *Abou Nouas*. Et celle-là, ajoute-t-il en pointant le doigt vers la nouvelle, fera de même. Elle s'appelle Noure El Houda, c'est déjà tout dire.

Slim regarde Noure El Houda. Comment peuvent-ils la comparer à Ihsane ? Si pure ! Celle-la a l'air de sortir droit d'une loge de théâtre.

Il se lève et va aux toilettes. Puis il compose le numéro de Judith sur son portable.

— Slim ? Sais-tu quelle heure il est ? répond-elle d'une voix endormie.

— J'ai besoin de toi.

— J'arrive bientôt à Marrakech. Dans une dizaine de jours. Rejoins-moi là-bas.

— Non, pas Marrakech. Arrange-toi pour venir d'abord à Casa. Chez moi.

— Chez toi ? Je croyais que nous avions déjà parlé de ça.

— Tu feras une exception.

— Que se passe-t-il, Slim ? Tu as un problème ? Demande-t-elle, inquiète.

— Je veux te voir. Tu me manques, c'est tout !

— Bon, bon ! Je m'arrangerai. Je te rappelle demain.

Abattu, le dos voûté, la mine déconfite, Slim paye sa note et s'apprête à quitter le *Abou Nouas* quand Nacer y fait une entrée remarquée ; éméché, accompagné de deux filles vulgaires et court vêtues. En voyant Slim, il s'immobilise.

— Mon très cher Slim ! Où étais-tu ? Ça fait un bail qu'on ne t'a pas vu.

— Tu as encore le culot de m'adresser la parole toi ? braille Slim. J'ai une envie folle de te cogner, ajoute-t-il en colère.

— Ne t'en prive pas, mon cher. Vas-y, cogne ! répond Nacer en le défiant.

Slim le prend par le col de sa veste et le secoue. Le frère aîné s'interpose, conciliant.

— Vous n'allez pas vous battre ! Vous avez toujours été en bons termes. Que se passe-t-il ?

— Ce type est un escroc, hurle Slim. Il m'a foutu ma vie en l'air.

— Allons Slim, rentre chez toi. Tu as l'air épuisé. Nous reparlerons de tout ça demain. Viens déjeuner avec moi, je t'invite, dit le frère aîné en le tirant vers la porte. Puis, plus bas : " Tu es fou ou quoi ? C'est un flic ! Tu t'attendais à quoi ? Je te pensais moins naïf. "

— Oui c'est ça. Je suis naïf. Je m'en vais. Pas de bagarre au *Abou Nouas*, dit Slim en se dégageant de la poigne du frère aîné.

Slim sort, puis revient. Il fait signe de la main à Camélia qui s'empresse de le rejoindre.

— Tu me veux, Slim ? demande-t-elle, aguichante.

— Dis-moi, Camélia, je voudrais savoir une chose. Ihsane ne t'a jamais rien dit me concernant ?

— Quoi par exemple ? demande Camélia.

— Je ne sais pas moi ! une confidence. Entre femmes, on se raconte certaines choses.

— Non Slim. Ihsane n'est pas bavarde. Elle ne m'a jamais rien dit sur toi.

Dépité, Slim quitte le *Abou Nouas*. " J'espérais quoi au juste ? " s'interroge-t-il.

VI

Slim est allé chercher Judith à l'aéroport, presque gai à la perspective de la revoir.

Elle lui est apparue derrière le comptoir des formalités, dans une robe en lin écru un chapeau assorti sur la tête, des lunettes de soleil sur le nez. Lointaine.

Le trajet de l'aéroport à chez lui, en grand taxi, s'est accompli dans le silence, la main parfaitement manucurée et douce de Judith sur la sienne qui tremble d'émotion.

Et maintenant, Judith est là. Dans son appartement.

Elle s'y promène avec aisance, comme si elle y avait toujours vécu.

Judith se verse un autre verre de vin — un Bordeaux qu'elle a ramené dans ses bagages —, boit une gorgée puis, sans un mot, avec une curieuse indifférence, comme si Slim n'avait pas été là, elle se déshabille.

Elle pose un long regard sur lui. Dans ce regard, ni coquetterie, ni défi. Plutôt une interrogation.

Slim, gêné, ne comprend pas. Il lui sourit de son sourire qui n'en est plus un. Elle ne le lui rend pas, reste encore immobile quelques instants, nue, le verre de vin à la main.

Slim se lève, s'approche, la couvre de baisers tendres. Elle le repousse, se retourne, les yeux rivés cette fois-ci sur la fenêtre entrouverte.

Ce sont les premiers jours d'été. Il fait chaud. Tous les rideaux sont baissés, sauf celui de cette fenêtre. À l'intérieur, règne une agréable fraîcheur.

Au loin, au-delà des terrasses, une mosquée. Cela ne peut pas être ça qui retient son attention, songe Slim. C'est alors qu'il s'aperçoit que ce qui retient l'attention de Judith, c'est leur reflet sur la vitre ; une femme nue aux côtés d'un homme jeune en jean et en tee-shirt noirs.

Judith lève les bras en arc comme une danseuse étoile qui s'apprête à exécuter les répétitions d'un ballet d'opéra. Ses seins irréprochables remontent encore plus vers le haut.

Dans le reflet, on ne voit plus qu'elle.

— Judith ! Parle-moi, gémit Slim.

— Chut ! Plus tard, répond-elle en le bâillonnant de sa main.

Puis elle l'entraîne vers la chambre à coucher.

— Oui, dit-il, fais-moi l'amour.

À califourchon sur Slim, Judith mène la danse. Elle semble prendre du plaisir. Elle va et vient sur son sexe, sans relâche. Slim transpire. Il est déjà épuisé. Elle s'acharne jusqu'à ce qu'elle jouisse, puis s'abat à côté de lui.

— Mmm ! quel pied ! soupire-t-elle.

elle se lève pour prendre une douche.

Elle revient, vêtue du tee-shirt XXL de Bouthaïna que Slim a lavé et rangé dans le placard de la salle de bain.

— Tu portes du XXL, toi, maintenant ? demande-t-elle en se vautrant sur lui et en secouant ses cheveux mouillés.

— Tu es toujours amoureuse de ton Espagnol ? dit-il tout à coup hargneux.

— Je croyais que tu t'en foutais.

— J'ai dit ça ?

— Oublions l'Andalou. C'est quoi, ton problème ? Tu as besoin d'argent ?

— Je ne suis pas ta pute.

— Ah bon ? Je l'aurais cru pourtant ! s'exclame Judith en riant.

— Tu es ignoble.

— Tu m'aimes, non ?

— Je me demande pourquoi.

— Contente-toi de m'aimer.

— J'ai besoin de toi.

— Oui ?

— Tu es trop loin de moi.

— Décidément, tu ne lâcheras jamais prise.

— Je souffre !

— Tu te la joues surtout. Que veux-tu que je fasse ? que je quitte tout et que je vienne m'installer avec toi ici ?

— Non, répond Slim, tout à coup conscient de l'incongru de cette éventualité.

— Alors fiche-moi la paix et prenons du bon temps, dit-elle en l'embrassant sur le front.

La sonnerie du portable de Slim retentit.

— Tout va bien, dit Jaouad à Slim. J'ai tout réglé. Tu peux revenir quand tu veux.

— Et la Direction de publication ?

— C'est une autre histoire.

— Judith est là.

— Dans ce cas, je ne te dérange pas plus. Dis-lui quand même que je voudrais la rencontrer pour une affaire personnelle. J'ai un service à lui demander.

— Je n'y manquerai pas.

— Dis-moi, Slim, cette petite qui est morte dans un accident de voiture, ce n'est pas ta Bouthy ?

— Je suis désolé, Jaouad, je dois interrompre la communication. Judith s'impatiente. Je te rappellerai plus tard.

— C'est Jaouad, dit Slim à Judith. Il voudrait te voir avant que tu ne partes.

— Je vais demain à Marrakech.

— Déjà ?

— Tu le savais. Je ne suis ici que parce que tu m'as appelé à ton secours. Et apparemment, tu n'as pas vraiment besoin de moi. N'est-ce pas ?

— Ça m'a fait du bien de te voir.

— Viens plutôt admirer les cadeaux que je t'ai ramenés, susurre Judith à Slim. La dernière fois que je suis venue, je me suis rendu compte que tu n'avais plus rien de décent à te mettre sur le dos. Tu te négliges.

— Il ne fallait pas, Judith !

— Ça me fait plaisir. Ne sois pas idiot, dit-elle en déballant des paquets cadeaux de toutes tailles.

Allongé à côté de Judith endormie, Slim palpe le tissu du pyjama qu'elle lui a offert. " De la vraie soie. Comme si j'étais habitué à porter des pyjamas en soie, moi ! Elle me prend pour sa vieille chochotte de mari. "

VII

Premier trophée. L'Enjôleuse, bijouterie à la mode, organise un tournoi de bridge au Sun life, club chic casablancais.

Le Sun Life bénéficie d'un magnifique site au bord de l'océan. Taillé dans les rochers, le club " le plus classe " de la Corniche offre une vue incomparable sur les hautes vagues de l'Atlantique. Sa piscine, eau de mer, ses cours de tennis, terre battue, son restaurant, fruits de mer, et ses salons, Roche Bobois, font la fierté de ses adhérents. N'y entre pas qui veut. Une sélection draconienne assure à ses membres de ne jamais se trouver nez à nez avec des nouveaux riches sans éducation ou des poules de luxe arrivées d'on ne sait où.

Mais aujourd'hui ses portes sont ouvertes à des invités de tous les horizons. Des créateurs de renom arrivent des quatre coins du monde, des marques prestigieuses parrainent l'événement. Les gagnants se verront remettre, à l'issue des compétitions, des bijoux de grande valeur signés des griffes les plus célèbres. Tout le gratin de Casablanca est présent ; les artistes, les mondains, quelques demi-mondaines

— ce sont les clientes les plus assidues de L'Enjôleuse, et les plus sûres aussi -, les excentriques, les riches à millions, les mécènes… Et les journalistes aussi bien sûr.

Slim arbore la veste Kenzo que lui a rapportée Judith. Il sirote un Gin en observant ce beau monde cosmopolite, fait de fastes et de frivolité, un peu snob, un peu maniéré.

Ce que Slim apprécie dans le luxe, c'est le confort et la facilité. Certainement pas le milieu, trop guindé à son goût. " Quels emmerdeurs ! songe-t-il, j'irais volontiers ailleurs si je n'avais pas rendez-vous avec Jaouad. Il doit être dans ses petits souliers maintenant que Judith lui a rendu ce fameux service. Ma Judith ! "

Laïla de Féminités, le magazine féminin le plus en vogue du moment, parade, habillée d'une robe Azzeddine Alaïa ajustée, qui met en valeur ses cuisses sans l'ombre d'une culotte de cheval, résultat miraculeux d'une liposuccion chère payée grâce à un salaire mirobolant et injustifié. En effet, Laïla a la réputation de gagner plus d'argent qu'il n'en faudrait et ce, en se contentant de passer la journée à mâcher du chewing-gum — ce qui lui donne mauvais genre —, et à fumer. On dit d'elle aussi qu'elle ne sait pas écrire et que ses éditos ne sont pas de sa plume. En réalité, c'est pour ces mêmes raisons qu'elle a été nommée directeur de publication de Féminités.

" Elle ne se doute pas qu'on l'appelle la pipelette de la presse, celle-là ", se dit Slim en ricanant.

Inopinément, la-dite pipelette s'approche de lui.

— Comment vas-tu, mon cher Slim ? On ne te voit pas souvent.

— Ne me dites pas que je vous manque.

— Et pourquoi pas ?

— Vas-y, Laïla, parle, qu'est-ce que je peux faire pour toi ?

— Je voulais juste savoir si tu vas bien. J'ai appris pour l'accident de Bouthaïna, je suis désolée. Tu étais avec elle ?

Slim virevolte et s'éloigne de Laïla comme d'une apparition aberrante. Il se fait servir un deuxième verre qu'il avale rapidement puis un troisième.

Il ne s'aperçoit pas que plusieurs personnes le scrutent.

À deux mètres de lui, une jeune femme esseulée semble égarée dans ce lieu où tous les convives se connaissent. Grande et mince, un peu gauche, le visage en forme de cœur, elle a un air un peu bêta qui retient l'attention de Slim. Elle le fixe comme s'il était l'objet de tous ses fantasmes.

— Je ne vous ai jamais vue auparavant, lui dit Slim pour engager la conversation. Qui êtes-vous ?

— Je crée des bijoux pour L'Enjôleuse. Ça ne fait pas longtemps que je suis rentrée des Etats-Unis. C'est fou ce que tout a changé ici.

— Vous trouvez ?

— Oh oui ! On se croirait ailleurs qu'au Maroc.

— Vous avez été absente longtemps ?

— En fait, je suis née en France. Mais, s'empresse-t-elle d'ajouter, je suis venue passer toutes mes vacances d'été au Maroc, à Oujda, chez mes grands-parents. Mon pays me passionne.

— C'est vous qui avez l'air d'être passionnante.

— Ne vous moquez pas de moi, dit-elle en rougissant, gênée. Je ne suis rien du tout.

— Et philosophe, avec ça ?

— Que voulez-vous dire ?

— Que diriez-vous de foutre le camp d'ici ? Je voudrais vous faire découvrir un endroit beaucoup plus intéressant que ce club de snobinards.

— Je suis venue avec Laïla. Il faudrait peut-être que je la prévienne que je m'en vais.

— Pas besoin. Elle a l'habitude qu'on la plaque en milieu de soirée. Elle comprendra.

— Ce n'est pas gentil, ce que vous dites.

— Taisez-vous et suivez-moi, dit Slim en la prenant par le bras et en la dirigeant vers la sortie.

“ Tant pis pour Jaouad, songe-t-il, il s’en remettra aussi. ”

Laïla, qui a suivi avec une grande attention la scène de loin, hoche la tête d’un air entendu et dit à son vis-à-vis en regardant le couple sortir — Slim trébuchant, et la jeune femme un peu déroutée, mais le talonnant déjà — : “ Décidément, il ne changera jamais, celui-là ! ”

Epilogue

Slim se réveille en sursaut et en sueur. Il tend l'oreille, se demande s'il a rêvé. Cela ressemblait plus à un cauchemar qu'à un rêve d'ailleurs, ce bruit apocalyptique de fin du monde. A côté de lui, une jeune femme dort tranquillement comme s'il ne s'était rien passé. Il la regarde, son visage est serein, innocent. Comme celui de Bouthaïna. Depuis qu'elle est morte, il y a deux ans, il lui arrive rarement de penser à elle. Si ce n'est quand il croit la reconnaître dans les traits d'une autre femme. Il a l'impression qu'elle est toujours vivante, mais loin de lui. Et ça, ça ne l'a jamais dérangé.

Tous les signes de l'insomnie sont là, bouche sèche, tachycardie, mal de tête, angoisse. Il avale une grande rasade de coca-cola, se dirige vers la salle de bain, met sa tête sous le robinet du lavabo. L'eau froide le ragaillardit définitivement. Dehors, le silence est total, mais il sent confusément que quelque chose est entrain de se passer. Il enfile rapidement son jean, un tee-shirt et des baskets et sort en claquant la porte derrière lui. Il y a des gens dehors qui ont l'air affolés. Il entend des bribes de conversations : " Plusieurs morts, bombes, islamistes, attentats... "

Ce n'était pas un cauchemar, c'est la réalité. La fin du monde, son monde à lui. Celui d'une pseudo liberté. Il se sent étouffer. Un homme lui explique brièvement ce qui s'est passé. Plusieurs attentats ont été commis à Casablanca. Dans un brouillard, il l'entend lui dire " on se croyait à l'abri de tout ça ". Slim avait été presque tout heureux de voir les deux tours s'écrouler. Le 11 septembre ressemblait à un film hollywoodien. La guerre de l'Irak l'avait écœurée. Et maintenant, Casablanca !

Il arrive sur les lieux de l'attentat. Ambulances, morts, flics, il n'a vu ça qu'au cinéma. Il a l'impression d'ailleurs d'être dans une autre dimension, irréelle. Enfin quelque chose qui se passe, pense-t-il. Toute cette léthargie, cette résignation, ce malaise diffus. Même la mort devenait banalisée. Ce n'est pas comme de la voir devant soi, victorieuse. Tous ces cadavres sont la preuve de sa victoire. Un flic lui demande de s'éloigner. Machinalement, il sort sa carte de presse de sa poche, pose des questions, écoute à peine les réponses, décide brusquement de rentrer chez lui.

La jeune femme dort toujours aussi paisiblement. Elle ronfle légèrement. Il s'approche d'elle, la touche.

Elle respire profondément. Il insiste, caresse lentement son corps nu. Elle ouvre les yeux, lui sourit.

— tu es habillé, tu es sorti ? demande-t-elle

— Embrasse-moi, lui répond-il doucement.

Il la prend dans ses bras. Son corps tiède, ses lèvres, ses cheveux, sa respiration. Sa main cherche son sexe. Elle est la vie. Il la mord dans le gras de la peau, là où c'est le plus tendre. Elle gémit. L'excitation monte. Slim se sent envahi par une violence inconnue. Il a presque envie de lui arracher la peau par lambeaux, de la dévorer. Elle le repousse, surprise et apeurée.

— Qu'est-ce qui se passe ?

— Il y a eu des attentats cette nuit à Casablanca.

— Attentats ? ? tu plaisantes ?

— Non. Dans plusieurs endroits différents. Il y a eu des morts.

— Tu es sorti ? tu m'as laissée toute seule ?

— Je te dis qu'il y a eu des attentats et c'est tout ce que tu trouves à me répondre ?

— Je dois appeler chez moi !

Elle se lève, nue et échevelée. Déjà ailleurs. Slim se lève à son tour, indifférent à son inquiétude. Il se rend à la cuisine, ouvre le réfrigérateur et en sort une bouteille de vodka. Le goût de l'alcool le fait grimacer et il se sent envahi d'une chaleur bienfaisante. Il continue à boire de la bouteille, lentement, concentré sur la sensation que lui procure la vodka. Il pense que c'est trop tard pour lui. Peut-être aurait-il du mourir avec bouthaïna dans l'accident. Sa vie n'a pas de sens, elle n'en a jamais eue. Qu'est-ce qui s'est passé au fond ? des attentats. Et alors ? se dit-il, tous les jours il y en a ailleurs, c'est devenu banal, on ne fait que se normaliser, c'est tout.

FLASHAGE QUADRICHROMIE

IMP. EL MAARIF AL JADIDA - RABAT 2004